# ROAD ROCKET

# ROAD ROCKET

BY HENRY GREGOR FELSEN

Octane Press, Edition 1.0, February 2024
Random House Edition, September 1960
Bantam Edition, September 1961
Bantam Pathfinder Edition, April 1963
GP / Books Edition, July 1990
Felsen Ink Edition, 2013

ISBN: 978-1-64234-132-4
ePub ISBN: 978-1-64234-166-9
LCCN: 2023945743

*On the cover: Cover art used with permission
of Bantam Books (Penguin Random House).*

Design by Tom Heffron
Copyedited by Faith Garcia
Proofread by Danielle Magnuson

octanepress.com

Octane Press is based in Austin, Texas

Printed in the United States

To my daughter Holly

# CHAPTER 1

SUDDENLY, STRIDENTLY, AT LONG-AWAITED LAST, seventeen buzzer bells buzz-rang simultaneously in seventeen overheated rooms. Immediately, 431 teenagers and twenty-five adults sighed, relaxed, and looked happier and brighter. Except for extracurricular activities and punitive detentions, James Audubon High School was through with its people for the next sixteen hours. Lively voices floated away on lively feet as freedom permitted flight.

One of the first to fly was Woody Ahern, a tenth-grade student aged sixteen years and two months. He headed for his locker on the run, sidestepping past slowpokes, matching shoulder bumps with oncoming traffic he couldn't (or wouldn't) dodge, and going right through groups of standers and talkers who were in his way. Arriving at his locker, Woody pulled open the metal door and carelessly threw his books inside. As he reached in to get his new red nylon jacket, an expression of disgust distorted his face. He snorted angrily, and slammed the locker door closed with a furious, clanging kick. Despite the urgent business he had elsewhere, Woody waited grimly for his locker mate to show up.

Moments later a tall boy with long black hair slouched out of the passing crowd. Woody blocked the locker with his body. "I want to talk to you, Graffan," Woody said ominously.

Graffan returned Woody's hostile stare. "What's eating you, Ahern?"

"I'm telling you now for the last time," Woody said, his voice rising with every word. "No more bananas!"

"You ain't telling me nothing," Graffan said contemptuously. "Get out of my way." He motioned as though to push Woody away from the locker but changed his mind when he saw Woody's hand clench into a fist. "Come on, Ahern," he said instead, "I need to get in the locker."

Woody thrust his jacket at Graffan's face. "Smell that," Woody ordered. "A brand new jacket, and it stinks like a rotten banana. The whole locker stinks like those rotten bananas you bring with your lunch. I'm telling you, Graffan. I've had it. No more bananas!"

"Listen, Ahern, what I carry in my lunch is my business, not yours."

"It's my business when it stinks up my locker."

"*Your* locker! It's just as much my locker as it is *your* locker."

"You park bananas in there again," Woody said grimly, "you'll locker on the hall floor."

"Yeah," Graffan sneered. "Just because your old man . . ."

"Never mind my old man," Woody broke in. "I'm just telling you . . . you stink up my clothes just one more time, and I'll bust you right in the nose!"

With that, Woody turned and strode away, pulling on his jacket with abrupt, angry motions. He could smell the heavy, garbage-like stale banana odor that his jacket gave off. Of all times to smell like the city dump! Maybe there would be time for the fresh outdoor air to blow away the smell.

Woody went out the front door and on another hundred feet, taking up a position at the head of a broad flight of stone steps that led down to the street. Three afternoons a week he met Dick Slater at this spot, then they walked together to Stonelee's Dairy, where both of them had jobs. Woody always had to wait for Dick, and often this annoyed him. But today he hoped Dick would be slower than usual in getting around and would not show up too soon to spoil everything.

Woody leaned against the cold black iron railing that bordered the steps and watched enviously as the boys with cars drove away from school. How many of them there were! And what a variety of cars they drove! They went by below him, taunting him with the heady music of glass packs as the drivers stayed in low gear and constantly revved up and backed off. The sounds rose and fell, the V-8s roaring and popping in bass tones, the occasional sixes snarling more shrilly.

There were boys who drove away alone or with one friend. There were boys who carried away a carload of buddies. There were boys who drove away with girls sitting close beside them, and there were even *girls* who drove their own cars. Only he, it seemed to Woody, was without a car. He and a few other unfortunates or misfits.

The cars came out of the parking lot by the dozens, and this afternoon there was an extra torment. In the morning the sky had been gray—there were skimpy patches of snow still on the ground—and the air had been cold. But now the afternoon March sun was warm, the snow had melted quietly into the ground, and even the air felt soft and warm. Green was replacing brown on the school lawns. Scarcely anyone wore a hat now, and some hardy souls had even discarded their outer jackets. And the boys who drove convertibles had the tops down, so all the world could see how much fun it was to have one's own car, and to drive away in the sunshine after the long day at school was over.

Woody turned his back on the scene below and watched the school entrance, listening to the sound of pipes and able to identify many of the cars by sound. Three afternoons a week he waited at this spot for Dick Slater, and three times a week Sandra Rowan came by alone while he was waiting. Woody pressed his back against the iron railing and rested his elbows on the cold pipe. She *had* to be first again today—and alone. Nervously he sniffed at his jacket and felt violent rage as he detected the sickish-sweet old banana smell.

Perhaps the most outstanding feature about Woody Ahern, seen as he leaned against the railing and waited in his red jacket, dark khaki slacks, and light blue sports shirt, was his lack of outstanding features. He was the kind of normal, average, ordinary-looking boy one sees by the thousands in hundreds of high school annuals, in crowds of teenage boys at dances, athletic contests, watching fires, or accidents, or joining the armed forces. Woody was just over five feet seven inches tall and weighed 138 pounds. As such, he was neither tall nor short, thin nor fat. His hair was darker than blond, yet lighter than brown, and although he kept it cut short to look straight and neat, it showed a tendency to wave or curl when it grew out a little. Woody had the kind of eyes that seemed to change with the light, the season, the clothes he wore, or the mood he was in. In summer, when his skin was tanned, his eyes seemed blue or green. When his skin paled in winter, his eyes appeared more hazel, and some of his friends would have sworn they were brown. His mouth was rather broad, his teeth were even and white. Head on, his nose looked broad and straight, but seen from the side it had a thinner look, and seemed longer, and turned up slightly at the tip. So, there were angles that made him seem compact and husky and other angles that gave him a more slender and slight appearance.

If Woody had an outstanding characteristic, it was his ability (shared with a million other boys) to be convincing in looking the way he wanted to. When he put on hunting clothes, he took on the appearance and quality of a young outdoorsman. When he dressed in his best for school, he was every inch and degree the neat and nice young boy. When in old denims, boots, and shirt with the sleeves rolled high and tight on his muscular arms, he looked and had the quality of a real young hard hat at odds with the world.

This afternoon, neatly dressed in casual school clothes, biting his lower lip, bumping restlessly against the railing, working his shoulders nervously, he also looked exactly like what he was—a tenth-grade boy waiting hopefully and uncertainly for a girl to appear.

At last, she came out of the school building, and fortunately she was alone. She walked out slowly, cradling her burden of books in both arms, her head bent forward and turned to one side, her face a picture of serious thought and concentration. She wore a yellow sweater, a dark brown skirt, and a lightweight tan coat, unbuttoned and pushed back on her shoulders, that swung behind her as she walked.

Sandra Rowan was slender to the point of being thin, with golden brown hair, dark brown eyes, and a pleasant mouth. She was lithe and graceful and walked with a slight willowy swaying motion. She was a good but not flashy student with a low, soft voice and an air of reserve that intrigued Woody. Many times when he had looked at her in class she seemed to be lost in some inner meaningful thought. Woody knew she wasn't going steady, and since she wasn't one of the wheels in school, and he wasn't one of the wheels, he felt they somehow had something in common, and that there was a chance she might go out with him. He had never really asked a girl for a date before and was thankful he wanted to go with a girl who wasn't too loud, sophisticated, or popular.

She approached the steps, books cradled, purse on top of her books, her expression gently remote and contemplative.

"Hi, Sandra."

It seemed to Woody he croaked the words out like an old frog. She walked on unhearing, unaware of his painful smile. Her foot felt for the first step. In a moment she would be gone.

"It sure is nice to have a real spring day for a change . . ."

He almost bellowed. She stopped, turning toward him, aware of him, and smiled. "Hello, Woody. Did you say something? I was listening to my radio."

Now he heard it too. The little transistor radio that was in the opened purse on top of the books. The song had ended, and a loud, shouting commercial had taken its place. With this he could compete.

Woody glanced nervously toward the school and was relieved to see no sign of Dick Slater.

"I was just wondering," Woody said, knowing he was pressed for time and had to get to the point quickly, "if you were going to the Teen Hop Saturday night."

"Are you going?"

"I was thinking about it," Woody said.

"How are you going?"

"In a car, of course."

It had happened so easily, so smoothly, that Woody wasn't even aware that they had switched roles, and that Sandra was doing the questioning.

Sandra moved a step closer, shifting her books in her arms. "I didn't know you had a car, Woody." Her voice and look were friendly. It was turning out better than Woody had dared hope.

"I don't have my own car yet," Woody said. "I . . . uh . . . haven't found one I wanted to buy. I guess I'm pretty hard to please."

"I'd imagine so," Sandra said. "All those talks you've given in Speech about cars and racing . . . how are you going to the dance?"

"I asked my father if I could borrow his car for the evening," Woody said. "It's not real new or sharp, but it's transportation . . ." He laughed apologetically.

Sandra smiled her friendliest and waited for Woody to continue. She liked Woody. He didn't take part in any of the school activities and didn't seem to care about getting good grades, but he always looked neat and clean and wasn't rowdy or dirty mouthed around girls. Actually, his aloofness from school life attracted her to him, and she knew it attracted other girls as well. It had kept him from becoming too well known, too common, and too ordinary.

"What did your father say about that?" Sandra prompted gently. "When you asked to use his car?"

"Oh, he was all for it," Woody said.

"That was very nice of him."

"Oh, Dad's a nice guy when you get to know him," Woody said with a chuckle. "He would let me use it, all right, if he didn't need it himself to get to some meeting. But he's going to drive me to the dance, and pick me up when it's over, so there won't be any walking . . ."

Woody's words hung in the air. It was the nearest he actually could come to asking for a date. He waited for Sandra to say she would be glad to go with him or give him another bit of encouragement so the direct question would be easy.

"That's very nice of your father, to take you places like that," Sandra said. "I hope you have a real nice time at the dance. Bye now . . ."

She went down the steps, and Woody didn't know what had hit him. For a stunned moment he thought she hadn't understood he was trying to ask for a date. He was about to run after her and explain, when he noticed a familiar, heavy odor in his nostrils. That was it! He stank of rotten bananas, and she had smelled it!

Woody whirled toward the school, his fists tight. He would go back in there, find Graffan, and knock the devil out of him . . . right now! But, as he started toward the building, the front door opened and Dick Slater strolled out in his customary nonchalant, arrogant, and provokingly slow way.

Woody turned his head and permitted himself one last regretful look at Sandra's retreating figure, then he forgot her as Dick approached. There was much more important business at hand than a date.

- - -

Dick Slater was a few months older than Woody, a few inches taller, and a few pounds heavier. He had wavy blond hair which he wore rather long, and a lean, fairly handsome but usually sullen face. He approached Woody dressed in faded denim pants, a black turtleneck sweater, and an unzipped war surplus navy leather flying jacket with a fur collar. An unlit cigarette dangled from his lips. Dick came as close as he could to defying the ban on smoking on school grounds while still remaining out of trouble. He sauntered toward Woody, his right thumb hooked in his belt, his left hand thrust in a jacket pocket. It was hard to tell which movie or TV star he was imitating. He imagined he looked like all of them and was apt to combine the sneer of one with the slang of another and the grooming habits of still another.

"You see the other guys?" Woody asked the moment Dick was in speaking range.

"Yeah, I saw 'em."

"Will they be at the meeting tonight?"

Dick smiled disdainfully. "Did you ever know them to miss?"

"This is the big one," Woody said. He reached in his pocket and pulled out a sheet of paper covered with neat figures. "I've worked out the whole thing. I think this will convince Dad I can afford a car. And if you guys back me up . . ."

"We'll back you up," Dick promised.

Walking, they reached the head of the stone steps. Instead of going down, Dick sat down on the top step. Woody stood beside him. "We'd better move on," Woody said. "I want to finish up early at the dairy."

Dick yawned. "There's plenty of time. Let's watch cars for a minute while I have a smoke."

*"Here?* You can't do that."

"I'll flip it in the street if anybody comes." Dick lit his cigarette and puffed smoke toward Woody. "I saw you making time with

Sandra Rowan," he said, a teasing edge in his voice. "That's why I didn't come out sooner."

"Uh-huh." Woody tried to kill this line of talk with a grunt.

"She sure took off in a hurry. What'd you say to her?"

"Asked her to the Teen Hop."

"Why her?" Dick wanted to know.

"Why not?"

"She going with you?"

"No." Woody held his arm in front of Dick's face. "Smell my jacket. That lousy Graffan brings bananas every morning and sticks them in the locker. She must have got a whiff."

"I can't smell anything," Dick said. "How were you going to go?"

"I wanted to borrow Dad's car, but he needed it. He would have taken us there and picked us up, though."

Dick shook his head in a pitying way. "You're dumber than you look, Woody. The girls who run this school don't date if the parents do the chauffeuring. That's so they won't be mistaken for junior high kids."

"Sandra doesn't run with that bunch," Woody said. "Must have been the bananas."

Dick laughed scornfully. "What's Sandra? Another one of the herd, that's all. Maybe she doesn't run with the wheels, but she's run by them. Just like all the other herd people in this dump."

"Maybe you're right," Woody said. He sat down beside Dick and yawned. "That old sun sure feels good. Boy, what I wouldn't give for a car of my own today."

They watched the cars go by. A dozen or more student-driven cars, without any better place to go at the moment, had been circling the block around school again and again.

"We must be the only guys in school who are on foot today," Woody grumbled. "Let's head for the dairy. This is the day I run acid through the lines."

"And I've got a million eggs to candle," Dick said without

enthusiasm. "Hey . . . maybe we can get a ride over. The Pooch is in the merry-go-round."

Dick pointed to a lone driver who was jockeying an unwashed dark green hardtop in the wake of the other cars. Though shabby and covered with dirt, the car was gaudy in a haphazard way. It had mud-caked spinner hubs, clusters of rusty chrome stars on all four fenders, and twin six-foot radio aerials slanting back from the rear deck. The car carried twin spotlights, and twin klaxon horns were mounted on the hood. The bumpers were covered with strips of red reflector tape that spelled out *The Pooch*. Thus did Freddy Calmon proudly display the derisive nickname he had been given.

"We can walk," Woody said. "Let's leave him be."

"Aw, come on," Dick, said, getting to his feet. "The simple jerk will think we're doing him a favor by asking."

Dick led the way down the steps, and they waited for the cars to come around again. When they did, Dick flagged down the dark green car. "Hey, Pooch!" Dick yelled. "How about a lift to the dairy?"

"Sure. Hop in." Freddy moved over so there would be room for all three in the front seat. Dick nudged Woody with his elbow as he got in first and sat in the middle. Woody got in and closed the door.

"Thanks a lot, Freddy," he said. "We *are* a little late."

"Any time," Freddy said. He put the car in gear and drove off, obviously pleased and flattered to have them as passengers.

Eleven years before, they had all been in kindergarten together. For a few years, Freddy seemed merely a happy-go-lucky boy with curly black hair, friendly black eyes, and a big smile for everyone and everything. But as they grew older and the work became harder, Freddy found it increasingly difficult to squeeze through with his class. He never lost his carefree smile or his good nature, but the mission and message of school somehow failed to connect with any terminal in his brain. By the time the others were in high school, Freddy was just starting (and spottily attending) junior high. By the time the others were in tenth grade, Freddy had drifted away from school for good.

But, in the freedom of his schoolless world, Freddy was lonesome. Although he had never been able to work up any interest in classes and studies, Freddy was devoted to his former schoolmates and made every effort to maintain his contact with other boys his own age.

Now that he wasn't forced to attend classes, Freddy never missed a day of school. Every morning he would make a dozen trips to school with a dozen different groups of cars, following each group onto the parking lot before driving off to find and follow another group, as though he personally were herding them all to their proper corral. During the noon hour he drove around and around with whoever happened to be driving around and around, and it was the same at night.

He not only went to all school games and functions, he seldom missed a practice session, and the school had no more a devoted fan than he. And, in order to bridge the gap between himself and the boys in school, he would go to any length to be friendly, or to be of service, just so he would be allowed to stay around. There was something doglike in the devoted way in which he waited for the boys and bounded off to run their errands or be helpful. At first someone jokingly referred to him as "man's best friend," and it was a short step from there to his final nickname—the Pooch. Naturally, he didn't mind. In fact, he was proud of it. It made him seem a definite person to the others. He was mercilessly exploited by the others. They begged rides from him, borrowed money which they never returned, and sent him off to buy cigarettes, or beer, or whatever else they wanted and weren't permitted to buy. Somehow, the Pooch always found a way. Also, he never objected. He was not concerned with the onerousness or illegality of a request. His only concern was to please the boys with whom he wished to associate, and no trouble, no risk, was too great a price to pay for this privilege.

"Say, Pooch . . ."

"Yeah, Woody?"

"You know anybody that's got a car for sale?"

"What kind of a car?"

"Well, Dick and me and a couple of other guys have got a car club, and we're looking for a cheap car to build up."

"Don't know anybody right now," Pooch said, "but I'll ask around for you."

"Don't go out of your way," Woody said. "I'm not sure yet I can buy it."

"It's no trouble," Pooch said earnestly. "I got nothing else to do."

Dick squirmed around and looked in the back seat. "What's all that junk, Pooch?"

Pooch gave Dick a merry smile. "Stuff," he said. "Stuff guys need for their cars. You know, they tell me what they need and I get it."

"What do you charge for a set of those Dodge hubs?"

"I don't charge anything," Pooch said. "The guys tell me what they need, and I get it for them. You know, for friends."

"Where do you get the stuff, that you can give it away?"

"I look around," Pooch said, "and I find what they want, and I get it for them. If you need anything for your car, Woody, I'll get stuff for you, too."

"Thanks," Woody said. Dick turned to him and winked, then indicated by rolling his eyes what he thought of Pooch's brain.

Pooch pulled up in front of a long, low building with a sign for *Stonelee's Dairy* painted across the front. "You want me to come in and give you a hand?" he asked hopefully.

"Can't," Woody said. "It's not allowed."

"You could help me candle eggs," Dick said.

"No, he can't, Dick," Woody said. "You know the rules."

"They're not my rules," Dick said. "I didn't make them."

"You're not supposed to. Your job is to obey them."

"Oh, get off my back," Dick grumbled. "You sound like a preacher."

"I need my job," Woody said. "I lose that, and there goes my chance for a car."

"Okay, okay," Dick said. "I give in."

"How about," Pooch said, "if I come back when you're through, and give you a ride home?"

"No, we can make it all right," Woody said. "We don't know when we'll be through."

"I could wait. I don't have anything else to do."

"I'll tell you what, Pooch," Dick said. "Pick me up in two hours. I'll be through by then. Okay?"

"Okay," Pooch said cheerfully. "Meanwhile, I'll look around for a car, Woody."

"Don't . . ." Woody began, but Dick shushed him. "Let him look," Dick muttered. "Don't you want him to have any fun?"

The Pooch drove off with a wave and a clatter. Woody was annoyed. "Why don't you leave him alone?" he said to Dick as they walked toward the dairy. "Poor guy . . . it isn't right to step all over his good nature."

"I tell you he loves it," Dick answered carelessly. "I told you he'd think we were doing him a favor if we rode with him."

"Well, he's a good guy," Woody said. "Don't work him for too much."

"Other guys do."

"We're not other guys."

"You asked him to look for a car, didn't you?"

"Yeah, but I didn't ask him to go get it and *give* it to me. If he finds me one, I'll pay him a commission."

"It's guys like you," Dick said, "who go around the world spoiling the natives."

"Well, I don't want him hanging around," Woody said. "You start up with him, and you can't get rid of him."

"I thought you liked him."

"I do, but I don't want another shadow."

They reached the dairy building. One of the delivery trucks was at the loading door, and as they came up, Mr. Stonelee came out carrying several boxes of ice cream bars. "Hi, Woody, Dick . . ." he called out. They returned his greeting. He put the ice cream bars inside the truck and came out again. Mr. Stonelee was a tall, thin, wiry man with bright blue eyes, sandy hair, and the wind-burned face of a farmer. He was dressed in white bib overalls and a denim jacket.

"For a minute I thought you were coming to work in your new car," Mr. Stonelee said to Woody.

"I wish I was," Woody said.

"I wish you had it, too," Mr. Stonelee said. "I can't let you drive the truck until you're eighteen, Woody. But if you had your own car and could make some of these special deliveries for me, I'd pay you for your time and your mileage."

"There's nothing I'd like better," Woody said with intense feeling. "Maybe when my dad hears that, he'll loosen up and let me get a car. I could tell him what you said, couldn't I?" Woody looked anxiously at his employer.

"I guess so. You wouldn't make more than your expenses as far as the car goes, but it would be a help to me."

"That might clinch it," Woody said firmly. "That might be all it would take. I'm sure going to tell him!"

Mr. Stonelee laughed. "You do that, Woody. You'll remember about the acid tonight, won't you?"

"I knew about it," Woody said.

"Good. I was sure you'd remember. And Dick . . . if you're in doubt about an egg, discard it. We had a couple of complaints this week. Look at every one, boy."

"Okay," Dick said.

The boys watched Mr. Stonelee drive away in the small truck, then went into the dairy. It was a small, independent operation, run by their employer, two other full-time drivers, and themselves—Dick as the egg candler, and Woody as the clean-up man in the milk room.

They stopped in front of Dick's work area. He had a corner that was curtained off from the rest of the room. Behind the curtain was a little table with his egg-candling light, a small scale for weighing the eggs as they were candled, and Dick's radio. In front of the table was a low chair on which Dick sat while he worked. On his right were the cases of eggs to be candled, and on his left an open case for him to fill with good eggs. Next to this case was a large white enameled pail in which Dick put the rejects.

"Want anything before we start?" Dick asked, motioning with his head toward the cold room where the ice cream was kept.

"I'll wait," Woody said. "I want to get through."

"Guess I will, too. Well . . . back to the salt mines." Dick took off his jacket and sat down on his low chair. "Four new cases," he said. "I'll have that done in two hours. Maybe less."

"The man said to look at them *all,*" Woody said.

"I do . . . most of the time." Dick laughed. "Of course, when I'm in a hurry . . . anyway, what's it to you? You only work here, like me."

"It's a lot to me," Woody said. "He trusts us to do our jobs right, that's all."

"Listen to the preacher! Trying to make something out of a couple of lousy jobs."

"If I didn't clean those vats right," Woody said, "the next batch of milk could be tainted, and people could get sick. That's not such a lousy job."

"I never heard of a rotten egg killing anybody," Dick said.

Before Woody could think up an answer, Dick turned his radio on full blast and reached for the first egg to be candled and weighed. Woody shrugged and went to his own job.

In the room where Woody worked were the big gleaming stainless steel vats through which the milk was run, the clarifier which removed impurities from the milk, and the bottling machine. As usual, since milk had been run that morning, the floor around the machine was littered with broken bottles.

Woody walked across the stone floor to his own radio, which sat on a high shelf, and turned it on. Then he took off his shirt, pants, and shoes and got into a pair of white bib overalls and a pair of rubber pacs. His job would be to sweep up the broken glass. Then he would clean out the clarifier, run acid through the lines, and scrub the vats with hot water and soap. Then he would clean out the vats with milk stone remover. After they were rinsed and dried, he would give the floor a cleaning.

Woody went about his job methodically, taking his time, listening to the blare of his radio. In a little while he was through sweeping and went to clean the vats. He was able to clean the two small vats by bending over the rims and reaching in. But he had to get inside the big vat to clean it right. Here, with his soap and brush, he scrubbed until his arms ached, and it was only a matter of minutes before he was soaked from head to foot by the constantly running rinse hose.

The radio blared in the steam-filled room, and Woody, crouched uncomfortably inside the big steel vat, scrubbed at the milk residue with might and main. His was not an easy job, but he liked it, even the getting soaked to the skin part. It felt good, after being cooped up in school all day, to do something almost violently physical and to splash around in the water. Also, it was the kind of job that allowed him time to think—usually about cars.

This particular afternoon, as Woody wielded brush and soapy water, he created the future scene in which he, backed by the club members, would ask his father for a car. The figures were all down in black and white to prove he could afford a car, and all he needed was to find some way to convince his father that he should have one. And why not? There wasn't another boy in school who was more interested in or devoted to the automobile than he was. He'd bet money on that. And as long as so many other boys had cars, it wasn't fair that he, who was serious about automotive work, should be without one.

Again and again, Woody ran through the coming scene in his mind. Again and again, armed with facts, figures, and good arguments, he saw himself talking to his father. And again and again, he saw his father remain unconvinced and shake his head.

Woody's ears rang as someone hammered on the outside of the vat. Woody stood up and saw Dick standing by with the white enamel pail in his hand.

Dick lifted the pail. "Let's go . . . rots for Cokes."

"Uh-uh . . . I don't want to quit in the middle."

"Come *on*."

"You know we're not supposed to," Woody said, shouting to make himself heard above the radio and the running water.

"So what? Stonelee's gone. Come on, don't be chicken about everything."

Woody looked around. It would only take a moment . . . He climbed out of the vat and turned off the hose. "Okay, but not too many. How many you got?"

"Eight each."

They went out behind the dairy building, and Woody shivered as the cold air hit his wet clothes.

"Set up the target," Dick ordered. "I'll get the eggs ready."

"They're already ready," Woody said. But he went to the tree.

Although they weren't supposed to do it, it was a custom of the dairy to throw rotten eggs at a target to see who would pay for the next Cokes. There was a large vacant lot behind the dairy with a great deal of tangled brush and one good-sized tree. The target was a square of cardboard that the boys kept hidden. Woody found the target and began to set it up firmly in the lowest crotch of the tree. Although the boys had thrown thousands of rotten eggs at the tree, there was no odor and no mess. The rains and snows washed the tree and the ground clean; weather somehow destroyed even the shells. Weather was aided in this work by birds, weasels, rats, and an occasional skunk.

Woody had the target almost placed when an egg sailed past his head and splattered against a tree limb. "All right, wise guy!" Woody yelled over his shoulder. "Cut the comedy!" Dick replied with a cackle of laughter.

Woody slogged back through the weedy lot to join Dick. "It's a good thing you missed me, Slater."

"Aw . . . it wasn't a rot. I wouldn't throw a rot at you."

"Oh no," Woody said. "Not unless you thought you could get away with it. I could tell it wasn't a rot when it didn't stink. But it's still a good thing you missed. If you'd hit me, I'd have pushed your head right in that bucket."

"Any time, any time," Dick said. "We'll see whose head gets in the bucket. Come on . . . give you first throw."

"I get a free throw," Woody said. "You had one just now."

Dick didn't agree, and they argued about it for a while, then Dick gave in and went back to get Woody an extra egg. Woody took a warm-up toss and hit the target.

"I'll take that for my first throw," Woody said. Again, Dick didn't agree, and again, they argued. Finally, grousing and griping at each other, they threw their eight eggs, splattering shells, gummy yolks, and sticky whites all over the unoffending and long-suffering tree. When they finished, they were tied with four hits each. By this time Woody was freezing in his wet clothes, and he was glad to run back into the warm steamy room, get his brush and suds, and climb back into the big steel vat. Hidden here, surrounded by the curving steel wall, in this gleaming, steaming, streaming nest, Woody grunted and puffed as he scrubbed and rinsed and planned just how he would convince his father that he could afford, and ought to have, a car of his very own.

# CHAPTER 2

WOODY AHERN TAPPED AN INTAKE VALVE against the side of a truck motor piston. "Gentlemen," Woody said gravely, "the weekly pit stop of the Road Rockets Auto Club is now in session."

As usual, the club was meeting in the back room of the Ahern basement, sharing its official headquarters with the furnace, a water heater, several old trunks and suitcases, some old household appliances awaiting repair, and an assortment of cardboard boxes. When Woody had been given permission to use this room for himself and his club, he had created an atmosphere that reflected his own intense devotion to the automobile and to automobile racing, repairing, rebuilding, and remodeling.

The walls were almost solidly covered with pictures of racing stock cars in action, prize-winning custom cars, sleek street rods, famous dragsters, and close-ups of outstanding modified engines. There were how-to picture stories that showed, in photographs and diagrams, how to make numerous mechanical or body work improvements over factory installations and designs.

As though reluctant to part entirely from his interests of a few years past, Woody had also pasted on the walls a few hunting and fishing scenes taken from outdoor magazines. And the faint shadow of the future could be discerned in one comer, where he had hung a pin-up modest enough to meet with his mother's approval. Along one wall was the club library—four orange crates filled with dozens of automotive magazines, each carefully arranged as to publication and date. There were copies of *How to Fix Your Ford*, *How to Fix Your Chevrolet*, and *How to Fix Anything on Any Car*. There were also some inexpensive car repair handbooks and a troubleshooting guide for mechanics.

Several shelves held the collection of auto parts and accessories the club had been able to gather for study purposes and which, displayed, added to the serious automotive atmosphere. These trophies included a number of discarded transmission and engine parts, the shaft of a floor shift, a broken (but shiny) electric fuel pump, a variety of burned-out spark plugs showing a variety of ills, a dead Mallory coil, the gutted hull of a Stromberg 97 carburetor, several impressively burned valves, half a camshaft, and assorted pistons, springs, gears, nuts, bolts, gaskets, and bearings—all worn or burned out.

Hanging from the rafters by strings were several examples of skill at a hobby he had not yet deserted. Over the past three years he had bought dozens of small plastic car model kits, but not one had ever been assembled in stock form or been made entirely from the parts that came in the box.

Woody had designed and constructed his own custom pick-ups from hardtop model kits and made dragsters from sedans and street rods from classics. His special pride was in his miniature stock car racers, which were complete down to their taped steering wheels, tiny shaker screens, roll bars, hood and rear deck tie-down lines, overflow hoses, sponsor's ads, team names, and even crumpled fenders, stove–in doors, and dented tops—those inevitable scars of cars that have seen action.

The final touch was provided by the decals that Woody had secured by writing to various equipment manufacturers. According to where he had pasted these decals, the water heater was Moon Equipped, the furnace ran an Iskenderian Roller Cam, the dehumidifier had an Offenhauser intake manifold, and a heavy old trunk had, running on pump gas, turned the quarter mile in 9.30 seconds, reaching a speed of 161.14 miles per hour.

This back basement room, with a door that could be locked to seal it off from the outside world, was the perfect headquarters for an auto club. It was so good that although the club met formally once a week, the boys usually gathered there on other nights as well. It was a place where they could talk and plan and dream in safety, and the talk, the dreams, and the wishes were always the same. The only difference was that on club nights they wore their uniforms and made an attempt to voice their longings in a formal and organized manner.

Seated at an old kitchen table directly under a bare overhead light, Woody glanced around the room to make sure all members were in uniform before he continued with the meeting.

The club uniform consisted of black shoes or boots, white socks, black cotton pants, a white shirt, and the official black nylon jacket. Across the back of each jacket the words *Road Rockets* had been sewn on in white letters. Below the club name was a white insignia that depicted a kind of wheeled rocket traveling at high speed. On the left front of each jacket, over the heart, each boy had his name sewn on in white.

The boys were proud of their jackets, and anxious for the day to come when they could be worn in public. But as long as the Road Rockets was a car club without a car, the club itself was kept a secret by its members, and the jackets were worn only in the basement headquarters and only during meetings. Everyone was in uniform.

"Gentlemen," Woody said, "I will now call the roll. Kindly acknowledge and signal as I wave you in."

Woody's voice flattened in imitation of the announcers at the racetracks. "In the red . . . number *sevvennty-sevvenn Ponntiiac* . . . Jim Bob Alton!"

Jim Bob, who was already seated at the table, held up his left arm and said, "Yo."

"In the blue . . . number forty . . . *Chevvrooolet* convertible . . ." Woody droned, "Sonny Mack!"

"Yo!" Sonny held his left arm high and, turning from the wall where he had been examining some new racing pictures, trotted to his place at the table.

"And in the black . . . number one hundred and one . . . Plymouth *Fury* . . . Dick Slater!"

"Yo." Dick answered, making a yawn out of his reply. He was lying on an old couch with his hands under his head, listening to a small radio, and he made no move to get up.

"Come on, Dick," Woody ordered impatiently, "signal and come in."

"I'm comfortable here," Dick said lazily, stretching his long, thin body to emphasize his point. "I'm only two feet from you," he continued as the three other boys stared at him with obvious irritation. "I can hear everything and take part from here. Besides, answering the roll like that makes me feel foolish. Little kids do things like that."

Dick closed his eyes, as though the last word had been said, and moved his toes in time to the music he was listening to on the radio. There was a faint smile of satisfaction on his lips, for this was the kind of situation he enjoyed. He liked to think of himself as being independent, different, and a nonconformist, but what he really enjoyed was being uncooperative.

It gave Dick a sense of pleasure to see things that should succeed, fail. The sight of an expensive new car that wouldn't start pleased him more than seeing an old car in trouble. He enjoyed the fumbles at football games and was always delighted when a majorette dropped her baton in front of several thousand people. He really wasn't objecting to the club ritual because it made him feel foolish. The purpose of saying that was to make the others feel foolish and spoil their fun.

The three boys at the table were neither surprised nor unduly disturbed. They had known Dick a long time, and they had learned to live with his negative approach. He had been the kind of small boy who always begged to play with their newest toys or most prized possessions and always managed to break or damage them before he gave them back. He was that kind of big boy, too. They expected him to behave the way he did and were always prepared.

"In the black . . . number one hundred and one . . . Plymouth *Fury*," Woody repeated unyieldingly, "Dick Slater."

"For crying out loud, Woody, there are only four of us here," Dick said.

"Four or forty," Woody said doggedly from the head of the table, "we abide by the club rules. In the black . . ."

"Okay, okay, I'm *coming*." Dick rolled off the couch with a bored, disgusted look on his face, gestured feebly with his left arm, and slumped into his chair.

The others had known Dick would give in, that he seldom held out very long. Besides, they knew Woody. He would have sat there all night repeating Dick's call until Dick either came to the table properly or walked out.

The moment Dick was in his rightful place, Woody finished calling the roll, a ritual whose function (like that of the pictures, the models, the auto parts, decals, and jackets) was to help make up for the fact that the club had no car.

"In the white . . . number twenty-two . . . Ford . . ." Woody called imperturbably, as though there had been no interruption, "Woody Ahern!" He held his left arm high, said his "Yo" in a firm voice, and lowered his arm. "All members being present and accounted for, the secretary will read the minutes of the previous pit stop."

Jim Bob Alton, the fifteen-year-old club secretary, rose to his feet and began reading his notes in a soft, precise, immature voice. Jim Bob was a small, neat, quiet boy who looked younger than his fifteen years. He was an only child whose father, a traveling salesman, was away from home most of the time. From Monday through Friday, Jim Bob lived alone with his mother, a gentle, affectionate woman whose major interest in life was bringing Jim Bob up to be "nice."

Jim Bob missed his father, but he enjoyed the amount of undivided attention he was able to get from his mother. He spent so much time with her that many of her teachings had become second nature to him. So that when he stood around with the other boys and smoked a forbidden cigarette, he never threw his cigarette butt down on the floor but hunted an ash tray. And while his vocabulary could be as profane as any other, he was never able to achieve the satisfactory ungrammatical profanity that came so naturally to the lips of others.

Because of his smallness and mildness, his neatness and his almost delicate manner, Jim Bob was always given the clerical jobs and those which called for a sense of order. And yet he too, with his shined shoes, his starched white shirt, his clean fingernails, his scrubbed, clear skin, and gentle manner, dreamed of roaring motors and screeching tires and of being master mechanic and daring driver rolled into one.

Woody and the club's fifteen-year-old second vice president, Sonny Mack, listened attentively while Jim Bob made his report. Dick Slater took a small mirror from his pocket and examined his long, bony face, in which his narrow, foxlike gray eyes seemed cramped for space between his high cheekbones and his eyebrows. A few months past, no less than eight downy blond hairs had sprouted at scattered points around and under his jaw. Immediately, he decided to grow a beard and waited for it to develop into a fierce, Viking-like growth. But so far, his chin, like the minutes of the previous meeting, and the minutes of all the meetings previous to the previous meeting, showed no perceptible change.

The minutes were approved as read. "I now turn the pit stop over to Sonny Mack," Woody said. "It's his turn to lead the technical discussion."

Sonny Mack stood up, holding a recent issue of an automotive magazine in his hand. Sonny was a chunky boy who was cheerful to the point of being jittery. He cleared his throat nervously but looked around with a confident grin. "Tonight, I'm gonna talk about the most important accessory a guy can have in his car . . ." Sonny's voice, a shrill blast at normal levels, rose to a piercing shriek as he delivered his punch line, ". . . girls!"

Woody tapped sternly for order. "Cut the clowning, Sonny."

Sonny rolled his bright blue eyes. "Who's clowning?"

"Name me something better."

He cleared his throat again, tried to look serious, and continued. "Tonight, I am going to report on the four-barrel carburetor." He bent his head until the tip of his nose almost touched the pages and began to read the opening paragraph in an uncertain voice.

"Wait a minute!" Dick interrupted. "Are you going to stand there and read the whole thing?"

"Sure," Sonny said, pointing his round, blue eyes at Dick. "That's what I'm supposed to do."

"I object," Dick said, turning to Woody. "We've all read that article by ourselves. What's the good of having Sonny take up an hour of our time trying to read it to us?"

"What do you mean, *trying*?" Sonny demanded.

"Just what I said. You can't even pronounce half the words in that article."

"Name one . . . just one."

"All right," Dick said, "how do you pronounce v-e-n-t-u-r-i?"

Sonny wrinkled his nose and scratched at his red-orange hair. "*Ventery*," he said.

"Ven*turi*," Dick said scornfully.

"Oh, *ven-tur-i*," Sonny cried. "I know *that*."

"That's not what you said."

"I mean I know what it is, and I know it when I see it on a carburetor," Sonny said brightly. "I just didn't recognize it as a *word*. But I know it . . . I know it . . . ven-tur-i. It's a hole . . . or a couple of holes . . . depending on the carb."

"You see what I mean?" Dick asked, turning to Woody. "Besides, why fool around with reports when we've got some real business on hand? I thought this was the night we braced your old man for your car."

"We'll do it," Woody said. "But let's have our regular meeting first. This is stuff we have to know about, especially if we get a car to work on."

"Aw, nuts," Dick said. "Let's go see your old man right now."

"What's your hurry?" Woody asked.

"What are you stalling for?" Dick countered. "You afraid to ask?"

"Why should I be afraid of my own father?"

"I don't know. He's *your* father."

"I'm not afraid of him," Woody said. "I don't have to be."

"All right, so let's go. Now."

Woody looked at Jim Bob and Sonny. They were watching him with hope in their eyes.

"We'll back you up all we can," Jim Bob said.

Sonny nodded. "You bet we will."

Still, Woody hesitated. He wasn't afraid of his father, but he was reluctant to approach him. Somehow, all his arguments seemed so weak when they were said aloud to his father's knowing face. And all the time, there would be that unspoken question in his father's eyes—the question that had been in them since junior high days.

"I don't know about you guys," Dick said, "but I'm fed up with hiding down here and playing cars the way little kids play house. If we can't have a car club as good as the other guys have, what's the point?"

Woody knew the next move was up to him. He had started the club when he and Dick were fifteen and the two younger boys fourteen. And when he was fifteen, it was a wonderful thing to have a car club, without asking for more. It made all their lives more interesting and exciting just to get together in his basement and talk about cars, study, dream, and make all kinds of plans for the future.

But now he was sixteen, and the future had arrived. Now he had a license and could drive and *could* have his own car. Now it was not enough to talk and dream the way they used to. Now, in order to feel equal to other boys their age, they needed a car, too.

And Woody was their only hope. Jim Bob and Sonny were too young to have cars, and Dick . . . when Dick had reached sixteen, he had been allowed to use the family car. Running true to form, he had been contemptuous of another's property and had wrecked the car driving carelessly on icy streets. Since that time, Dick had been denied use of his family's car and wouldn't be allowed to drive it again until he was eighteen. Woody was their only hope, and they couldn't wait any longer.

Woody sat frowning at the truck piston before him on the table, tapping it nervously with the intake valve. He thought of the fun the club could have rebuilding a car, of the date he had missed because he didn't have a car, and of the extra money he could earn at the dairy if he had a car of his own. He thought of the dozens of other boys who drove to school, belonged to car clubs, and who had rebuilt old cars into admired customs. Boys no better, no wiser, no worthier than himself.

He thought about what it was like to be on foot walking to school; not only passed up by dozens of boys who drove but ignored by them as they roared past. He remembered the hundreds of times he had waited to cross the street to school and, although pedestrians were supposed to have the right of way, the many cars that had swept arrogantly around the corner and forced him back to the sidewalk. To be on foot was to be a helpless swimmer in shark-infested waters. There was only one way to be safe, and equal, and *somebody*—and that was to have a car.

Again, he thought of the date he had missed, and of Sandra walking down the steps, away from him, because he had to be chauffeured by his father, like a junior high kid.

"All right, you guys," Woody said. "I've got all the facts and figures. I'm counting on you to back me up. Let's go see my dad."

CHAPTER 3

WHEN MR. AHERN HEARD WOODY and the boys coming up the basement steps, he automatically reached into his pocket for his car keys. The last item of club business was for Woody to drive the others home. The arrangement Woody had was that he was allowed to use the family car for approved purposes and definite missions but was not permitted to take it merely to drive around. Driving the boys home after a meeting was an approved purpose.

"Well," Ahern asked as Woody entered the living room, "how did the meeting go?" He held out the car keys without looking up from his paper.

"Not very good, Dad," Woody said. Instead of taking the keys, Woody sat in a chair near his father, and leaned forward. The other boys stood in the doorway, waiting.

"That's the way meetings go sometimes," Ahern said.

"The fact is," Woody said despondently, "it looks like the club is dead."

Ahern put down his newspaper and looked at the four unhappy faces that were turned toward him. "What happened? Did you fellows have a quarrel?"

"No," Woody said with a sigh, "but when guys get to be our age, we look pretty silly trying to have a car club without a car. Especially when other guys our age have cars. Now if I . . ."

"Maybe other guys have richer parents than you do," Ahern said. "Or better jobs."

"But they don't," Woody said. "I know people who are a lot poorer than we are whose kids have cars."

"Unfortunately, the fact still remains, Woody, that you can't afford a car, and I can't afford to buy you one."

"But I *can* afford one," Woody said. "I've got one hundred and ten dollars saved up already, and my job pays me seven dollars a week. And just this very afternoon, Dad, Mr. Stonelee said he wished I had a car of my own so I could make the extra deliveries he has to make all the time. Didn't he, Dick?"

"He sure did," Dick said. "He said he'd be glad to pay for the use of your car as well as your time. I heard him say it, Mr. Ahern."

"You see, Dad?" Woody said anxiously. "A car would help me out on my job, too. And in the summer I could earn a lot more if I had a car. The dairy really gets busy in the summer. So, the car would be like an investment in getting a better job."

"I appreciate that, Woody," Ahern said. "But you still can't afford a car. Do you know how much a reasonably good used car would cost?"

"You don't get the picture yet, Dad," Woody said earnestly, sensing a possible chink in his father's armor. "We don't want a *good* used car. I mean, Dad, we don't want a car just to rat around in. We're all real serious about cars. We want to buy an old car that we can fix up by ourselves, like the other car clubs at school have done. That's the whole idea of our club—to build up our own car. And I'm the only one in the club who can get a car now. Jim Bob and Sonny are too young for a while, and Dick has to wait."

Ahern looked from one hopeful face to the other. "I don't know, Woody. There's more to fixing up an old car than you realize."

"We know how much work it would take, Mr. Ahern," Jim Bob said. "We know other boys who have done the same thing."

"And we know just as much about cars as they do," Sonny added. "Maybe more."

"The reason we want to get an old car," Woody continued, leaving his chair to stand directly in front of his father, "is because old cars are easier to work on, parts are cheap, and you don't need many tools. Dad, we've been studying factory manuals that tell you how to do everything step by step, all illustrated with drawings and photographs. With an old car, if you can read and use a wrench, you're in business."

"Guys at school do it all the time, Mr. Ahern," Dick said solemnly.

"And it would be wonderful experience for anybody who might want to study engineering," Woody said, not exactly pointing at himself with his words, but not exactly pointing away from himself, either. He just knew how much his father wanted him to attend college. "All we want," Woody pleaded, wriggling like a nervous dog in his anxiety, "is an old car that doesn't cost very much. Just something to work and *learn* on."

"We know guys at school who've found real good old cars for twenty or thirty bucks," Sonny said. "Sleepers that the square Johns walked right past. They find them all the time, the guys at school."

"We'd take an old car like that," Woody said, "and we'd go to work on it. We'd tune it, make sure the running gear was in top shape, and then go to work on the body. We know how to adjust clutches, set brakes, smooth out dents, fill holes, paint and . . . *everything.*"

"A few bucks and a little work," Dick said, "and we'd have practically a new car."

"You see, we're all specialists," Woody said, almost sitting on his father's lap. The other three boys came in close, their natural shyness around other parents overcome by their desires. "Sonny is a carburetion specialist. Jim Bob knows all about the electrical system. Dick is our transmission man. I kind of troubleshoot all over the car."

"What I can't understand," Ahern said wryly, "is why, with all this talent, you've never shown any interest in fixing up *my* car. Or even washing it, for that matter."

"We're not interested in modern cars," Woody said. "We're only interested in old cars. We know our limitations, Dad. We're not dummies."

"I realize," Ahern said, "that all this sounds easy, but . . ."

"It *is* easy, Dad," Woody said. "Gee whiz, all we want is a chance to do the same thing that dozens of other kids at school have done. We're no worse or no dumber than they are."

"Heck no," Sonny said. "Joe Brisbee fixed up a beaut of a car all by himself, and he's so dumb he's going to flunk out of school."

"That's another thing," Ahern said. "The amount a car would interfere with your schoolwork. That has to be taken into account."

"We'll be very careful about that," Woody promised, giving Sonny an angry look. "We'll just budget our time, and not try to do everything at once. Dad, I'll study twice as hard if I can have a car."

"That's good news," Ahern stood up. "But before we go any further, I want to show you some figures about the cost of a car." Ahern went to a small desk in the corner of the living room. The four boys followed close on his heels, as though afraid he would disappear if he got a yard away.

"It would be a lot nicer for the whole family if I had a car," Woody said, his dark eyes burning with noble thoughts. "We wouldn't have to wait until you got home with your car to go shopping. I could run all kinds of errands for Mom any time of the day. I could even take her shopping. Not only that, Dad. If I had a car, I could take Cheryl to all the places she has to go, so you and Mom wouldn't have to be bothered with the extra driving. I . . ."

"I hear every word you're saying, Woody," Ahern warned as he took paper and a pencil from a desk drawer. "Be careful."

"I mean it, Dad. I mean it. It would make things a *lot* easier for the family if I had a car. I'm around when you're gone, Dad, and I could help in a lot of ways if I had my car."

Woody's father returned to his chair. "All right, boys," he said. "How much for an old car?"

"Twenty-five dollars," Sonny said. "At the most."

"If we're lucky," Woody said. "But let's suppose the worst. Let's say we can't get a good car for less than . . . fifty dollars. If it's more than that, it's too much for us."

Ahern wrote down that figure. "Now," he said, "how about insurance?"

"I've thought about that, Dad," Woody said. "I've got it all figured out." He enjoyed the expression of surprise on his father's face.

"When I got my license," Woody said, "your insurance went up one hundred dollars. Right?"

"Right. That's what it costs me extra for having a teenage boy in the house with a license."

"And you're paying that extra hundred," Woody said, "yourself."

"That's right. It's on my car, and I figure it's one of the extra costs that comes along as your children grow. Although, Woody, I won't have that cost with Cheryl. The rate only goes up for teenage boys. And it stays up until they're twenty-five."

"How about that," Dick said.

"Now if I get a car," Woody said, "you can put that hundred on my car instead of yours. Right?"

"Right. But there's more."

"I know," Woody said. "I found out it would cost me one hundred and sixty-eight dollars to insure a car of my own."

"A fifty-dollar car," Ahern said, shaking his head.

"Now," Woody continued. "If you pay the hundred you pay anyway, that leaves sixty-eight dollars a year extra. Now . . . add the license to that, and it comes out eighty dollars a year I have to pay. Now, if you will pay that . . ."

"Wait a minute, Woody!"

"I mean advance it, Dad. If you advance me that much, I can pay you back out of my salary. A dollar and fifty-five cents a week is all it will take. And that leaves me five dollars and forty-five cents a week left over from my job pay to buy gas and oil and extras. I've figured out that I can get by for two dollars a week for gas and oil and do all the driving I have to do. That leaves me three dollars and forty-five cents a week free and clear. I put a dollar a week in savings and spend two dollars and forty-five for things I need. And I still haven't touched the sixty dollars in savings left over after I've bought the car!"

"Boys," Ahern said, "I understand how you feel, and I'm in sympathy with your interests. But I don't think you've been very realistic about your plans."

Woody groaned. "Oh, Dad . . . we've thought it all out."

"Have you? You've thought out an ancient car for fifty dollars that will run like a new car after a wash and a dry. What's realistic about that?"

"We said we were going to do the mechanical work it needed. We said all that. We don't expect a miracle."

"You bet, Mr. Ahern," Sonny Mack said. "A car for our club is the thing we need. Us boys will work day and night to make it as good and safe as any car on the road. That's what we ache to do, Mr. Ahern, to work and work and *work* on a car."

"That's fine," Ahern said. "But what if this old car has something wrong that you can't fix? You know what an hour's labor in a garage costs, don't you? What about that?"

"What about what?" Woody yelled. "What's to go wrong that we can't fix? What's to go wrong?" In Woody's mind the car had already been bought, driven into his garage, and put in running shape. Whatever he looked at in this car of his mind was old, to be sure, but still running—or needing a touch here and a touch there. The car was as real to him as the shoes he stood in, and here was his father thinking up insults about it.

"I ask you, Dad," Woody said, trying to be calm and reasonable, "to name just one thing . . . just one thing that's going to go sour on our car and that we can't fix ourselves. One thing . . ."

"It could be anything, Woody. You know that. But even if you find a good car for fifty dollars, and only spend two dollars a week on running expenses, you have to allow some money for parts and supplies. Even if you do all your own work."

"We *know* that, Dad," Woody said, almost insultingly polite. "But we don't walk into a retail store and buy new parts. We go out to the salvage yards and find what we need there."

"What the salvage yards do, Mr. Ahern," Jim Bob put in softly, "is to let you prowl through the wrecked and junked cars to find the parts you need. If you know how to look, you can buy a good coil for fifty cents, or a radiator for a couple of dollars."

"You can even get a used transmission for ten dollars plus your old one," Woody said. "Maybe less, if you take it off the car yourself."

"And we can do that," Dick said, remembering he had been introduced as a transmission specialist. "We yank a trans off a junker, take off the side plate, and check the gears. If there aren't any broken teeth, and the gears move the way they should, we've got a buy. We save fifty or sixty bucks."

"Guys at school," Sonny Mack said, "they do it all the time."

"And we're no worse than they are," Woody added. "It's like I said, Dad, I don't want to buy a car just to rat around in and waste money. We've been studying cars for a long time, and now we need some practical experience. We're serious. It doesn't even matter to us if the car runs or not, or how long we have to work to get it running. The important thing is the work and the learning."

The other members of the Road Rockets nodded solemnly.

"If the car doesn't run," Woody continued, "we wouldn't have to insure it, and there wouldn't be any running expenses. We'd just take our time, and work, and shop around for bargains when we need parts, and get a lot of practical knowledge. I know I can afford that kind of a car. And the club is dead if we don't get one."

Ahern looked at their serious, hungry faces. It was true that other boys bought and built up old cars, and it was possible that these boys were just as interested and just as capable as some of the others. "Have you seen any good old cars for sale for fifty dollars or less?" he asked Woody.

"We've seen the cars that other guys have bought," Woody said. "We didn't look for our own club. There didn't seem to be any reason." Suddenly Woody had an inspiration. A great, sunny smile spread over his face. "I've got an idea, Dad. Why don't you put your shoes on and take the club on a tour of used car lots? Let's just see what they've got to offer. I promise not to put any pressure on you to buy *anything*. All we'll do is look around and get a rough idea of what's available and for how much. So we'll know, just in case things ever . . . work out."

Ahern felt himself weaken as he looked at the hopeful, trusting faces of the boys around him: Woody burning with eagerness, Dick with his face set for disappointment, Jim Bob young and wistful as a family pup, Sonny glowing an excited orange-pink and clutching nervously at his ear.

Yes, they were as good as any other boys. Certainly they deserved whatever other boys had that they hadn't—even unto hazard, discouragement, toil, dreams dreamed and dreams broken, plans made and plans smashed.

He didn't think Woody needed a car and could cite facts and figures to prove it—from an adult point of view. But from the boys' point of view, perhaps they did need one. Perhaps, Ahern thought as he studied Woody's expression of longing and need, they did know what they were doing, and what was necessary to them. Each generation had to be judged by its own standards, as well as by those of the past. And who was to say, because the standards and interests were different, that they were worse?

Ahern remembered his own boyhood, how in those years when people wanted to portray a shiftless, worthless teenage boy in the movies or a story, they pictured him carrying a baseball glove and devoted to sports. Now the baseball glove was the badge of the good boy, and the no-good kid of the present was the one who wore motorcycle boots and gave his time to hot rods. And tomorrow? Would tomorrow's adults be raising money to attract boys to community car clubs and buying them boots and leather jackets while there was some new kind of teenage villain for them to deplore?

"We wouldn't have to be gone very long, Dad," Woody coaxed. "An hour would do it. I just thought," he added wistfully, "that it would be a real nice father-son activity."

Woody's father grinned at that, but he also reached for his shoes.

— — —

Woody's father pulled the black family sedan in toward the curb and parked in front of WHEELER THE DEALER'S PRE-TESTED MOTOR SALES. By *pretested*, Wheeler the Dealer meant *used*.

The boys were out of the car before it had come to a complete stop and, slamming the doors in Ahern's face, dashed on to the used car lot. They ran past the newer models parked in the front row without a glance and made for the back of the lot where a line of old cars were huddled in the semidarkness.

"So, this is a father and son activity," Ahern said. "I'll toss you to see who gets to be the son." He spoke to a gruesome replica of a South American Indian shrunken head that hung by a cord from the rear-vision mirror. The head was a birthday present from Woody, given in the hope of providing the family car with a touch of "class." Ahern didn't have the heart to refuse it hanging space. It didn't make him self-conscious to have it there. Day in and day out he saw other men and women, some of them with white hair, driving cars in which the rear-vision mirrors served as gibbets for baby shoes, miniature boxing gloves, giant dice of all colors, a variety of dolls and toys, skulls, and various unidentified swaying objects made of fur or feathers. Compared to some of these other ornaments, the shrunken head wasn't too bad.

Ahern saw a man come out of the sales office and size up the boys. He thought it might be a good idea to let the man know the boys were with an adult, so he got out of the car and approached him. "The boys are with me," Ahern said. "They won't bother anything."

"They looking for anything special?" The salesman was a stout man in his forties who wore a tan, broad-brimmed Western hat, a brown suit, a pale green sports shirt, and a dark green string tie.

"Yes," Ahern said. "A miracle. They're ready to pay twenty-five dollars cash for anything in that back row that's better than a new car."

"They're welcome to look," the salesman said, hunting in his pocket for a card. He found one and handed it to Ahern. "I'm Sid Wheeler, cousin to the fellow who owns this place. How about fixing you up with a good car? Give you a real deal on the one you're driving. Surprise the little woman with that nice red convertible over there, or that baby blue hardtop."

"She's the one who picked out the black sedan," Ahern said, smiling and shaking his head.

"Buy that car new?" the salesman asked, trying to get a line on Ahern from his answers.

"Two years ago. And it's almost paid for."

"No trouble about getting that taken care of. Two years is a long time. She'll like a change. Why don't you take that red convertible for a little spin while you're waiting for the boys? Or that hardtop."

"I'm just chauffeuring the boys tonight," Ahern said. "That's all."

He said it quietly, but Sid Wheeler knew he meant it. "You've got my card there," Sid said, "in case you ever change your mind." He seemed to relax now that he wasn't trying to sell Ahern a car and made no move to leave. "Those all your boys?" he asked.

"Just one," Ahern said.

"The tall blond boy?"

"No, the shorter, chunky one. The one trying to get the hood of that car open."

Ahern was close to six feet tall, slender, and almost completely bald. What little hair he had left looked light in color. Sid guessed him to be in his late thirties. "I guess I picked the blond because he's tall," Sid said, pushing his big hat toward the back of his head.

"You work around here?"

"I coach and teach over at Central Junior High. I'm Darrell Ahern."

"How do you like coaching in junior high?" Sid asked.

"They're good kids at that age," Ahern said. "Full of spirit."

"Your boy an athlete too?"

Ahern shook his head regretfully.

"That's the way they are," Sid chuckled. "If you owned this car lot, he'd be a football nut. It never fails. I know a guy that runs a pool. It's full of kids all summer. The only kid that never uses it is his own. That kid spends all his time playing golf."

"It's easy to understand," Ahern said. "They want to be themselves, not carbon copies of their parents."

"My kid's a man now," Sid said. "And you know something? He was the same way, and I thought he didn't want to be like me. But that wasn't the case at all. He wanted to be like me, but he wanted to be like me while he was doing something different from what I was doing. Get me?"

"I do indeed," Ahern said. "I never thought of it quite that way before."

Sid was pleased. "Well," he said, "the used car business being what it is, I have a lot of time to think about things. Especially when it comes to kids."

"I suppose you do see a lot of boys here," Ahern said.

"I see them all," Sid replied with a sigh. "Every day. They come just like your boy and his friends. They look at everything, want everything, and can't buy anything. They've got to look at every car and touch every car and ask a million questions about every car. Sometimes I get so fed up with the parade I want to keep out everybody under twenty-one years of age."

"I can see where it would get on your nerves."

"A boy like yours I don't mind having around," Sid said. "He's a nuisance today and a customer tomorrow. But he's no trouble. And those younger kids don't cause trouble. But you take that tall boy, the one I thought was yours . . ."

"Dick?"

"I don't know anything about him. Only what I see by looking. He's the trouble kind. Notice he's been easing toward the new cars, and looking over this way a lot? That's a bad sign."

"Dick's a good boy," Ahern said. "I've known him almost all his life."

"I don't say he's a bad boy. But he doesn't have his head stuck under the hood like your boy, and he's not in love with the cars like those two little boys. Look at how he moves around by himself. He doesn't have that interested look or that wanting look. He's just along. I bet when that kid goes I've got another busted knob, or cut upholstery, or I'm missing something."

"That's pretty harsh talk about a boy you don't know," Ahern said.

"I could be wrong," Sid said, the cigar protruding from the corner of his mouth. "But I'm here every day and every night. I see these kids by the millions, it seems like. I get a feeling just by the way they look at the cars and move around them."

"I think you're wrong about Dick," Ahern said firmly.

"I hope so. Look . . . your boy is sure stuck on that junker over there. He's telling the others all about it. I can tell by the way he waves his hands what he's talking about . . . all the things he'll do to change it. You can read their hands like it was a real sign language."

"The boys have a club," Ahern said. "They want to buy an old car and fix it up. They meet every week, study up on cars, and have convinced themselves they can restore an old car to perfect condition."

"A lot of them do it," Sid said, the salesman in him responding to a slight lead. "Maybe your boy can, too. You really planning to buy him a car?"

"If I let him have one, he'll buy it with his own money. But I don't know. I don't know if I should."

Sid pulled his hat down over his eyes. "You ever buy your boy anything like an electric train when he was younger?"

Ahern nodded. "Don't think any father misses that. He was seven years old."

"How much did it cost you?"

"I got a buy on a good train set. Forty dollars for the works."

"All right. If you spent forty dollars on him when he was seven, it won't kill you to spend another forty on him now. Particularly if it's his own forty. Look at it this way, Mr. Ahern. Your boy doesn't want a car, he wants a big toy. If he wanted a car, he wouldn't be looking in that back row. Believe me, sir, there isn't anything that will keep a car-crazy boy off the streets better than an old car in his garage. Instead of ratting around at night with some older kid who has a car, he'll be home, working on his own little pride and joy. I don't think it makes any difference to kids like yours if their cars ever run or not. What they want is a real car to work on, with real gears, and real transmissions, and real engines. That way, they can tell themselves they're working and not playing. And maybe they are. Maybe he'll learn more from an old car that won't run than you can ever guess. One thing, he'll find out whether he likes to work on cars or just thinks he likes to work on cars. Think of it like an electric train, or an erector set, or some big toy like that. Let him have it."

"That's a very persuasive sales talk," Ahern said.

"I'm not trying to sell your boy a car," Sid Wheeler said. "We've got ten or twelve forty-dollar cars in that back row. Only, we've got to get a hundred for them. But if your boy looks around, he'll find some private party that has an old car who'll be glad to get thirty or forty bucks for it. Maybe less. When he finds one, let him drag it home and tear it apart. When he's done, if it won't run—and it probably won't—you can have it towed away for a couple of bucks. Call me, and I'll tow it away for nothing. Your boy will have had his fun, learned something, and stayed off the streets. Maybe he'll get cars out of his system and be ready to listen to your idea of what he might do in life. That's a lot to buy for forty dollars, Mr. Ahern. And it can be done." Sid chuckled hoarsely. "The worst that can happen is that the boys know what they're doing and make it run."

"Yes," Woody's father said, laughing to himself as he remembered the recent session in the living room with Woody and the boys. "The school is full of guys who do it all the time."

Ahern looked at his watch, shivered, and zipped up his jacket. "I'd better pick up my boys and go home. Looks as if you've got some customers." He nodded toward a car that had just driven onto the lot. It was an old maroon car filled with boys who poked their heads out of the windows and looked around curiously, like chickens peeking out of a crate.

"I can starve to death with customers like them," Sid grunted. "That kind do all their serious shopping at the Midnight Auto Supply."

"Where?" Ahern looked at Sid curiously.

"You know . . ." Sid hunched over, looked furtively over his shoulder, and pretended to snatch the hub cap from the car he had been leaning against.

Ahern looked troubled and gazed across the lot to where Woody was crawling all over an old coupe. "Wonder if Woody . . . he's always been an honest boy, of course . . . but I wonder . . ."

"I wouldn't worry about your boy," Wheeler said. "If he's been honest, he'll probably stay honest. But having a car does funny things to the way they feel. I mean, trust your boy as you always have, but keep an eye out for too many bargains. A twenty-dollar set of spinner hubs for two or three bucks is hard to pass by, Mr. Ahern, even for an honest kid."

Ahern turned up the collar of his jacket. "*If* I let him have a car, I'll watch out. But to have to think of Woody like that . . . it leaves a bad taste in my mouth. It makes me ashamed."

"I didn't mean to turn you against your boy," Sid Wheeler said, touching his green cowboy tie to see if it was straight. "If he's always been an honest boy, there's no reason he should change now. Boys are no different from the rest of us. I get grown men in here every day who try to cheat me in a trade." Sid's round face looked like a dark, smiling melon. "Of course, I'm happy to say that very, very few of them succeed." He winked at Ahern.

"I do trust my son," Ahern said. "There's no question about that. But what you said gave me something to think about. I wonder if it's fair to place a young boy in a position where he's subjected to extreme pressures and temptations and then expect him to be a saint."

Wheeler shrugged his heavy shoulders. "We've all got to learn how to live without getting everything we want."

"Well, I'll think it over," Ahern said, starting away. "Thanks for letting the boys look at the cars."

"Come back any time," Sid called after him. "Tell your boy he's welcome here too. And whenever you get around to a better car for yourself, give old Sid a chance to wheel and deal. I'll treat you right."

Sid erased Ahern from his mind as a shabby brown car halted in front of his lot. He bided his time as a young man in work clothes got out of the car and walked slowly toward the front row of cars, followed by a young woman wearing a scarf over her head and carrying a baby in a blanket. Sid waited while they looked all the cars over once. The moment they picked one for a second look he hurried forward with a smile as wide as the brim of his hat.

"Evening, folks," Sid greeted them heartily, sizing up the couple and their old car in one practiced glance. "Take a good look at that red convertible. You won't find another one like it in town. I'd swear in court to the miles on the odometer."

The mileage on the odometer was correct. But what Sid knew and failed to mention was that most of it had been put on flat out with the car in first and second gear. The previous owner had taken beautiful care of the car's finish, but he had also run his car regularly on every drag strip within a hundred miles.

# CHAPTER 4

AHERN THREADED HIS WAY BETWEEN THE ROWS of used cars until he reached Woody and the boys. They were clustered around an ancient Chevrolet coupe that was being offered for a hundred dollars.

"It's getting late, Woody," Ahern said. "Time we moved along and got everybody home."

"We've found a real good car, Dad," Woody said, gazing hopefully at his father's face. "Want to look it over? They're asking a hundred, but I'll bet we could get it for ninety."

"I'm sure we could," Ahern said with a brief glance at the junker. "But we won't."

"Take a good look, Dad," Woody urged. "The body isn't rusted out, there's tread on the tires, and the motor looks tight. If we made an offer tonight . . ."

"Remember your promise, Woody. No buy-me pressure."

"I know, Dad. But when I promised I didn't know we were going to run across a buy like this. It's a real bargain, Dad."

"What about your fifty-dollar limit?"

"I didn't know about this car, Dad."

"Or the one we saw at the last lot, and the one before that, eh? We've been to three lots, and you've found the perfect car on each one, and each one was priced at a hundred dollars."

"Let's face it, Dad," Woody said. "You're not going to get a good car for less than a hundred." Woody kicked at the front tire. "I should have known it would be like this," he complained. "You'll find something wrong with every car I want. That's how you'll keep me from getting one without saying no."

"Come on, Woody," Ahern said calmly. "Now you're talking like a spoiled brat."

"I'm sorry," Woody grumbled. "But if you only knew . . ."

"I know," Ahern said, "but this isn't the time or place to argue about it." He turned and walked toward the car. Woody and the boys followed, looking back at every step. Ahern drove each of the boys home, then headed back toward his own house. Woody sulked on the seat beside him.

"Want to drive?" Ahern asked, hoping that would lift Woody's spirits.

"No, thank you," Woody replied. "That car was worth a hundred dollars!" he burst out.

"You're sure of that?"

"I wouldn't say it if I wasn't sure."

"I was talking to the salesman," Ahern said. "He told me there wasn't a car in that back row worth more than thirty dollars."

"I know what I know," Woody said stiffly. "It was worth a hundred dollars."

Ahern grinned as he looked at Woody in the light cast by the instrument panel. "Woody, a famous old American humorist once said, 'It ain't what you don't know that hurts you. It's what you know that ain't so.'"

Ahern stopped his car for a red light. Another car pulled up even with them on Woody's side. It was a mud-caked car with a cracked left front window and a raked front end. The driver gunned his motor again and again, just to hear his glass packs roar, and looked over at Woody with a bold challenge in his eyes.

Woody leaned forward as the light turned to green. The car alongside took off with a great roaring and smoking but not too much snap. Woody was sure the family sedan could out-drag it without trouble. A low gear start, a shift to drive range, and back into low, to hold second gear. Even a slush pump could be hot if you knew how to use it. At the moment of the start, Woody looked hopefully at his father, but his father seemed deaf to the arrogant challenge.

"It's bad enough to fool others," Ahern continued as Woody sank back disappointed, "but it's tragic when you fool yourself. That's what you're doing. That car we saw isn't worth a hundred dollars. You aren't fooling anyone but yourself. The point is, you want a car so bad that you're willing to kid yourself about its worth just so you can get your hands on it right now."

"I'm not kidding myself," Woody said. "I know that to you, or anybody with your ideas, there's only thirty dollars' worth of machinery in that car. But it's worth seventy dollars to me and the club. That's what I meant when I said it was worth a hundred dollars to me. It's a car that's worth building up, and that makes it worth a hundred. I saw other hundred-dollar cars I wouldn't touch. And the way it is, if the club's going to have a car to work on, we either pay a hundred bucks or we get nothing."

"Maybe not," Ahern said. "The salesman told me your best bet was to find a private owner and deal with him. He said *you* could buy a car for forty dollars that he'd have to sell for a hundred to make any money."

"Where am I going to find a private owner?" Woody asked mournfully.

"Advertise. You can put a notice on the school bulletin board, can't you? And watch the classified ads in the paper."

Woody thought over his father's words. "Does that mean I can buy a car?"

"I don't know, Woody. It's a big decision to make. Not only the expense . . ."

"I mean a forty-dollar car, or even a cheaper one? If I hold out for that?"

"You won't get much for that kind of money. You realize that."

"We don't want much," Woody said. "What we want is something old enough that we're not afraid to tear apart and put together again. The fun is getting a car that won't run and putting it in shape."

"I'll tell you, Woody," Ahern said, turning in at his driveway. "If you can find a car for forty dollars or less, I'll let you buy it for a club project. But that's the limit."

"Oh, boy," Woody breathed as they drove into the garage. "Wait until I tell the guys! Dad," he said in a serious voice, holding out his hand, "it's a deal. A forty-dollar top. And I'll really shop around now that it's for real. I might even find one for thirty, or twenty. All we want is something to work on. Wait until I tell the guys . . . Wait until I tell Mom!"

"That's another thing, Woody," Ahern said as they got out of the car and Woody hurried to close the garage door. "You'd better let me tell Mom. We need her okay on this deal too, you know."

"Why?" Woody demanded. "You're the boss of the family, aren't you? You're the one who makes the living. The next thing you know, we'll have to ask Cheryl's permission."

"You know we always talk over the big decisions," Ahern said. "And this is a big decision." He recognized, in Woody's outburst, a kind of personal tribute, a "Long live the king!" declaration of loyalty and support.

"It sure is," Woody said, breathing deeply. "Boy!" He was overwhelmed by feelings of joy, love, and comradeship. He was a boy who fought selfishly to acquire, but who, once in possession, was quick to share generously.

"Maybe you could work along with us sometimes, Dad," Woody said. "We'd be glad to have you."

"Thanks, Woody. I might just do that. But first we'll have to get past your mother."

Woody darted ahead to open the door for his father, and as Ahern passed they exchanged affectionate, conspiratorial grins. On the way in, Woody walked as close as he could to his father, looking eagerly for some small service to perform for him, some small courtesy that he could show.

Ahern was delighted and touched. For the first time in years, it seemed, Woody was running to and not from him, and they were close without trying to be and without strain. It was, perhaps, the first moment in their lives when they had been two men, with friendship taking precedence over all other ties.

Ahern liked it. It was the kind of moment and the kind of relationship that he had sought with Woody down a hundred dead-end paths and activities. He liked it, but he was troubled and wondered about his motives. He recalled his own words to Woody: "It's bad enough to fool others, but it's tragic to fool yourself." Was he fooling himself? Did he really believe it was right for Woody to have a car, or was he, in his own way, and for his own selfish needs, buying forty dollars' worth of his son's friendship for a hundred dollars?

Whatever the reason, and it would take time to learn the truth, he was on Woody's side and would plead his case.

When Woody and his father walked into the living room, with Woody sticking closer to his father than a shadow, Mrs. Ahern was working on Cheryl's ponytail. Eight-year-old Cheryl sat in a chair where she could watch television and complained.

"Mom," Woody said at once, a tremendous grin spreading across his face, "Dad's got something he wants to discuss with you."

Mrs. Ahern took one look at Woody's grin and Ahern's uneasy expression. "You bought a car," she said.

"Owwww!" Cheryl yelled as her hair was pulled. "When do I get my ride, Woody? Can I have it now? You promised!"

"Bought a *car*?" Woody cried, as though he had never heard of the idea before. "What makes you think we did anything like that? We didn't buy any car, Mom. Dad says I can't buy a car until I get your permission, too."

"Too . . ." Woody's mother said. "In other words, you already have his permission."

"Why . . . uh . . . I *think* so . . ."

"And now you want mine."

"That's right, Mom."

Mrs. Ahern turned toward her husband, who sat on the couch with a resigned look on his face. "Tell me, dear," she said, "what was it you wanted to discuss with me?"

— — —

"Well," Woody's mother said when she was alone with his father, "Woody's done it again."

Cheryl was asleep. Woody was in his room, listening to his radio and reading a car magazine, too excited to close his eyes. Woody's parents sat at the dining room table. Ahern was making out questions for an English test, and his wife was painting a watercolor from a pencil sketch she had made of their house and yard.

"Done what again?" Ahern asked innocently.

"Wrapped you around his little finger."

"No, he hasn't," Ahern said, toying with a pencil. "I thought this car thing out very thoroughly before I gave any permission."

"Woody's always been able to get anything he wanted out of you," Mrs. Ahern said. "I could see this car business coming a mile away." She bent over her painting and examined it with a solemn, uncertain look on her pretty face. She had Woody's wide mouth and direct expression, and her face was framed by a mass of soft, dark brown hair.

"I wouldn't say that," Ahern protested quietly. "Just what have I ever let him have—other than a car—that you would have denied him?"

"The back basement room," Mrs Ahern said promptly. "We agreed to let him use it, but we forgot to have him agree to let *us* use it. He raises an awful fuss every time Cheryl or I go near the place, and I have to do the laundry there. Anyway, I'm against sixteen-year-old boys owning cars."

"So am I," Ahern said. "But they do. And younger boys than Woody. You'd be surprised how many junior high kids have school permits and drive to school. And not old junkers. Some of them drive better cars than mine."

"That's no surprise," Mrs. Ahern said tartly. "The way teachers are paid . . . Even so, that doesn't justify Woody's getting a car. It's hard enough to support one."

"Woody's going to pay all the costs," Ahern said. He smiled a little. "After a while, maybe he'll get tired of pouring all his hard-earned money into a car. But that's something he has to find out for himself. Besides, he's not getting a real automobile. His budget has a forty-dollar limit. The best he can buy for that kind of money is a broken down automobile to use for a big toy."

Mrs. Ahern carefully began painting the rose bush stalks that grew beside the back door. "Where do you and he intend to park this big toy?"

"Why . . . uh . . . the back yard, I suppose." Ahern grinned painfully. "I never thought . . ."

"Obviously. And I can imagine what the back yard will look like. You've seen the way Woody throws his clothes and possessions around his room. Imagine what our back yard will look like when he starts throwing old car parts over his shoulder. And I can see what his clothes will be like . . . and the oil and grease he'll track in . . . You men haven't any heart!"

Ahern pushed his work away. "We can tell him no, Karen. Parents can change their minds. Only, you know what Woody's like. He's been living cars for the past three years. And he wants to spend his life working on them, or driving them, or something."

"I know," Mrs. Ahern said. "I did have higher hopes."

"So did I," Ahern said. "And I'm not losing them. Woody's only sixteen. He'll have a dozen interests before he finds the right one. I thought getting him an old car would keep him from daydreaming about cars all the time. You know, it might ease his tensions and free his mind. And if it does turn out that he's slated to be a mechanic, or a race driver, it *is* his life. Who's to say it's a worse life than sitting at a desk, or . . . teaching school? We've got to give him a chance to find out about himself."

"I agree with you," Karen Ahern said quietly. She frowned at her painting and shook her head.

"You say you agree," Ahern said, looking at her across the table, "but you're angry, aren't you?"

"No. But the picture you've drawn of Woody's future doesn't fill me with joy." There was a tightness, almost like that of tears, in her voice.

"Look at me," Ahern said, passing his hand over his tanned bald head. "When I was a kid, I was wild about sports. My folks raised the devil because I liked to play ball and hated math. They wanted me to be an accountant or a lawyer. Well, I stayed with sports. I was cut out to be a coach. And I happen to like working with the younger kids. They need the help and attention. Is there anything wrong or bad about my life?"

"How can you compare teaching to being car-crazy?" Mrs. Ahern demanded bitterly. "What's Woody going to teach later on? Junior high drag racing?" She dabbed violently at her colors with a wash brush. "Somehow the boys you associate with cars are always loud and hostile and rude on the street and *dirty*."

"I don't think the car boys are any worse than the others," Ahern said. "A car just gives them a chance to expose their adolescence to more people and in tense situations. And as for being dirty—I see the way it is even in junior high. These days a little axle grease smeared on a boy's face is more glamorous than a football scar."

"I don't think Woody's interested in glamour," Mrs. Ahern said, looking more pleased with her painting. "To the best of my knowledge, he's never looked twice at a girl—except in certain magazines."

"Don't underestimate the boy," Ahern said. "He's not bad looking and he's just reached sixteen. It wouldn't surprise me if the real reason for all this car interest turns out to be some little blonde or brunette that Woody hasn't looked at twice—that we know of. He did ask to use my car to go to the Teen Hop on Saturday night."

"Did he have a date?"

"He didn't say. I needed the car, but I offered to take him and pick him up. I guess he decided to go to the movies with his club friends instead. Most of the kids go stag and make connections at the dance. If he didn't go, he can't be very interested in girls yet."

Suddenly Mrs. Ahern laughed. "If Woody goes overboard for a girl the way he's done for a car, I dread the day he looks up from a motor and notices big blue eyes. He'll be absolutely *impossible*. Well, I suppose a sixteen-year-old boy has to have a crush on someone or something—and maybe it's best that it be a car."

Ahern nodded. "Imagine how we'd feel tonight if Woody was after permission to quit school and get married. It happens two or three times a year at the high school. And we have kids who are practically engaged in junior high. Alongside that, Woody's interest in cars seems awfully young and healthy."

"Yes . . . the little Taplinger girl in Woody's class is getting married next week. Had you heard?"

"Of course. The husband and father was my star tackle in junior high three years ago."

"There goes that boy's life," Mrs. Ahern said. "Still, I don't want Woody to marry a car in high school either. If it takes up all his time and attention and he devotes himself to it to the exclusion of everything else, it's like getting married. The others will graduate and go on to better things, and he'll not be fit or qualified for anything but playing with dirty old cars. There goes his life, too!"

"It doesn't have to be like that," Ahern tried to reassure her. "Plenty of boys with cars graduate and go on to college. One of the conditions for Woody having a car ought to be decent grades."

"They couldn't be much worse," Mrs. Ahern said. "He just won't *try*."

"If his car hangs in the balance, maybe he'll try harder."

"Look, Darrell, you don't have to justify getting Woody a car if that's what you want to do. It's not like you."

"I have to justify it to myself," Ahern said. He got up and wandered around the room, his hands thrust in his golf jacket, his face troubled. "I think my being a teacher and a coach has been hard on Woody." He went on, picking his words carefully, as though not quite sure of the thought he wanted to express. "I know other teachers and coaches whose kids have been active in school and in athletics, but Woody couldn't do it. I think he has a very strong sense of self, and that's why he's run from me and everything I stand for. Otherwise, I'm sure he'd have taken part in sports and worked harder at his studies. But I've felt him run from me every time I've come near. And since I'm part of the school system, he's run from that too, in trying to be his own individual self, and not merely Coach Ahern's kid. Now, if he establishes himself as a young mechanic, that's as far from me and my world as he can get, and he can meet me on even terms. In a way, he has a world of his own in which I can visit without stealing his identity."

"Somehow," Mrs. Ahern said, "you've added the wrong numbers to get the right answer."

"What do you mean?" Ahern sat down again and prepared to go back to his work.

"I think the opposite of what you said is true. The trouble with Woody hasn't been wanting to avoid your world. The trouble is, he's always been jealous of your job."

"In what way?"

"You ought to see his face when you come home after a game and talk about 'your' boys doing this, and how 'your' boys did that, and how good 'your' boys are. You not only talk a lot about other boys, but you spend most of your time teaching them to do things, being with them, and thinking about their problems. I know Woody has resented that. I think the reason he wouldn't be on your teams is that he wants to be your own special boy and not just another one of 'your' boys. If Woody has felt hostile toward school and athletics, I think it's because they've stolen you from him, and other children have stolen you from him."

"Maybe that explains it," Ahern said thoughtfully.

"Explains what?"

"The first thing Woody did when I told him he could have a car was to invite me to help him work on it."

"The poor thing," Mrs. Ahern said. "He does want to be your friend."

"And I want to be his."

Mrs. Ahern sighed. "It's hard to know what the right thing is, isn't it? I mean, there are so many things to choose from. I suppose it would be all right to let him buy an old car and let him play at being a mechanic. I just hope he isn't foolish and doesn't go out and get killed in his car."

"He's always been steady and trustworthy with the family car," Ahern said.

"That's *your* car, and he drives it *your* way. It might be different with his own."

"I'll talk to him," Ahern said. "I'll let him know that I won't give him a second chance to play the fool. I think he'll be careful if the price of carelessness is his car. Besides, for his money he won't be able to find a car that runs, and I doubt he'll ever get a forty-dollar car on its feet so it *can* run."

"I hope you're right," Mrs. Ahern sighed.

# CHAPTER 5

WOODY AHERN STOOD IN FRONT of the school bulletin board and read, for the tenth time that day, a notice that was neatly typed on a white card.

**WANT OLD CAR!**
**The Road Rockets Auto Club needs an old car**
**for a club rebuilding project. Prefer car in**
**running condition, but will consider others**
**if no major vital parts are missing.**
**Contact Woody Ahern in 10A-2, or at home.**

Although the notice had been up for a week, and he had read it at least a hundred times, Woody still felt a thrill of pride and satisfaction when he looked at it. It hadn't brought him the results he had hoped for, but it was there in black and white, for the whole world to see.

Woody Ahern was in the market for a car. And that had brought about at least one positive result. Now, instead of his red nylon jacket, he wore his official black Road Rockets jacket, and so did the other members of the club. Nobody laughed at them. After all, they had given public notice they were in the market for a car, and that made a difference. In fact, a few boys had asked about the club in such a way as to indicate they were interested in joining. It was such a good feeling to be in the open as a car club that, although Woody wanted a car, he felt he could almost get along in his present status.

Woody scanned the bulletin board hopefully, looking for a message that answered his. But among all the "losts and founds" and "wanteds" and "for sales," there was nothing for him. In spite of himself he began to worry. It seemed that the moment he was ready to buy an old car, all the old cars disappeared from the face of the earth.

Woody moved aside to let another boy look at the bulletin board. Dan Ilder was a senior Woody knew by sight, and the sight of him filled Woody with envy. He had already accomplished everything Woody dreamed of doing. Dan wore a white jacket with the legendary Newton Racing Team lettered on the back in red. He belonged to a three-man car club that called itself the Three Musketeers. The boys drove cars they had rebuilt into simple but powerful automobiles. There was another reason why Dan aroused Woody's envy. During the summer months, Dan and his two buddies worked as a pit crew for Bart Newton, who raced late model stock cars throughout that part of the country. What more any boy could ask of life, Woody didn't know.

Dan turned to look at Woody, reading his club jacket and noticing the *Woody* sewn on the front.

"Are you the boy who put up that notice?" Dan asked. He was a husky boy with clear skin, light eyes, and a deep, friendly voice.

Woody nodded.

"Have any luck?"

Woody looked rueful. "Lots of guys want to sell, but all guys with a lot of time and money in their cars. I can't meet the prices."

"What kind of car are you looking for?"

"You'll laugh when I tell you," Woody said, suddenly ashamed, and looking down at the toes of his boots. "We're looking for a car we can buy for . . . well, all the money we've got for a car is forty dollars. The rest is for . . . stuff . . . tools . . ." Woody's face felt hot.

"Why should I laugh?" Dan asked. "You've seen my car, haven't you? I bought that for twenty-five bucks. Of course, it didn't look the way it does now. I've got fifteen hundred hours of work in that car and more dollars than hours."

Woody heard about the hours, but his ears refused admittance to the words about the dollars.

"That's a sweet car," Woody said with admiration, but without envy. "I don't expect to build up anything that nice." But in his heart, he really did expect to.

"I could sell it any day in the week for double what I've got in it," Dan said.

Woody looked horrified. "Sell that beautiful car? You *wouldn't!*" A vision of the car rose before Woody. It was a restored 1932 Ford coupe, painted a flawless, mirror-like rich blue, with white Naugahyde upholstery and trim. The little car was powered by a late model blown Chrysler V-8 engine on which almost everything that could be seen was chromed.

How could anyone sell a car like that!

Dan said, "Tell me, what have the guys tried to sell you?"

"Albert Johnson wanted two fifty for his Merc . . ."

"It's worth it. I helped him put it together."

"Bob Jones wanted nine hundred for his Olds."

"Too much—the way he drives it."

"Jerald Harmon wanted four hundred for his Ford."

"He's got over a thousand in it," Dan said. "It would be a terrific buy if you could raise the money."

"Only I don't have it," Woody said. "Anyway, I wouldn't want to buy a car somebody else had already built up. I want the fun of doing that myself. Even if I had the money . . ."

"There's always work to be done," Dan said, a glint of amusement in his eyes. "If I were you, I'd save my money until I could buy a good rebuilt car. Like one of those. You'd miss an awful lot of headaches."

Woody would not yield. To do as Dan said would almost be an admission that he wasn't as good as the others. Pride made him stick with his original plan. He would begin, as they had begun, with an old car. And he would end up with the kind of car *he* wanted, not somebody else's castoff. Although he didn't want to be rude to Dan—and Dan *knew* about cars—it occurred to Woody that if the others' cars were so good, the owners wouldn't be so anxious to sell them. But he didn't say what was in his mind.

"If it was for myself," Woody said diplomatically, "I'd think about waiting and getting a better car. But the guys in the club are real anxious to get an old heap for a project. You know . . . something to learn on."

Dan nodded, but his mind seemed to be on something else. There was an air almost of disappointment about him. "Well," he said philosophically, "that's the picture, you would be better off with a heap. I . . ."

"Say," Woody interrupted, anxious to prolong their talk, "are you going to pit for Bart again this summer?"

"Maybe," Dan said casually. "I'm not sure yet."

"Are you planning to drive your own car . . . ?"

"Me?" Dan looked at Woody's shining face and shook his head genially. "Why, do you want to pit for me?"

Woody felt giddy. "C-Could I, Dan? I mean, be one of your pit crew? Oh . . . gee . . . I want to drive stocks myself someday.

That's my ambition." Woody blurted out the information, then felt childish and ashamed as he saw Dan's level, amused look. What a way to talk to a guy who worked the races and knew all the tracks and drivers!

"No reason why you can't drive someday if you want to," Dan said in a man-to-man tone, restoring Woody's shattered pride. "They need new drivers all the time. Meanwhile, though, I think I've got a lead for you. That's what I wanted to see you about."

"You . . . *wanted* to see me?"

"Yeah. If you want an old heap, that is. I've got a buddy who's out of school and started building up a '47 Ford two door. Well, he's enlisted in the navy, and he wants to sell. I don't know the exact amount he'll take, but it ought to be around forty. It's not much of a car right now . . ."

"I don't want much of a car," Woody said fervently, spurred on by the immediate availability of the '47 Ford. "Like I said, I want the fun of building it up."

Dan grinned. "You ought to get your money's worth out of this one, then. It needs building up about as bad as any car I've ever seen. I'm not sure, but I think it can move a little under its own power."

"That's it!" Woody exclaimed. "That's *it*! And if you think it's okay . . ." By way of a gesture of faith, Woody reached up and pulled his notice off the bulletin board.

"Okay," Dan said. "Meet me after school and I'll run you over to take a look at it. You don't have to buy it, you know, just because I'm taking you. Well, see you later. Say hello to your father for me. Glad I met you."

"Uh . . . I . . . glad I met you, too," Woody stammered. And as he strolled away from the bulletin board, hands in his jacket pockets in imitation of an easy, rolling walk, he strolled on air. He had the feeling that at last he was finding his proper place in the world and that he would no longer be an outsider at school. He would enter, as he had held out for, in his own way, and on his own terms.

It all went back to his first years at school, when the teachers started telling him that they expected neater work, better conduct, higher standards, better grades, more interest, and greater respect from "the son of a teacher in our school system." It sometimes seemed to Woody that they thought they had his father for a pupil, rather than him, and that they expected him to be a cutdown version of his father. He began to show them that he was himself. When Woody reached junior high, he had already established himself as an indifferent student who "could get wonderful grades if he would only try, Mrs. Ahern."

In junior high Woody wanted to go out for sports, and at first, he dreamed of making his junior high letter. But he soon turned his back on sports, too, because of his father. It wasn't that he had anything against his father. But it was bad enough to hear what the other kids had to say about his dad as a teacher; he couldn't stand hearing what they had to say about him as a coach. The worst thing of all was to see some boy who was being critical shushed by an elbow and having a meaningful look cast at him, Woody. He felt that his presence on the squad embarrassed the others and made them feel awkward. He tried to overcome this by being loudly critical of his father, but that only shocked the others as well as embarrassed them, and they shunned him more than ever.

Nor was Woody's life on the field any less miserable. He never knew, when he got to play, if it was because he was good or because his father was the coach. He never knew what the other kids thought about it, and the uncertainty made him nervous and inept. Also, he never knew, when he warmed the bench, whether it was because another boy was better, or because his father was bending over backward to show that he was fair. There was no way, in this situation, for Woody to be one of the team or to know exactly where he belonged. Finally, it was easier to pretend disinterest in sports and to drop out rather than to continue. But he'd never explained why to his father. It was something that couldn't be explained. He'd just faced his father's disappointment with a hanging, sullen face, and said nothing. Someday, when he was a man and his father was old and retired, he'd explain, and things would be close and all right between them, the way they'd been when he was little.

So, he wound up as a boy who didn't, or wouldn't (or couldn't), belong to any of the high school crowds or cliques. He just came to school, sat in his seat, earned his C average, and got along.

Since he wasn't an athlete, a brain, a school politician, or a social leader, he needed something to interest him, and it was natural that he should discover cars. Having an interest in cars and racing and arraying himself in greasy clothes seemed about as far away from being a teacher's kid as he could get. And he got himself there.

At first, he had planned to associate with the boys who built their lives around cars and be one of them. Although he wore boots and denims and studied and talked about cars, these boys did not welcome him either, for he was not, despite his costume, one of them. To them he was a teacher's kid who lived in a teacher's house. Other than cars, they had nothing in common with him, and they were ill at ease when they came to his home and saw his father, their old coach and teacher. And so, he was denied this kind of life and this companionship, too.

He retreated into dreams and plans. He studied, he read a great deal, he went to races and hung around garages, he built little cars. He was, in many ways, mentally ahead of his contemporaries. He understood more and had learned more. But because he had cut himself off from team life and the normal group life in school, he was also, socially, less grown-up and less experienced in everyday group living than were his classmates. He became an odd mixture of wisdom and naivete, a husky boy born for action who lived in dreams and did nothing, a boy who longed for companionship but who closed himself off from friendships that he couldn't establish on his own terms.

Finally, he found kindred souls and organized the Road Rockets. Dick Slater came in because he was so openly contemptuous of the school and everyone in it that no other group wanted him. Jim Bob and Sonny came in because they were both young and car-crazy and belonging to a club with two older boys made it seem like the real thing. And the club, like its members, alternated in great sweeps between book knowledge and practical ignorance, plans and play, mature objectives and childish dreams . . . and none of its members knew for sure which was which.

Well, Woody thought as he walked proudly to class after his talk with Dan, now their car club was going to be as good as—if not better than—any car club in school. And he had done it. He had held out until he could have his own car and be his own self, and now he had accomplished both at once. Now he would emerge as himself, not as his father's son.

Woody went into the classroom and took his seat. For once he didn't confine his attention to his own desk or to the car books he usually had hidden behind the texts. He looked around openly and proudly. He saw Sandra Rowan, looking pensive and pretty, as though deep in some secret thought, and knew she was listening to her radio through a tiny earplug. He looked at her until she met his gaze. He held his eyes steady, to prove that he felt no humiliation because she had turned him down for a date. *She didn't know he might buy a car today*. He was pleased that she was the one who looked away first.

Fifteen minutes later, to the astonishment of the teacher and his classmates, Woody's hand was in the air as he volunteered to answer a question. Once, even knowing the answer, he would have kept silent, not caring. But now it seemed important to show that the president of the Road Rockets Auto Club, present and in uniform, was no dummy.

Woody bounded into the house at noon, his face shining with joy. "Guess what, Dad! I've got a line on a car!"

"Where?" Cheryl cried excitedly, running to the window. "Where's your new car, Woody?"

"I don't have it yet, Sis," Woody said expansively, every inch the kindly big brother as he publicly acknowledged that Cheryl existed. "But when I get it, I'll take you for a little spin."

"Did you hear what Woody *said*?" Cheryl shouted happily at her father and mother, her ponytail whipping about as she bounced up and down with joy. "Woody's going to give me a ride in his new car!"

"Lots of rides, Sis," Woody promised, overflowing with benevolence. His father and mother exchanged unbelieving looks.

Woody sat down at his place and picked up a fork. He put that down, picked up a spoon, put that down, grabbed a knife, looked at it and put it down, picked up a sandwich in his hand, opened his mouth to take a bite, and put down the sandwich. "At last," he said with a manly sigh.

"Tell us about it," his father said.

Woody turned to his mother as she approached the table. "I recited in English today, and I got an A on my recitation. And I got a B in a surprise algebra test. You know, I think my marks are going to be real good on the last report."

"I hope so," his mother said. "There's no reason why you shouldn't get wonderful grades . . . a boy with your brains. Your teachers have told me that for years. All you ever needed was to try, and work a little harder . . ."

But Woody had already turned to his father. "About the car, Dad," he said seriously. "Dan Ilder found it for me."

"I remember him," Ahern said.

"He remembers you too, Dad. You ought to see his car. It's a beautiful blue Deuce with white upholstery and a blown Chrysler mill."

"Don't tell me you're planning to buy *that* car," Mrs. Ahern said, sitting beside Woody. "Even I know you need more than forty dollars for that one. You'd be surprised how much I've learned, picking up your automotive magazines every day, Woody."

"Of course not, Mom. What do you think I am, an idiot?" His tone softened. "Dan saw my notice on the bulletin board, and he knows a guy who's going into the navy and has a car to sell. Dan's taking me over after school to have a look at it."

"Can I go with you, Woody?" Cheryl pleaded, taking advantage of Woody's unexpected friendliness toward her. Out of habit Woody started to give her a hostile answer, but he caught himself in time. "Not this time, Sis. But you'll see it when I bring it home . . . if I buy it. We're going over right after school." Woody sighed and began to eat his lunch, not really knowing, tasting, or caring what he stuffed into his mouth.

"Don't forget your job," Woody's father cautioned.

"I won't, Dad," Woody said with his mouth full. "It will only take a minute to look it over. I'll rely on Dan's opinion. If I like what I see, we can talk business tonight. Well, I'd better be on my way. I want to tell the club members what's in the wind. See you all later." Woody got up with a sandwich in one hand, scooped up some cookies with the other, and strode toward the door. There he stopped and turned around. "Did I tell you I got an A in English recitation this morning?" he asked anxiously.

"Yes, dear," Woody's mother answered. "And a B on your algebra test. We're very proud, and we want you to keep up the good work."

"I probably will," Woody said carelessly. "See you." Then he was gone, and they could hear him running.

Ahern chuckled. "I haven't seen Woody act so bright and cheerful for ages. If just the chance of getting an old car does that, what do you suppose actually having the car will do?"

"I'm afraid to wonder," Mrs. Ahern said, clearing away Woody's dishes. "I know one thing it will mean. With Woody's hungry friends camping here all the time, I'll have to order hot dogs and Cokes in wholesale quantities."

"Hamburgers too, Mama," Cheryl said helpfully. "I heard the boys say they got tired of having hot dogs all the time. And find some old clothes for me. I'm going to help Woody work on his car too. Then, when I'm bigger, and have my own hot rod, I'll know how to fix it by myself."

"Forgive me, forgive me," Ahern said ruefully to his wife. "I didn't know I was starting an avalanche."

# CHAPTER 6

WOODY OPENED HIS LOCKER AT SCHOOL, stuck his head inside, and sniffed. Graffan hadn't brought any more bananas to school since the day Woody had warned him, but it seemed to Woody that he could detect a slight banana odor. He would have risked his red nylon jacket, but he wouldn't take the chance with his club jacket. Besides, he hated to take it off in school, where so many people could see it.

Sandra Rowan was in Woody's first afternoon class three seats ahead and two rows over. When he entered the room, she was already there with her head resting on her books, her brown eyes wide, dreamy, and unseeing.

Woody took his seat and looked at Sandra. She was nice. There was something about her that made him feel as though a huge ball of wax was melting in his stomach. While he watched her, he saw the spellbound look leave her eyes, replaced by a glaze. That meant a commercial was on. The glaze gave way to a focused look, and she saw him. For a moment they merely looked at each other, and then, just as Woody was about to look away in confusion, Sandra smiled at him. It was a small, slight, friendly, shy smile that pierced him like a knife. He smiled back and blushed.

He had to do something. He did the first thing that came into his head. Silently, exaggerating with his lips, he tried to mouth the words, "I'm going to get a car," hoping she would be able to make out the words from the way he moved his mouth. But although she looked, frowning, trying her best to decipher his signal, she couldn't make out the message and gave a helpless little shrug.

"Do you have something stuck to the roof of your mouth, Ahern?" The teacher's voice hit Woody's ears like a bomb. Mr. Manbarg, seated behind his desk, was looking at Woody with a questioning expression.

"Uh . . . no, sir," Woody answered in a low, embarrassed voice, shriveling as every face in the class turned toward him.

"What is the matter? I thought you were having a fit."

"I . . . uh . . . I was practicing the vowel sounds the way you taught us yesterday," Woody said, inventing quickly.

"Oh. Well, I'm sorry I jumped you," Mr. Manbarg said. "Keep on."

"I'm all through now," Woody muttered, sliding down in his seat. When he was no longer the center of attention, Woody hunted up a small piece of paper and, for the first time in years, wrote a note to a girl. "What I was trying to say," he wrote in his cramped handwriting, "is that I am getting a car of my own." He folded the note, awaited his opportunity, and had it passed to Sandra.

He watched while Sandra read it. For some reason, it seemed terribly important that she be informed of all the details concerning his getting a car. It was almost as though if *she* didn't know, it hardly mattered. Why it happened, he didn't know, but Woody's heart beat faster the moment he saw her begin to write a reply. He could hardly wait for the message to arrive. It said, "I know. I saw your ad on the bulletin board."

He sent her another note, much to the annoyance of the people who sat between them and had to be part of this bucket brigade. "I mean I might buy one *today*. I'm going to look it over after school."

Her note came back. "Oh! Hope you like it."

He wrote a reply which said, merely, "Me too!" but the boy on his left wouldn't take it to pass along. So, Woody had to content himself with smiling proudly at Sandra and enjoying her friendly little smile in return.

Woody opened a book and began to dream about the car he was going to look at, trying to envision it. Somehow, it kept looking like a two-door version of Dan Ilder's Deuce. He was startled out of his dream by a note that bounced on his desk. He opened it and quivered when he recognized Sandra's neat, open handwriting. "Did you have a good time at the Hop Saturday night?"

Woody scribbled his answer below her question. "I didn't go. Did you have a good time?"

He watched again as she answered, getting a thrill out of knowing that what she was doing was for him. She had written under his question, "I didn't go either." He couldn't explain his sudden surge of happiness.

He wanted to write back but noticed Mr. Manbarg looking too suspicious. It was the teacher's custom to read aloud notes that he intercepted. Woody folded Sandra's note and put it in his pocket. There was something warm and cozy about both their handwritings being on the same small piece of paper.

Woody didn't know it, and wouldn't have believed it if someone had told him, but Sandra was happier than he that they had established, really for the first time, direct communication. She had turned Woody down for the Teen Hop because his father was going to drive. At the time, she had been proud of her action, for it made her feel very womanly and grown-up. No girl in school who was *anybody* would ride with a parent, and she wasn't going to be different.

But she had stayed home Saturday night and had been miserable. All she had done, she realized, was to deny herself a date with a boy she liked. And why? Because she didn't have the courage to defy a custom set by a group of girls who weren't even her friends and who really didn't care where she went, or how, or with whom. She had let what others *might* think rob her of freedom to live her own life.

And yet, it wasn't easy for a girl to go against what was "done." It was easier for a boy to be independent and a nonconformist and to go his own way. The society of boys wasn't as dictatorial as the society of girls. Boys just ignored a boy who refused to join their fads and fancies. Girls couldn't tolerate an outsider by choice. They'd destroy her, even if she was insignificant, for being a "traitor." But thinking back to her lonely Saturday night and her surrender to what "girls might think" if she went on a parent-chauffeured date, Sandra was filled with resentment. If Woody would only give her the chance, she'd defy the silly custom and let the others say or think what they pleased. But would he?

For days after she had turned Woody down, he had avoided looking at her. She didn't know that he was ashamed to look at her because he had been refused a date. She thought he was angry with her. She wanted to explain and let him know she was interested, but she *couldn't* make the first move. For all she knew he wasn't interested anymore, and she couldn't risk being humiliated.

Boys didn't know how lucky they were, she thought. They were allowed to be ordinary without being penalized. They didn't know what it was like to be judged on their looks. There was always some beauty contest going on at school, some queen being chosen, some competition for popular standing. A boy didn't know what it was like to be caught between a choice of humiliations.

The first and most common humiliation was sitting in one's seat pretending to be unconcerned while other girls were nominated as worthy competitors in beauty or charm and one was passed over without a second glance. Not even to be nominated as one of many! Year after year . . .

But as bad as it was to be passed over, there was an even greater fear that one would be nominated and have to face the humiliation of being rejected in an early round or, finally, of being publicly and formally identified as being less pretty, less charming, less popular, less attractive, less liked than ten or fifteen other girls in the school. Boys didn't have to submit to that kind of torture. They matched their muscles, speed, and skill in games and races, but that was about all.

No, there were too many contests, too many comparisons, too many public humiliations to face without risking the final, crushing blow of making overtures toward a boy and being rejected. If there was ever going to be anything between Woody and herself, he would have to make the first move. She felt that it was the boy's place, even if he had been turned down once. But as the days passed, Woody ignored her. She lost hope and turned to her radio for the constant sad consolation of the love songs that came out of it twenty-four hours a day.

And then Woody sent his first note.

Somehow, and neither of them to their knowledge did anything to make it work out that way, they reached the door together when class was over. Since they both went to the same room for their next class, it seemed natural that they walk together.

In responding to Woody's note, and now in walking with him, Sandra was showing, in her girlish, roundabout way, that she considered the turndown as part of the dead past. If Woody had any sense at all, he would know that she had flashed him a signal anyone should recognize. She was making it as plain as a girl could, while still keep her dignity, that she wouldn't mind being asked again and that her answer would be different.

But Woody didn't have any sense when it came to girls. He

didn't know they could be just as uncertain, insecure, unhappy, and lonesome as boys, make mistakes, and be as sorry for them.

It never occurred to Woody that Sandra might have changed her mind. She was a girl, and girls, as far as he knew, were "like that"— odd, demanding, incomprehensible, self-contained, self-sufficient people who always seemed to know what they were doing and were always doing what they wanted to do.

All Woody knew was that he had been turned down for a date because he didn't have a car. The answer, obvious to him, was not to ask again until he had a car. Meanwhile, he would try to keep Sandra interested in him by talking about cars and letting her know what progress he was making toward getting one. The closer he came to having a car, the more interested she would be. That was the way Woody saw it.

"You know that car I wrote about in my note," Woody said as they matched steps down the hall. "My club is going to rebuild it. We've got real good plans."

"That sounds awfully exciting," Sandra said, although the idea seemed very dull to her.

"Dan Ilder looked me up to tell me about it," Woody said, proudly dropping what he thought to be a big name with everyone in school. "He's taking me over in his car . . . you know, the sharp blue Deuce with the white upholstery?"

"That's nice of him."

Woody could tell she wasn't interested in Dan or his car, and that confused him. Everybody knew that girls liked boys who had cars, and that the nicer the car, the more choice the boy had among the girls.

And here was Dan, a good-looking senior with the best car in school, and Sandra acted as though she barely knew who he was and cared even less. Yet this was the same girl who wouldn't date *him* because he didn't have his own car. Girls just didn't make sense!

Doggedly, however, Woody began to court Sandra in what he thought was the most effective way to arouse her interest in him.

He began a lengthy rambling account of all the mechanical changes and modifications he intended to make in the car he hoped to buy. Sandra walked at his side, pretending interest, smiling, being friendly, and doing everything she could to show Woody it was all right to ask for another date. That *was* the reason for the notes and for their walking together, she assumed. Why was he so slow in coming to the point?

She came as close as she could to asking Woody for a date. "Do you see that poster?" she asked, in the middle of an explanation about carburetors. "I designed it. Do you like it?"

It was a huge poster announcing a spring dance for couples only and specifying that no stags would be admitted.

"It's pretty nice," Woody said. "You're a pretty good artist. Maybe you could help me with some of the pin-striping on my car."

Sandra forced a smile. "I'd be glad to, if you think I'm good enough."

Woody studied the poster, and she waited expectantly. He wanted to ask her to the dance, but he knew his father had a coach's meeting that night and would need the car. Without a car, there was no point in asking. She'd made her feelings clear enough once before.

"Oh, you're good enough, all right," Woody assured her. "You're . . . real good. That's perfect lettering."

*Read what it says!*

Sandra looked up at Woody, waiting . . . waiting . . . She saw Woody's face light up with a sudden, happy glow but he was looking over her head. "Say . . . Sandra . . . excuse me a minute, but I see Dan Ilder, and I need to talk to him about that car. See you around . . ." He didn't even look at her as he flew off down the hall, chasing Ilder.

Sandra felt as though she had been struck in the face. She didn't know the real reason why Woody hadn't asked her to the dance, or that his rushing off to see Ilder was meant to impress her with the fact that he had senior friends. As she saw it, and felt it, she had practically asked Woody for a date when she pointed out the poster. And Woody had got his revenge for what she had done to him. That was it . . . she had turned him down, and he had done the same thing to her, just to get even and humiliate her. It had all been a trick on his part. A clever trick.

Without thinking, Sandra turned to her usual source of consolation. She opened her purse and switched on her little radio, fitting the plug in her ear. The radio responded faithfully with a sad song about how it felt to be unloved. It was as though the vocalist had heard and seen everything and had put her own sad situation into song. Her eyes blinded by tears of shame and disappointment, Sandra walked slowly down the hall to her next class.

Just as the late bell rang, Woody dashed into the room and flopped down in his seat, breathing heavily. He was so happy he wanted to shout. He had become friendly with Sandra, walked with her, and made it clear he would soon have a car to drive her around in. And he was all set to see the car as soon as school was over. What more could he ask?

Woody looked around until he saw Sandra. Her look of unhappiness reached him as a pensive, reserved expression that he found very appealing. Their eyes met, and Woody, trying to show his happiness, gave her a big, exultant grin.

To Sandra, Woody's grin of triumph was for his triumph over her, its purpose to mock her. Her eyes almost black with anger, she struck back in the only way she knew how: She made a terrible face and stuck out her tongue at him.

Woody's jaw dropped and a look of stunned surprise came over his face. He was so obviously shocked that Sandra knew at once she had made a terrible mistake. She turned her back to Woody, unable to face him, feeling horribly sick and hating herself for being a stupid fool. How could she ever face him again?

Woody couldn't figure out what had happened. Her violent expression had been such an uncalled-for surprise that he couldn't believe it was meant for him. After all, they had been practically going steady for over an hour. Looking around, Woody realized that Graffan, his banana carrying locker mate, sat behind him in this class. Graffan sat hunched over his desk, his long black hair falling over his forehead. He had seen everything, and he sniggered as Woody turned to face him.

Graffan's presence there explained everything to Woody. He guessed that Graffan had seen him walking with Sandra and had been teasing her about it. That mean look and protruding tongue had been for that creep Graffan! Satisfied, Woody turned around again and looked at Sandra. He wanted her to turn around so that he could let her know he understood, but she wouldn't. And when class was over, she was gone before he could intercept her. He was disappointed but philosophical. After all, she was a girl, and girls were impossible to figure. Anyway, he had no time to spare. He had to get outside, meet Dan Ilder, and take a look at what might become his first car.

## CHAPTER 7

WOODY SETTLED HIMSELF HAPPILY on the white Naugahyde upholstery in Dan's car and, following Dan's example, fastened his safety belt. He watched hungrily as Dan switched on the key and touched the starter button. He knew the car was powered by a big, blown engine, but he wasn't prepared for the glorious sound of power that filled the cockpit of the Deuce.

Dan put the car in reverse, backed around until he was pointed at the street, then shifted into low. They moved forward to the throbbing music of massive, fine-tuned horsepower. Woody had never in his life ridden in a car that felt so alive, so agile, and so powerful. He hoped that Dan would pour the coal to the car and wrap up his pipes. But Dan drove easily, with deft, gentle hands and feet.

"Like the way she runs?" Dan asked as he shifted into high gear.

"Mmmmm," Woody said, his eyes glazed with pleasure. "I'll bet you're really proud, having a car like this."

"It was a lot of work."

"But it was worth it," Woody lectured. "It was worth every minute of it, I'll bet . . ."

"I suppose so," Dan said casually.

Woody could hardly believe his ears. How could anyone be matter-of-fact about a car like the Deuce?

"I just hope mine will be a tenth as good," Woody said.

"No reason why it can't be just as good or better," Dan said. "If you've got the time, the know-how, the money, and the tools, you can build anything."

"That's what I told my dad," Woody said. "I suppose you learn a lot while you work, too."

Dan glanced at Woody's trusting face and grinned. "Oh, you learn, all right. Mainly, you learn how many ways there are to do things wrong."

"I'll stick pretty close to the book on my first job," Woody said.

"Cars and motors are funny things to work with, Woody," Dan said. "Especially when you're modifying. They don't always behave according to the book. You can build up two cars that seem identical in every respect, and they can be different a hundred ways. They can ride differently, perform differently, and handle differently. No matter how hard you tried to make them alike, you'd find they had to be set up differently and tuned differently. One might need hotter plugs than the other, or different carb jets and settings, or different ignition or valve timing. There's no end to it. You just have to find the best combination of everything for each car."

"I know there's a lot to it," Woody said. "But I'm ready to give it a whirl."

"Mind if I give you some advice?"

"I want it," Woody said, expecting some inside technical tip.

"Don't try too much your first time out."

"I wasn't planning on much," Woody said. "Just to get it running, keep it running, and have it looking nice. Maybe some bolt-on performance boosters."

"That's the ticket," Dan said.

Dan slowed down. They had arrived near the edge of town, an area of small bungalows, large vegetable gardens, and chicken houses. Dan turned in at a dirt driveway and parked beside a small white house with green shutters. There was no sign of a car, but at the end of the driveway there was an old, sagging white garage with the doors closed. Outside the garage, in the weeds, were a few old wheels, a torn-up front seat, odd pieces of battered and broken chrome, and a rusty old muffler with jagged holes in it. Woody's heart began to beat a little faster. He unbuckled his seat belt and got out, joining Dan in front of the shiny blue car.

A moment later the back door of the house opened, and a big, shaggy, sleepy boy stepped out, pulling on a jacket over his skivvy shirt. He was wearing a pair of skintight faded denim pants and, despite the chill day, was in his bare feet. Seeing Dan and Woody, he scratched his unruly hair and yawned noisily. He picked his way toward the car with mincing steps, like a huge bear with sore feet. "What gives?" he grumbled good-naturedly. "Can't you let a guy get a little rest?"

"Come on, you sack rat," Dan said, "I've got a guy who wants to look at your heap. He's Woody Ahern . . . old Coach's kid. Woody, this is Sam Rizzell."

"Glad to meet you," Sam said. "How's Coach?"

"Pretty good," Woody said.

"You want to see my car?"

"I sure do."

Sam stared owlishly at Woody, amused by the fervent note in Woody's voice. His big round face looked like a good-natured moon. "Come on," he said, chuckling to himself. "I'll show it to you."

Sam led the way in his bare feet, watching carefully for nails, bolts, small car parts, and other hazards that might be in his way. Despite his caution, he stepped on a bolt and grunted with pain. He held his sore foot off the ground and hopped ahead on his good foot. "You'd better get used to wearing shoes, Sam," Dan kidded. "Everybody in the navy has to."

"Not all the time," Sam said.

"Sure, all the time."

Sam winked at Woody. "Not in the sack, they don't!" He slapped his heavy leg and laughed.

Sam opened the garage doors. Woody's first impression was of some kind of great gray beast kneeling at rest, with a high, curved back. Then he recognized a humpbacked 1947 Ford two door. Woody followed Sam into the garage and slowly walked around the car. There was so little room between the car and the walls, and the light was so dim, Woody couldn't *see* too much of the car. He did see that it was mostly a dull black, with big patches of gray primer paint. He noticed that Sam had removed some of the chrome strips and had sanded, but not yet filled, the holes that were exposed. He also noticed there was no front bumper, and the hood did not close all the way. Looking inside the car, he saw (and smelled) the musty, moth-eaten, drab, plush upholstery and the sagging, pushed-out-of-shape seats.

All in all, Woody beheld a high, huge, clumsy, ancient, and battered car that seemed to defy repair. He walked around it twice, making an effort to discover how it sagged and leaned, what was missing or falling off, and what didn't fit or work anymore.

"Want me to start it up for you?" Sam asked.

Woody looked at him in amazement. "You mean it . . . *runs?*"

"Sure it runs," Sam said jovially, chuckling at Woody's expression. "Just listen."

Sam climbed behind the wheel. The old front seat went flat beneath his bulk, and the back of the seat tilted rearward in a spiritless, strengthless way. Sam unlocked the ignition, turned it to "On," pulled out the choke, pumped the gas pedal, and pressed the starter. The battery turned the motor with agonizing slowness, and the entire mechanism seemed to groan and whine in protest against the call to start. The engine coughed feebly and uncertainly a couple of times, and then, to Woody's pleasant surprise, roared into life.

And what a roar it was! In a second the old garage was filled with an ear-splitting racket and clouds of blue smoke as the rich mixture burned away. Sam throttled down to a high idle, looked at Woody, winked, and smiled with sleepy satisfaction. Woody's head rang from the high-pitched explosions and the harsh rasp of the pipes. Sam let the car ease down to a slow idle, but the sound that came from the car was still the aggressive, cracking thunder of a track racer. Suddenly the engine sputtered and quit.

"About time you shut that thing off!" Dan yelled, his hands over his ears.

"I didn't shut it off," Sam said, getting out of the car. "It must have run out of gas." He looked at Woody. "How do you like it, boy?"

Woody was almost too overcome to speak. He gestured helplessly and blissfully. "Oh, it's just *exactly* what I was looking for. It couldn't be better."

"What makes it a little loud," Sam explained, "I got a motorcycle muffler on it. There's another one that matches it that I could let you have. Gives it a tone, eh?"

"Perfect," Woody said.

"Of course, it needs a little work here and there . . ."

"That doesn't matter," Woody said. "I want it for a club project. We'll try to take it from where you left off. I figure I'll paint it white, with red trim. Reverse and chrome the wheels, lower it and rake it, put the stick on the floor, build my own grille . . ."

"That's a lot of work there, boy," Sam said dubiously, rubbing his matted hair with the palm of his hand.

"We can do it all right," Woody said. He tried to appear well-informed. "I meant to ask you about the mill. Is it stock?"

Sam stared at Woody with an incredulous look on his broad face. "Is it *stock*, you ask?" When he saw how deadly serious Woody was, he repressed a delighted giggle. "Why . . . yeah, it's stock," Sam said, having trouble keeping his face straight. "What's left of it, that is. Have a look."

Directing Woody how to help him, Sam opened the hood and braced it with a section of broomstick. "The stick goes with the car," Sam said. "Most important accessory it's got."

Woody looked in and saw, in the dim light, an ancient flathead covered with dirt and grease. There were two bright spots in the engine compartment. There was a new chrome air cleaner on an old, discolored carburetor and a thin, cheap chrome cover around the generator.

"You can see I only just got started on it," Sam said.

"I'd rather have it that way," Woody said. "It leaves more for the club to do. It's just perfect for what I want, all right."

Woody took a step back and looked at the car. Already, he could see what it could become; could see it in gleaming white with red trim, mirror-like chrome, spotless and powerful. A little sanding, a little painting, a little work on the engine, and it would be like a new car. And even the way it was it was a real car, with a real motor that *ran*, and it could be his if he wanted it. *This* car could be his. *Would be his!*

There was a moment of awkward silence. They had come to the point where an offer had to be made or a price asked, and neither boy knew quite how to begin. Woody didn't want to seem cheap, yet he had his forty-dollar limit. Sam was anxious to get rid of the car, but he didn't want to seem greedy.

Woody gently slapped a front fender with his open hand. "Solid," he said. "They don't make them like this anymore."

"They sure don't," Sam agreed, looking at the lines of the car.

"What do you figure it's worth . . . ?"

"Oh, I don't know." Sam hit the fender with his hand and laughed. "What do you figure it's worth to you?"

"Would you let it go for thirty?" Woody said it and held his breath.

"That's pretty low," Sam said. "I was kind of hoping I could get around forty-five out of it. Them tires are good for a lot of miles."

"Forty-five is more than I can spend," Woody said regretfully. "I have to stay inside a budget. You know . . . the club and all . . ." He looked at Dan Ilder, who had been standing by, listening.

"Why don't you guys split the difference?" Dan asked. "That seems fair all the way around. Thirty-seven fifty."

"It's okay with me," Woody said.

Sam looked at the car, shook his head, and laughed. "It's okay by me, too. It's a deal. You've bought yourself a car."

When the full impact of Sam's words hit Woody, he felt a strange, gnawing sensation in his stomach. *He had bought himself a car!* Suddenly, he felt like laughing or yelling at the top of his lungs, or sitting down and crying. He owned a car!

He realized they were waiting for him to make the next move. The car wasn't bought until it was paid for. "I've got my money at home," Woody said, having difficulty controlling his voice. For no reason at all, he was trembling.

"I think," Sam said, "I have to deal with your old man, on account of your age. I could put a drop of gas in the tank and bring it over tonight." Sam blinked and looked alarmed. "Hey . . . this *is* all right with your old man, ain't it? I mean, he won't get sore or nothing when he sees it?"

"It's all right," Woody said. "He knows all about it. I mean, the whole idea of finding a car like this was his idea."

"Okay, I'll bring it over. I just didn't want to tangle with the old coach. Man, he's tough." Sam shook with pleased laughter.

"I was just wondering," Woody said hesitantly, not wanting to sound childish, "if I could ask you a favor."

"What?" Sam asked.

"Would it be all right if I came over with my club members, and we rode with you to my house? I thought you could give me some pointers on how to handle the car on the way over."

"Oh, sure thing," Sam said genially. "Be glad to have you. It's better that way, in case we need pushers." He winked at Woody and laughed again. "See you then." Hands in his pockets, huge shoulders hunched, Sam picked his way back to the house, stepping as lightly on the gravel with his bare feet as he could.

"Old Sam's a good egg," Dan said as he and Woody got back in Dan's car. "And you got a pretty good deal."

Woody nodded. He'd thought so, too, until he was in Dan's car again. He wondered if his car would ever look as beautiful and be as good as Dan's. At the moment, it seemed hopeless. And, for a moment, as a reaction to the excitement, Woody regretted his purchase. But only for a moment.

"You've got the makings of a good custom in that old car," Dan said as they drove away.

Woody brightened. "You really think so?"

"You should have seen this when I started. It wasn't half the car you've bought."

"I don't have too much money to put in it," Woody said. "Mainly, I want to get it running good and looking good."

"You're wise. Too many kids try too much and wind up nowhere."

"Not me," Woody said. "I've got it all figured out on paper. I know just how much I can spend to run it, and how much I can put into parts and so on. It's all down on paper."

"That's a good idea," Dan said. "Just one thing you want to be sure of when you start figuring a car on paper."

"What's that, Dan?"

"Be sure you start figuring at the top, and that you've got a *long* sheet of paper."

CHAPTER 8

"HERE THEY COME!" CHERYL CRIED EXCITEDLY. "Here they come!" She had been watching out of the dining room window for half an hour, and her vigil was at last rewarded. Ahern came in from the living room to watch beside her, and Mrs. Ahern came in the kitchen.

"Woody made me drop them a block from Sam's house," Ahern said. "He wanted me to get my first look at the car when they drove up."

"Oh, heavens!" Mrs. Ahern exclaimed. "That *can't* be Woody's car!"

But it was. Creeping along with an exhaust blast that was loud even inside the house, the ungainly car followed its dim, yellowish lights down the street and under the streetlight. Members of the Road Rockets had their heads and arms protruding from every window, arms waving, heads bobbing, and mouths shouting. Just opposite the house the driver turned his face toward the dining room window. Even at that distance, and in the artificial light, Woody's face showed a proud grin as he steered his car around the corner and turned in the home driveway.

The Aherns headed for the back door, and, as they approached it, they could hear the loud, uneven roar of Woody's car as he gunned it again and again for the benefit of the club members.

"He'll have to get over that habit," Mrs. Ahern said, "or the neighbors will run us out of town. There are four babies within a block of us, and I'll bet they're all awake *and* howling."

Woody had shut off the motor by the time his parents and little sister reached the driveway, but he and his friends remained in the car. He poked his head out of the driver's window. "Here it is, Dad!" Woody cried. "Do you like it?" Beside him, Sam Rizzell laughed heartily.

"Well," Ahern said, looking at the car very dubiously, "I can see that it runs. That's more than I expected." He thought, but did not say aloud, *or wanted.*

"You just have to know how to look," Woody said proudly, for the benefit of his club passengers.

"Well," Ahern said, "Sam and I had better hunt up a notary to witness the change in title."

"Sure, Dad," Woody said. "Hop in. Mom, you and Sis squeeze in, too, if you want to."

"I think we'd better take my car," Ahern said. "You want to come with us?"

"No," Woody said. "I think I'll stay home and get acquainted with my car." His voice shook with pride as he said the last two words.

Sam got out of the car and walked around it to join Ahern. "Hello, Mr. Ahern," he said. He glanced at Mrs. Ahern and Cheryl. "Evening, Mrs. . . . and . . ." He didn't know how to finish and solved the problem by nodding a few times and giving out a hearty, friendly laugh.

"Hello, Sam," Ahern said. "I hear you're going into the navy."

"Yes, sir, that's true."

"I think you'll like it, Sam. It's a good outfit."

"That's what they say, Coach." Sam looked around at Woody and laughed.

"Now," Ahern said, "just what am I buying from you with Woody's money?"

"My own personal car, Coach," Sam said, his large body shaking with repressed laughter. "He won't get in no trouble with it. It uses up all its strength making noise. She's got a safe top speed of about fifty miles an hour right now."

"What do you mean, *safe*?" Mrs. Ahern asked suspiciously, eyeing the hulk of a car with distrust.

"Any faster," Sam said politely, "she'll probably throw a rod or two. Mainly, though, the clutch. It won't hold tight enough to go any faster."

"Well," Mrs. Ahern said uncertainly, "I suppose that's a good thing. Is there any way to keep it from making such an awful racket?"

"Yes, ma'am," Sam said. "Don't start the engine." Once more he shook with quiet, pleased laughter.

"Well, come along, Sam," Ahern said. "We've got work to do. Woody . . . let your car roll back toward the street so I'll have room to back out of the garage and go around you."

"Will do, Dad," Woody said cheerfully. He took the car out of gear and let it roll back down the gentle slope. Near the end, he brought the car to a stop and put it in gear again to hold it. His mother, after a final head-shaking look, went into the house, taking Cheryl with her. His father and Sam drove off to find a notary public.

Woody turned to face inward, his left arm resting on the steering wheel, his right arm on the back of his seat. Dick Slater had come up to the front seat with him. Jim Bob and Sonny shared the spacious back seat.

"Now this," Woody said, "is more like it. The Road Rockets Auto Club is finally meeting in a car."

"Why don't we hold all our meetings in the car?" Sonny asked. "It would be more fun than in your cellar. There's lots of room to stretch out back here. And it's really private."

"Uh," Jim Bob added softly. "It is good to own our car at last."

Woody's eyebrows raised. That 'our car' statement didn't set too well with him. It was *his* car. But he let the remark pass.

"Well," Dick Slater said impatiently, "now that we've got a car, what do we do?"

"I'll run it in the garage," Woody said. "We can look it over in a good light and figure out a plan of action. No reason why we can't start work on the car tomorrow . . . or even tonight."

"We've all got our good clothes on," Dick objected. "We can't mess around on a car in good clothes. Since we've got a car that runs, let's run it."

"That's a good idea!" Sonny cried, bouncing up and down on the back seat. "Let's cruise around a little, Woody. Let's see how it runs. Maybe we'll see some girls."

"We can talk while we drive around," Jim Bob said. "Like the other guys do."

Woody wanted to ride around as much as the others, but he felt he had to make a responsible start with his car. "I don't want to drive around too much until I've got the title and my insurance policy is delivered. It's safer that way."

"You're covered the minute you ask for insurance and the agent agrees to take you on," Dick said. "You don't have to wait."

"Even so," Woody said. "I want everything in order, just in case we're stopped or something happens. I'll tell you what, though. I think it would be all right to go get gas. I think Sam only put in enough to run a couple of miles. I've got two fifty in change from the forty I paid him, and I'll put that in the tank. It's better to have a full tank anyway. Less chance of condensation and rust."

"Well, let's go, go, go!" Sonny cried exultantly. "Me, I want to hear them lovely pipes again."

"There's only one pipe," Dick said, just to deflate Sonny.

"Who cares?" Sonny demanded. "It makes as much noise as two!"

"Okay," Woody said. "I'll tell my mom we're going." Woody ran into the house to let his mother know they were leaving.

"Can I go, too?" Cheryl begged. "Can I ride in your car, Woody?"

"Not tonight," Woody said impatiently. "I've got all the guys with me."

"You *promised*!"

"Some other time."

Mrs. Ahern tried to make herself heard over Cheryl's cries of protest. "Woody, I wonder if you could run a little errand for me while you're out. I need . . ."

"Next time, Mom," Woody yelled, already out of the door. "I'm late now. Be back soon." He ran for his car, climbed in, and settled himself behind the wheel.

"Hang on, men!" Woody called. "Here we go!"

In the back seat, Sonny let out a shrill rebel yell and pounded both feet on the floor.

"Will you cut that out!" Dick turned in his seat and raised his hand as though to hit Sonny. "You're worse than a little kid."

"Killjoy," Sonny muttered.

Woody switched on the ignition, eased the choke out a little, and pushed the starter button. A groan, as from a dying cow, came from under the hood. Woody waited a second, then tried again. This time the groan was weak. The third time Woody tried, there was a little clicking, like a death rattle, and then silence.

"That was a short trip," Dick said. He tried to be flippant but could not conceal the disappointment in his voice.

"Battery's down," Woody said. "We're still not stuck. Let's shove the car out on the street and aim it down the hill. I think that's all it needs."

The club members piled out of the car to perform their first club task. Two on a side, they pushed at the old car and got it rolling. Woody pushed with one hand and turned the wheel with the other. When they were in the street, the boys prepared to push forward.

"Hey," Sonny panted. "How do we all jump in when it starts rolling? There's only two doors."

"You don't, stupid," Dick said. "Woody jumps in alone. When he's got it started, he can back up and pick us up."

"I never thought of that," Sonny admitted airily. "Let's push!"

Woody stayed by his door, ready to jump in, pushing with one hand. The three others got behind the old car and put their backs into it. The car didn't budge.

"I thought this was downhill," Jim Bob gasped. "You sure it's out of gear, Woody?"

"It's out of gear," Woody said, feeling indignant at the question. "There's just a little reverse slope before the hill starts down. Let's try again."

Again, they pushed, leaning forward until their bodies were almost parallel with the ground, grunting with effort, their feet slipping on the pavement. Slowly, a reluctant inch at a time, the old car began to move forward. It picked up a pinch of speed and got its front wheels on the down slope. In a moment it was under way. Sonny, pushing with all of his might, his eyes closed, fell flat on his stomach as the car moved away. Woody jumped behind the wheel and began a frantic search for the ignition switch. The car was rolling down the hill, eating up distance, and he was still fumbling in the darkness for the switch. He also had the lights off and had to divide his time between hunting for the switch, keeping his eye on the dark street, and steering straight.

At the last minute he found the switch, flicked it to the On position, shoved in his clutch, and shifted into second gear. Slowly he let out the clutch pedal until at last it was engaged. A million gears seemed to grind beneath his feet before the car coughed a few times and caught. Suddenly, so that he was off guard, the car was rolling in high gear, picking up speed, and running without lights. Shaking with excitement, Woody had sense enough to shift into neutral as he braked to a stop and turned on his lights. He adjusted the choke until the car was running smoothly and gave it enough throttle to rev at a healthy rpm. He had done it. He had started the car. He breathed in and out deeply and noticed that he was clinging to the steering wheel so tightly his fingers hurt. He unbent his fingers and stuck his head out of the window to look back. He could see the other boys watching him from the top of the hill, under the streetlight.

Woody put the car in reverse and started back very carefully so as not to stall the engine. He went back up the hill at a snail's pace, slipping his clutch and racing his engine as he veered from one side of the street to the other. So much smoke came out of the exhaust that his vision kept getting obscured, and he ended by backing straight at the boys and almost running over Sonny, who was so interested in watching he barely got out of the way.

"All aboard!" Woody called, a big confident grin on his face. "We're ready to roll."

"I hope we don't have to do this every time we start," Sonny groaned as he squeezed into the back seat. "I skinned my hand and knees when I fell down."

"I hope we can make it to the station," Woody said, with a worried look at the gas gauge. "The needle has been below the empty mark ever since we left Sam's place." He slipped the car into low and eased forward, an ear-splitting racket coming through the motorcycle muffler.

"Listen to that beautiful tone," Sonny Mack sighed, leaning back contentedly in the back seat. "Just like the first lap at Ranger Park Raceways. *Vrrrrrooooommmmmm!*"

"When you get gas, Woody," Jim Bob said hopefully, "maybe we could go through town once and watch the drags on Main Street."

"What do you mean, *watch*?" Sonny shrieked. "Man, we'll go down and *choose*!"

Woody smiled to himself as the car rang to the happy talk of his club members. It was a glorious feeling to be driving his own car, with his friends as passengers. Never before had driving been such a thrill or such pure pleasure. Because this was his very own car, the wheel felt different in his hands, and the accelerator had more meaning to his foot. Every motion, every pressure, every action was a brand new delight. No sir, there was nothing, *absolutely* nothing, that could take the place of having your car. Oh, how he loved this old car! His very own, his very own, his very own . . .

# CHAPTER 9

WOODY TURNED IN AT LOU JOHNSON's service station and came to a shuddering halt beside twin gas pumps. Lou Johnson stepped out of the station wiping his hands on a rag, looking warily at this noisy, unfamiliar customer who had come to call. Some of the stations had had trouble with carloads of strange roughnecks who ordered gas and oil, then threatened to beat up the attendant and wreck his station if he asked for payment. When he saw Woody at the wheel, he relaxed and grinned broadly. The Aherns were old customers at the station.

"What does it eat, Woody?" Lou asked as he approached the driver's window. "Gasoline, diesel fuel, nitro, or oats?"

"Runs just fine on regular," Woody said. "I suppose when I drop in an ohv, I'll move up to the premium tank, though. How do you like it? I just bought it from Sam Rizzell."

"Sounds loud enough to satisfy any boy," Lou said. "Want to shut it off while I pump gas? It's dangerous to pump while it's running."

"I know," Woody said. "But if I shut it off, I don't think it will start again without a push. The battery's down."

"I'll give you a push with the truck, if you need one."

"Thanks. I guess I'd better see if I need any oil. Whatever money I have left, I'll put in the gas tank."

Woody shut off the motor and got out to help Lou lift the hood. "My right side hood bolts are missing," Woody explained. "It takes two guys to open the hood and three to close it. I'll hold it up while you check the oil."

Lou wiped the dipstick clean, measured, and showed the results. "Down about a quart, Woody."

"I'd better add, then," Woody said. "I don't know what Sam used, but I can't go wrong with a heavy duty, non-detergent twenty weight, can I?"

"Ought to do just fine," Lou said. "If you hold the hood up, I'll check your radiator and battery water."

"I can hold it," Woody said, getting a new grip. He looked past the hood toward the windshield and grinned at his club members. It was really something, buying gas and oil for his own car. Really something. He was a customer in his own right now, not merely a customer's son. He looked on proudly as Lou serviced his car with as much care as he used on any new car that came to his station. He was a customer, and his business was important to Johnson.

"The oil comes to sixty cents," Lou said. "How much gas did you want?"

"That leaves me a dollar and ninety cents," Woody said. "I'll take that much."

He watched while Lou started the pump. His dollar bought him a fraction under six gallons. The pump didn't stop, and Woody gestured in alarm. "I'm giving you a gallon on the house, Woody," Lou said, "since this is your first visit as a new customer."

Woody was moved. "Thanks a lot, Mr. Johnson," he said earnestly. "I can use every break I get. It will probably cost me a little something to restore this car."

"I imagine it will," Lou said with a straight face. "The main thing is to keep it running. You can always add the fancy work later."

"That's the way I figured it," Woody said, giving Lou the two fifty he owed him. "You can't rebuild a whole car with a few hand tools."

Lou chuckled. "Not anymore, you can't. But if you run into trouble and need a special tool once in a while you can borrow one from me. I don't usually lend tools, but I know your dad so well, and since it's you . . ."

Again, all Woody could say was "Thanks a *lot.*" His head spun with all the good fortune that was his. Free gas, an offer to lend tools . . . How could he fail, with the whole world on his side?

"Tell you what, Woody," Lou said. "Things are pretty slow tonight. You and your friends push your car around by the side of the station, and I'll stake you to a battery charge. You'll never get that battery up by just driving."

The boys pushed Woody's car around to the side of the station. "I'll set it for an hour," Lou said as the boys watched him hook up the charger. "After that, it wouldn't hurt if you drove it around for about half an hour. It helps hold the charge."

Lou moved off, and the four boys got back inside the car. It was their natural den, and they felt comfortable and at home in it, insulated from the outside world.

"You know something," Sonny Mack said, "we don't have a name for the car. It ought to have a name."

"I've got one," Woody said.

"Shouldn't the club pick the name?"

"Why? It's my car, isn't it?"

"It's the club's car too, isn't it?"

"Not when it comes to naming it. I mean, when you guys get your cars, they'll be club cars too, won't they? Still, you'll want to name your own car yourself, won't you?"

"I guess so," Sonny said reluctantly. "What name did you have in mind?"

Somehow, Woody felt embarrassed. "Well, I didn't want to name it after some pop songs, like some guys do, or make it anything mushy . . ."

"How about Road Rocket, after our club?" Jim Bob suggested.

Dick Slater hooted derisively. "With a top end of fifty miles an hour?"

"That won't always be the top end," Woody said, offended.

"I like Hell's Angel," Sonny Mack said.

Suddenly, Dick was on Woody's side. "What did you have in mind, Woody?" he asked.

"I thought . . . well, I thought Sidekick might be a good name."

"I like it! I like it!" Sonny yelled. "That's what it is . . . our sidekick."

"It's better than My Buddy," Jim Bob said. "That sounds like a boat."

"I like it," Dick said. "Not too sticky."

At once, the car was one of them. The name brought the car into the club as a fifth living, individual member, and not as a machine. It made the car seem to belong with, and not merely to, them. With this name, the car assumed definite character and moved into its own special place in their hearts.

"Now another thing," Woody said, laying down the law as owner and chief spokesman for the car. "Nobody is to refer to Sidekick as she, or her. This car is a *he*."

"Well," Dick said in a strangely friendly tone for him, taking something from his jacket pocket, "I would like to present Sidekick with a little gift . . . his first custom accessory."

Dick held out his hand toward Woody. "There it is, Mr. President.

A genuine chrome gearshift knob. It's for the floor shift Sidekick will have some day. Meanwhile, I think it will fit the column."

"Well, thanks a lot, Dick," Woody said. He was pleased and surprised. "When did you buy it?"

Dick laughed out loud. "Buy it? Man, I didn't buy it . . . I acquired it."

"In other words," Woody said, "you swiped it."

"In other words," Dick answered, gleefully mimicking Woody's tone, "I guess I did."

Dick waited with an expectant grin for Woody to laugh with him and acknowledge his gesture. For, despite the way he had got the knob, he was giving it to show his affection for Woody as a friend. He waited for the thanks and praise he felt he had earned.

"Why'd you do that?" There was annoyance in Woody's tone, and he made no move to take the knob. Dick was shocked and hurt, but he covered his feelings with his usual cynical behavior.

"The same reason they climb mountains," Dick said. "Because it was there. Who needs a reason? Kicks." He laughed mockingly. "I'll bet that guy really flipped when he found the knob was gone. I wish I could have seen his face."

"What guy?" Woody asked.

"The guy at the used car lot your dad took us to," Dick said. "That fat slob Wheeler."

Dick looked at the chrome knob in his hand. He hadn't known, when he stole it, that he would offer it to Woody. He had taken the knob because, as he had said, it was there. He didn't have any use for it. What gave him pleasure in taking it was the thought that it would be missed, that Wheeler would be angry, and that something had been damaged. This ability to hurt someone seemed to ease some of the angers he felt; angers he couldn't quite understand, but which tormented him. Even now, he felt angry toward Woody because Woody had been able to buy a car. And, even though Dick would get to ride in the car, he resented the fact that he didn't have the car instead. He was older than Woody and deserved one more than Woody did. It was just more proof of how the world was fixed against him.

"That was a lousy thing to do," Woody said slowly.

"Since when did you get religion?" Dick sneered. "You used to swipe as much as anybody else."

"That was when we were little kids," Woody said. "Most little kids swipe stuff. But that's been over for years."

"You're right, Woody," Jim Bob said. He leaned forward, his head between Woody and Dick. "The purpose of our club is to uphold the law and help people, not steal things."

"Nobody asked you," Dick said nastily. "And stop leaning on me, will you? I don't need you breathing all over me."

"Aw, what's a knob," Sonny Mack said. "All the guys with cars visit the midnight auto supply once in a while."

"It was a lousy thing to do to my dad," Woody said to Dick. "How do you think that makes him look? Hauling around a bunch of swipers."

"Aw, nobody saw me," Dick grumbled. "Who's to know it was us? Besides," he added, wanting revenge for the way Woody had hurt him, "since when did you start caring how anything made your dad look?"

"Just what do you mean by that remark?" Woody asked, his voice edgy.

"What I said. What's your old man ever been to you?"

"He's been my father!" Woody exclaimed. "And he's been a good friend, too. And I've been his friend."

"That's not what the guys used to say," Dick said.

Suddenly it was very quiet in the car. The two younger boys in the back seat hardly dared breathe.

"What guys?" Woody asked in a voice so calm it seemed unreal.

"The guys in junior high with us," Dick said.

"What'd *they* say?"

"They said you couldn't think very much of your old man if you wouldn't even be on his teams."

"They said that?"

"Yeah. They said he couldn't be much of a father if his own son wouldn't play for him. Or much of a coach, either . . . if a guy's own son wouldn't stick by him."

Woody's throat was so tight it hurt him to talk. "For your information, Slater," he said in a choked voice, "the guys were wrong. My father's the best coach that school ever had. You guys know him. You know he's a good guy. He let me have a car, didn't he? He hauled us around, didn't he?" Woody's voice rose and strained to the breaking point as a savage fury took possession of him. "Where's *your* car, Slater? If your old man is so much better than mine . . . where's your car?"

"I didn't say my old man was any good," Dick said, his jealousy of Woody eased by Woody's perturbation. "And I didn't say anything against your father myself. All I said was what the guys used to say. They just thought there must be something wrong with a guy whose own son didn't think enough of him to be on his teams."

Woody felt numb and confused and stricken with guilt. He had never dreamed that anything he did could hurt his father. His father was a man, a teacher, and a coach. How could he be affected by anything his young one did or didn't do? Woody had left the team because of the way he felt about *himself,* not his father.

To find out now that it was his father who had taken the blame, who had been criticized, who had lost status in the eyes of the boys, was a jolt. He had always thought of *himself* as the victim of the coach/father situation, and now he saw that it was his father who had been the real victim. Woody wanted to jump out of the car and run to his father and beg his forgiveness for what he had done by being so self-centered and so blind. But he didn't move from behind the steering wheel, and he knew he would never say anything about it to his father; it would be too painful and too humiliating to let his father know he knew.

For a long time, not a word was said inside the car.

Finally Jim Bob leaned forward, cleared his throat, and said timidly, "I think the hour's up, Woody."

Dick made a big show of looking at his wristwatch. "You're right, Jim Bob. Just up." Dick looked across at Woody. His face, illuminated by the service station lights, was taut and stern. Dick could have kicked himself for what he had said about Woody's father. Woody was his friend, and he liked him, but it was hard to resist a chance to make lucky people like Woody know what it felt like to hurt a little.

"Come on, Woody," Dick coaxed, "forget what I said. It was a long time ago, when the guys were kids. They know better now."

"It doesn't mean anything, Woody," Sonny Mack said.

Woody turned so he could look at the others and they could see his face. To their surprise, he was laughing. What Dick had said had been so painful to Woody that he was frantically eager to wipe the words and meanings from his mind and pretend they had never been spoken. "What's the matter with you guys?" Woody cried. "You're acting like a bunch of old women. Do you think I care what anybody said way back in junior high? For crying out loud, cut the gloom and have a little fun."

"You mean ride around?" Sonny squeaked hopefully.

"Give that man a fifty-cent *see-gar* or his choice of prizes on the second shelf!" Woody said. "That's exactly what I meant."

"I thought you wanted to go straight home," Jim Bob said. Sonny and Dick groaned and threatened Jim Bob good-naturedly.

"The man said we ought to ride around for half an hour," Woody said. "So, we'll show Sidekick our town."

"I'll tell you what," Jim Bob said eagerly. "Let's cruise around and see if we can help anybody in distress. That's one of our club projects, and it would be a swell way to start out."

"We don't have any cards yet," Dick objected. He referred to a card the club had designed for itself. On one side was the club name and emblem. On the reverse side was a message which read:

*You have just been assisted by members of the*
*Road Rockets Auto Club,*
*an organization of teenage boys interested in automotive mechanics,*
*sportsmanlike driving, obedience to the laws, and helping motorists in*
*distress. Our only fee is your good will.*
*Thank you.*

"How about it, Sonny?" Woody asked. "You volunteered to draw the emblems and type the message. What happened?"

"Nothing happened," Sonny said. "As long as we didn't have a car, I didn't see any reason to rush. I'll get them done now, though."

"Get cracking," Woody said. "We ought to have a couple of dozen made up this week."

"A couple dozen!" Sonny bleated. "Man, that's work!"

"We might need that many," Woody said. "We'll need a card for everybody we help. We can build up a good name for ourselves in a hurry."

"Well, I'll try," Sonny said without enthusiasm.

"Since that's out for tonight, what's next best?" Dick asked.

"Oh," Woody said casually, "I thought we might take Sidekick for a look at the Main Street drags."

The car rang with happy shouts. The boys tumbled out of the car, removed the charger cables, and cooperated to close the hood. Woody waited until they were all back in the car again before he tried to start. When Woody pressed the starter button, the motor roared to life almost at once. He was so surprised he kept pushing the button after the motor was going and produced horrible grinding noises under the hood.

Woody revved the engine to hear it roar, then turned on his

lights. Even at the station, he could see they were much brighter. "Are you ready?" Woody sang out.

"Ready!"

"Here we go!" Woody pushed the clutch pedal to the floor, shifted into low, fed more gas, and let up slowly on the clutch. Sidekick went into gear with a severe case of clutch chatter, but managed to lurch forward, gagging and choking as it was called upon to haul a load. Woody shifted into second, urged the car forward at a higher speed, and shifted into high.

Sonny bounced on the back seat and chanted, for no apparent reason, "Cheer, cheer for old Notre Dame," over and over again. Jim Bob looked out of the window with a tight smile. Dick lounged back toward the door on his side, the look of a hunter in his eyes. Woody gripped the steering wheel with both hands and guided his car through light traffic as he headed toward the downtown area.

The boys knew about the Main Street drags at night, and often they had watched them while on foot or riding with a parent. But to watch from a car that rolled along the same street would be like taking part. It moved them from the ranks of the lookers and wishers to the ranks of the fortunates who drove and rode.

And who could tell? Perhaps, while they were trailing and watching, they would find another car like Sidekick; another ancient vehicle that snorted fire, roared fiercely, and, under the whip, trotted laboriously from traffic light to traffic light.

It was not beyond reason that there were cars (or a car) slower and weaker and sadder than Sidekick that would also be on Main Street. And while the thoroughbreds raced on in the front rank, who could tell? Perhaps, going against other old humpbacked Fords, heavy-jawed, old Stovebolt Chevys, ancient slope-backed Oldsmobiles with automatic transmissions, or aged boxy Plymouths and Dodges, Sidekick might rise to the heights hinted at by the bass scream of his motorcycle-mufflered engine. He might, just *might*, on his very first night as a member of the Road Rockets Auto

Club, an organization of teenage boys dedicated to safe driving, obedience to the law, courtesy, and respect, win his first official drag race down Main Street!

# CHAPTER 10

MAIN WAS A ONE WAY STREET, just wide enough for four cars to run side by side. And that was how they ran. There was very little normal traffic at this hour. Ninety percent of the cars were driven and occupied by boys and young men. Only a few had girls along or had the look of having a destination or a goal. Most of them were very obviously on hand to compete in the stoplight *grand prix*.

Four rows wide and three rows deep, with a few stragglers behind the main pack, the cars waited impatiently for the light to change to green. There were, in this tight jam-up, cars of every age and description. There were brand new convertibles with continental kits, cars that had been lowered, raked, dechromed, or adorned with original chrome arrangements. There were cars with factory power packs and cars that carried, under old, conservative exteriors, powerful engine and transmission swaps from original equipment.

The one thing all these cars—new and old, modified or stock—had in common was their ability to make noise. If nothing else had been done to a car, the owner had at least replaced stock mufflers with glass or steel packs.

Situated roughly in the middle of the pack, Woody pressed his clutch pedal to the floor and revved his engine as the others were doing. Sidekick's harsh blast joined the deafening mixture of mellow pipes, throaty pipes, high-pitched pipes, and snarling pipes.

"EeeeeYOWeeeee!" Sonny screamed from the back seat. "This is like a start at Ranger Park Raceways!"

Woody permitted himself a tight grin. That's just what it was like, he thought. It was like waiting for the green flag with engines revving and roaring, a duel of cars and drivers. If he had ever had any doubt about wanting to be a race driver, that doubt was gone now.

A dozen engines wound up tight. Tire screeches cut through the deeper engine noises. Clouds of smoke rose up. They were off!

Woody gave Sidekick the gas and eased out the clutch. The old car lurched forward, yielding to no other machine in the amount of noise it made per mile per hour. The newer and more powerful cars shot ahead. Woody found himself bringing up the rear in company with two other old cars that breathed more smoke than fire. His engine screaming as though ready to fly apart, Woody engaged in a grim duel with a 1948 Chevy on his left. He went all out in low, snap shifted awkwardly into second, and gunned his car. For a moment he and the Chevy ran a dead heat, and then slowly but surely Sidekick nosed ahead.

"You got him!" Sonny yelled as Woody pumped his brake. The pack ahead had come to a stop. Woody roared up to it in low gear and eased his way into a hole, ready to choose another car. His heart pounded, his mouth was dry, and his palms were sweaty.

"What do you mean, *him?*" Dick said to squelch Sonny. "There was a woman driving that Chevy."

"The *car* wasn't a woman," Sonny protested.

"How do you know she was racing with us? Maybe she wasn't even trying."

"She was trying, all right," Woody said. But the edge had been taken off his victory.

He glanced to his left. He had pulled up even with and close to a rough looking car with four boys in it. They were in their late teens or early twenties, and they were looking back at him as though sizing him up. They looked contemptuous and hostile.

Woody took a firm hold on the wheel. The front seat was so loose that every time he accelerated, the seat sagged back as though it were going to topple over.

"Watch me take these guys," Woody muttered to Dick.

"Watch out for them," Dick said. "They look mean."

"Yeah," Woody said. "You think they're the ones who've been going around beating up people?"

"They've got that look. Don't crowd 'em."

"We've got as much right to be on the street as they have," Woody said stubbornly.

"You're asking for it, Woody . . ."

The light changed, and all the cars charged ahead. Woody charged with them, but they pulled away from him with ease. The car on his left stayed close, trying to force him over, but Woody held a straight course. He thought, for a moment, he was holding his own. Then the other car shot ahead and cut in front of him, braking immediately. Woody hit his brakes, but they weren't good enough. His car weaved as the brakes grabbed unevenly, squealed, and then faded. Helpless, Woody bumped into the other car.

"Now we're gonna get it," Dick said. He took hold of the door handle, ready to run. The boys in the car ahead looked back threateningly, but they stayed in their car.

"They did that on purpose," Woody said. "They're looking for an excuse to rough us up."

Sonny's voice came unhappily from the back seat. "Let's get out of here, Woody. We're no match for those guys."

"I'll try to steer clear of them," Woody promised. When the light changed, he started up very slowly. The car ahead pulled away and to one side, and he lost it in traffic. "They're gone," Woody said. "You can relax." But when he looked in the rear-vision mirror, he saw that the other car had come in behind him.

"Let's get out of here," Sonny said again.

"Can't," Woody said. "They're trailing us. They're waiting for us to get on a side street so they can head us off and work us over."

"What are you gonna do?"

"Stay on the merry-go-round. As long as we stick with the other cars and stay on the big streets, they won't dare jump us."

*"You hope."*

Woody stayed with the pack as best he could while it dragged up Main, turned left at Twelfth, went a block, turned left at Locust, dragged back on Locust to First, and then turned left to Main again. There were so many sections to the races that he was always surrounded by cars, catching up to those held by a light or being overtaken by faster cars behind him. Around and around he went, and all the while the other car stayed close behind him, waiting for him to break away.

"How long are you going to keep this up, Woody?" Jim Bob asked anxiously. "I have to be home soon."

"I've got to stick with it until they give up or we run of gas," Woody said. "Unless you want your nose flattened."

"I wish we'd never come down here," Jim Bob said dolefully. "I don't want to get beat up for nothing."

"Who does?" Dick said impatiently, his own fear making him belligerent and intolerant. "What's so special about you?"

Woody kept on driving slowly, but the car behind stayed with him. The fellows in it had chosen their victims. Woody had read about groups of older boys attacking cars, but it had never entered his mind that anyone would want to attack *him*. But they were after him now, and he could see why he and his friends were good game. They were smaller boys in an old car, and they would be easy to knock around. All the bullies needed for an excuse was an imagined insult, and they were ready to do violence.

Woody cruised steadily, watching for a chance to escape. And when he was almost ready to abandon hope, chance came. Another car pulled up alongside the boys who were trailing him and shouted a challenge at it. Then it pulled ahead, the boys in it shouting derisively, the very sound of their car's exhaust insulting and gloating. It was more than the boys following Woody could stand. Being hit by Woody was enough of an excuse to get tough, but it couldn't compare with being shouted at and *passed* by another car. And being passed with a mocking shout was too much to ignore. The car pulled from behind Woody and gave chase. Woody waited until it was lost to sight among other cars, then quickly turned off Main Street and headed for home as fast as he dared travel.

Now that they had escaped, what had been fear became excitement, and they were able to shout and laugh about it and feel brave. It had been a real thrill.

"Old Sidekick here is a pretty fair automobile," Woody said. "All he needs to hold his own on Main Street is a clutch. What do you say we put one in tomorrow night?"

"Man, I'm with you all the way!" Sonny exclaimed. "It's about time we got down to some real work on a car."

"The way I see it," Woody went on, "a new clutch will handle an ohv without any trouble at all, so we can prepare for the future while we fix for the present. About all we'd have to do would be to put in roll bars, double shock, and lower, and we'd be ready for real racing over at Ranger Park."

"That'll be the day," Dick said, both envious and unbelieving. "I can just see your dad letting you drive a modified on the track."

"We've talked about it," Woody said. "He said I could do it when I was old enough."

Jim Bob leaned forward. "Really, Woody? No kidding?"

"Really. You guys want to pit for me?"

"Why can't we drive, too?" Dick demanded. "Why do you always have to be the guy who drives, while the rest of us look on and cheer? I've got a license, and I was driving before you were. So, how's about giving me a shot at driving right now?"

Woody was outraged at the idea of anyone but himself having control of Sidekick, but he didn't know how to turn Dick down. After all, they were a club, and Sidekick was the club's car, and he supposed Dick had a right to drive. Yet the thought of Dick at the controls of Sidekick was unbearable.

"How about it?" Dick persisted.

"I'm thinking about it," Woody snapped.

"Sonny and I both have permits," Jim Bob said in Woody's ear. "We're allowed to drive if there's a licensed driver in the front seat with us . . ." His voice, filled with soft hope, trailed off into silence, leaving the way clear for Woody's reply. Woody was physically incapable of letting go of the wheel or giving up his seat, even though he recognized the justice in his friends' requests. Sidekick was the club's car in a way, but Sidekick was his. Couldn't they understand that?

"You expect us to work on the car," Dick argued. "We know you've spent money on it, but labor is worth something too, you know. I mean, we're not going to work and fix up a car for you to drive around all by yourself. We want some kicks, too."

Woody slowed down reluctantly. "All right," he said ungraciously. "If you can't wait two minutes . . . I just hope you'll be as anxious to work as you are to drive."

"I'll work, all right," Dick said. "Don't you worry about that." Woody pulled over to the curb and stopped with the engine running. "Are you sure you can drive this car?"

"I can drive it better than you can," Dick said insultingly. "My dad's car had a stick." He got out and went around to the driver's side and opened the door.

"Come on, Woody, move. Give a guy room. I can't drive sitting in your lap."

Woody gave way, but with a warning. "Don't try driving this the way you did your old man's car, Slater. Take it easy."

"Who asked you?" Dick brushed Woody's words aside. He sat behind the wheel for a moment to get the feel of his new position, his long face twisted into a kind of secret, progressively arrogant half grin. Without warning, and with the car still in neutral, he pushed the gas pedal to the floor. The engine responded with a wild, tortured shriek, the car shuddered, and the clamorous exhaust broke into a series of sputtering explosions as the engine misfired at high, unloaded rpm.

"Hey!"

Before the indignant Woody could move, Dick let up on the gas. "Just testing," he said. "Just getting the feel of it."

"I'll get the feel of your neck if you try that again," Woody threatened. "Now take it easy, or you'll tear out the clutch. And if you do . . ."

Dick had intended to floorboard the gas pedal and let the clutch pop, but Woody sounded too angry. In order to keep his place at the wheel, Dick decided to take off easily. He kept a light foot on the gas pedal and started to ease out the clutch. The moment he felt it engage, he let the clutch out all the way, then tried to feed a big charge of gas. The car bucked and stalled.

"Now look what you made me do!" Dick complained angrily. "I was doing all right until you had to butt in." He tried to start the car again. The lights dimmed and almost went out, the starter ground hollowly, and nothing happened. A smell of raw gas became strong in the car.

"Cut it, cut it," Woody said, reaching over to turn off the ignition and switch off the lights. "You've flooded the carburetor."

"I can clear it," Dick said. "Hold the gas pedal to the floor and push the starter."

"You'll only wear down the battery that way," Woody said. He flicked on the dash lights for a moment. "Just as I thought . . . overheated. We're vapor locked. The best we can do is raise the hood and sit here until it cools off."

"That's your fault, not mine," Dick said. "You got it hot dragging."

"All right . . . give me a hand with the hood."

"It going to take long, Woody?" Jim Bob asked, his young face squeezed into worried wrinkles. "I've got to be home soon. I should be home now."

"It won't take long," Woody assured him. Woody and Dick got out and raised the hood, holding it open with the broomstick. Woody put his weight on the fender and rocked the front end, hoping to spill the gas from the carburetor and help rid it of its lock. The motor was so hot that it gave off little ticking and sizzling noises.

"I hope those guys don't find us here," Dick said, joining Woody.

"They've probably forgotten all about us," Woody said. "I hope."

Jim Bob and Sonny got out of the car and came forward. The four boys stood around in the darkness, hands thrust in the pockets of their uniform jackets. They felt strange and different. Their club had only had the car a few hours, and yet their lives seemed to have taken another step up. They had cruised around in their own car, joined the drag races, and had a brush with violence. They had known, from hearing others talk and reading stories in the newspaper, what went on in their town at night, but this was their first time as part of it. It made them feel more mature, yet somewhat uneasy. They were still strangers to the new level of life and not sure of their place in it.

"Once we get Sidekick tuned right, we won't have this kind of trouble," Woody said. "And if we can find a good buy in an electric fuel pump, we'll really have it licked."

"Nothing's going to help very much until we get that clutch adjusted," Sonny said. "I could hear it over-revving from where I was sitting in back."

"It's just as easy to put in a new clutch as adjust the old one," Woody said. "We'll have to pull the transmission anyway. Tomorrow afternoon I'll buy the parts we need, and we can install it tomorrow night. Then we can fine tune and call it an evening."

"That sounds like a good plan," Jim Bob said seriously.

"A little at a time, and first things first," Woody said. "That's the way we'll get things done."

"Look alive, you guys . . ." There was a note of warning in Dick's voice. "There's a car coming."

They watched tensely as a car came slowly up the street toward them.

"Looks as if they're looking for somebody," Sonny breathed. "If it's those guys, I'm gonna be long gone . . ."

"Not me," Woody said grimly.

"You want your head pounded in?" Sonny demanded.

"If we run, they'll smash up the car," Woody said. "Nobody's going to smash up my car without getting a fight from me."

"You won't catch me losing any teeth over an old car," Sonny said. "Not while I can run fast. Anyway, they'll pound you and smash the car too. You can't stop four big guys."

"I can try," Woody said, taking a firm stance in front of his old car. His heart was beating painfully, and his legs trembled with the desire to run. But he was ready to stand and die to protect Sidekick. It was *his* car.

The others moved about nervously, wanting to run, yet reluctant to abandon Woody.

"You guys can go," Woody said. "You don't have to get caught."

"Let's *all* go, Woody," Jim Bob pleaded urgently.

Woody shook his head. He couldn't have run if he tried. His place was where he stood, in front of his car.

Suddenly Dick laughed with relief. "Everybody relax. It's the Pooch."

"Whew!" Sonny's exclamation spoke for them all. Dick waved the

Pooch down, and he pulled in behind them. He got out of the car and approached them with a friendly but uncertain look on his face.

"Are we glad to see you!" Dick shouted.

The Pooch's face beamed with surprised pleasure. "You are?" He added, naively, "I was following you on Main and then I lost you. I thought you were trying to get away from me."

"We wouldn't have any reason to do that, Freddy," Woody said. "We were ducking some big guys who were looking for trouble."

"I saw them too," Freddy said in his open, childish way. "I know them. I'll tell them to leave you alone. They will. I get things for them too, sometimes." The Pooch noticed that Sidekick's hood was up. "You having trouble, Woody?"

"Vapor lock," Woody said.

"I'll give you a push," the Pooch said. "That'll start you."

"Good deal. Hop in, guys."

Sonny and Jim Bob jumped back into the car, but Dick stayed where he was. He had an odd feeling. Up until now, he had liked being with Woody and the others because they had been have-nots and outsiders. But now that Woody had a car and was talking like a serious property owner, now that the Road Rockets was a *have* club, he wasn't as interested as he had been. It seemed natural for him to be an outsider, and he wanted to stay that way. He wanted the painful pleasure of being different and apart. There was something about accomplishment, and success, and belonging, that seemed a threat. If he became like everyone else, what was he?

"Pooch lives over my way," Dick said. "Maybe I can ride with him and save you a few drops of gas. How about it, Pooch?"

"Sure," Pooch said eagerly, almost falling all over himself in his eagerness to have company. "Ride with me."

Woody sensed Dick's withdrawal from the group. "Be glad to take you, Dick. You know that."

"Let him ride with me," the Pooch begged. "You've already got two guys with you."

"Okay," Woody said. He felt troubled. "You'll be over tomorrow night to help with the clutch, won't you, Dick?"

"Wouldn't miss it," Dick assured him heartily. "Man, I'm just as eager to get the club car in shape as you are. I'll be there."

"See you then," Woody said. He got behind the wheel of his car. The Pooch came up behind him and nudged his back bumper. Woody signaled that he was ready, and the Pooch began to push, accelerating rapidly until they were sailing along at thirty miles an hour. Woody slipped into high gear, switched on his ignition, and let out the clutch. Sidekick roared into life at once, exhausting a rolling cloud of thick smoke. "Men," Woody called cheerfully to Sonny and Jim Bob, "I will have you home in a couple of minutes. Meanwhile, why don't you climb up front?"

Sonny and Jim Bob accepted the invitation eagerly, for to be in the front seat was to be up where everything was going on. It was the next best thing to driving. They were glad to be there, and Woody was glad to have them. With Dick gone, he felt the need to have the others close, to reassure himself that they were still together, and a club. "As soon as we get that clutch in and the tuning done," Woody promised, "I'm going to give you both a chance at the wheel."

Woody's car pulled away, and the Pooch slowed down, watching Woody's left taillight, which was the only one working. It glowed a faint purple color.

"Do you have to go home right away?" the Pooch asked Dick, looking at him with pleading eyes.

"I don't know," Dick said noncommittally. "What do you want to do?"

"I've got to get some gas," the Pooch said, eyes busy looking from side to side up the dark street. "Want to help me?"

"I don't have any money," Dick said.

"You don't need any." The Pooch looked at Dick, his eyes shining with doubt and loneliness. "Could I trust you with a secret?"

"Sure," Dick said. "What?"

"You won't tell anybody?"

"Cross my heart."

"Even if it's not . . . honest?"

"What do I care about *that?* You're my friend, aren't you?"

"I hope so," the Pooch said longingly. "I'd like to have good friend like you."

"I'm that," Dick said. "What's your secret?"

"Feel over the visor . . . where there's a slit in the overhead lining."

"Found it," Dick said, sliding his hand around.

"Take out what's in there," the Pooch said mysteriously.

Dick pulled out a long, thin, coiled rubber tube. "Got it," he said.

"That's how I get my gas," the Pooch said shyly. He waited for Dick's reaction.

"I know a siphon when I see it," Dick said. "I'll help you."

"You're not mad?"

"Why should I be mad?" Dick laughed contentedly. "I can't think of a better way to get gas. Anybody who buys it is nuts."

"I can't afford to buy much," the Pooch said. "And I drive around a lot."

"Find a car in a good dark spot," Dick said. "We'll fill your tank." He was excited. This was more like it . . . to find a car hidden in the shadows, sneak up, and siphon out its gas. In the morning, when the owner came out to drive it away, what a surprise! *This* was more like it!

They cruised along the dark residential streets until they found a car hidden by bushes. The Pooch shut off his motor and his lights and coasted for a couple of hundred feet, coming to a quiet stop. He waited for a few minutes, listening. The street was quiet. No one seemed to be outside. "Now," the Pooch whispered.

He got an empty five-gallon gas can from the back seat, and quietly opened his door. Dick, still carrying the siphon tube, slipped out on his side. Crouched over, keeping in the shadows, they approached the car. Staying as low as possible, the Pooch lifted the cover of the car's gas tank and unscrewed the cap. He took the tube from Dick, put it in the gas tank, and sucked gently on the other end, intently trying to sense when the gas would come through. At the last moment, expertly, he pulled the end of the tube from his mouth and shoved it into the opening of the gas can. A steady stream of gas flowed into the can.

Dick, his chest tight, kept looking around nervously, ready to fly at the slightest noise. But the Pooch seemed at ease. He squatted by the gas can and grinned at Dick, obviously overjoyed at having a friend along to keep him company at his once-lonely labors.

When the can was full, Dick expected the Pooch to rush it back to his car. But the Pooch was in no hurry. He capped the gas can, put the rubber tube in his pocket, and then examined the car they had just robbed.

"Let's go," Dick whispered, his nerves on edge.

The Pooch shook his head. "Need the hubcaps," he whispered. "Promised a set like these to Shorty Lewis."

"Forget Shorty Lewis!" Dick whispered frantically. "Let's go before our luck runs out."

"In a minute," the Pooch whispered calmly. He took a taped screwdriver from an inner pocket, dragged himself around the car, and, with the muffled blade, pried the hubcaps loose. He took off his jacket and packed the hubcaps in so they wouldn't rattle, then signaled for Dick to take the gas can and follow him back to the car. Dick hurried with his load, crouching over, his body soaked with sweat. The Pooch tossed the hubcaps in back, set the gas can on the back seat, and got behind the wheel. Lights off, he started his motor and took off gently, going slowly and quietly until he reached the corner. Then, lights on, he gunned his car and fled the area. A few blocks farther on, after a couple of turns, he stopped where it was dark. He got the hubcaps and slipped each one into a concealed hiding place in each of his four door panels. Then he got out and poured the gas into his tank. When this was done, he got back in the car again and started up.

"You work smooth enough," Dick said, reaching for a cigarette with a shaking hand as he tried to relax. "But you sure take your time! That's dangerous."

"I've never been caught yet," the Pooch said. It was obvious, from his tone, that he never expected to be caught.

"What's Shorty giving you for the hubcaps?" Dick asked.

"They're a present," the Pooch said. "The reason the guys ask me to get stuff is that they can't afford to buy all the things their cars need. So, I give them the stuff free."

"You're nuts," Dick said, and instantly regretted the words. But the Pooch was smiling, his eyes wide and innocent. "I mean, you ought to get something for your trouble and risk. If they can't come up with a few bucks, let 'em go without."

The Pooch laughed. "I like to do it for the guys. It makes them friendly." He looked hopefully at Dick. "Want to help me again?"

Dick hesitated, but his fear was overcome by the thrill of what he had done. He had stolen plenty of small things in his life, but this kind of operation was different. This was big.

"What do you need to get?"

"I need a two-barrel carb for a Chevy six. It shouldn't be hard to find."

"I'm not sure," Dick said, watching the Pooch closely. "I don't know if I want to."

"Don't you like to be with me?" Pooch saw everything in the most simple, personal terms.

"Sure I do," Dick said. "You're a swell guy, and that's why I'm not sure. I mean, Pooch, I think you ought to get paid for the stuff you get. And I hate to risk *my* neck for nothing."

"I'd hate for the guys not to be my friends," the Pooch said. "They might not be friends if I wanted money."

"You want me for your buddy, don't you?" Dick asked.

"Sure, Dick. It's been swell having a buddy."

"All right. I'll be your buddy and help you on one condition. You let me handle the business end. I mean, Pooch, you'll still be getting the stuff for the guys free, and I'll deliver it to them, and ask for . . . expenses. That's all, just expenses. You let me handle that end. Okay?"

"Okay," the Pooch said. "Anything you say, partner."

Dick looked thoughtful. "You know, Pooch, I want to be an equal partner, share and share alike. Risks and everything."

"That's swell, Dick. Gee, it sure is swell to have a partner."

"I think," Dick said carefully, "I ought to share the work of driving too, don't you? So, we can take turns looking and turns driving?"

"That sounds fair enough," the Pooch said. He brought the car to a stop. "You can drive all you want to, Dick. And I'll have more time to look. I think," the Pooch added with a touch of pride, "I'm a better looker for parts than you are."

"Oh, I know you are," Dick said, getting behind the wheel. "You're the best."

He started up and drove off, feeling as though the car belonged to him, and he could do anything he wanted with it. And crouched beside him, looking for a car that might have the right Chevy carb, the Pooch hummed contentedly to himself as he reveled in his new good fortune. It was so nice to have a friend of his own. So nice not to be alone anymore.

— — —

Woody delivered Jim Bob and Sonny to their homes, made sure they remembered about putting in the clutch the next night, and turned toward his own home. He was wonderfully happy and contented, and suddenly he realized, with a pang of shame, that the reason he was so happy was that he was alone in his car. There was no doubt about it. It was more fun, more . . . *personal* to drive alone in his car. *His* car.

He saw that the lights outside the garage were on as he swung into the drive. He drove up to the garage on the side his father didn't use and stopped. Holding the car with the foot brake, he slowly revved it until it began to pop, then backed off, watching his ammeter. He revved again and again, soaking in the powerful gutty sound of his motor. At last, reluctantly, he eased up and, with just a quick touch of rev-up, shut off his engine. He turned off his lights and gulped. Just before the dash lights went off he saw his gas gauge. It read *below* empty! For a moment he was stunned. Two dollars' worth of gas gone. He'd have to check at once. There must be a leak in the gas tank or line . . . two dollars in one evening, and his budget for a week was a dollar and a half. As Woody got out of his car his father came around the end of the garage, waving his hands. "Woody . . . Woody! Take it easy! The neighbors are calling. You've awakened their babies. It's eleven o'clock!"

"It's *what* time?" Woody asked.

"Eleven o'clock," Ahern said severely. "Look, Woody, I won't kid you. I'm pretty burned up about the way you behaved tonight. Your mother has been worrying herself sick. Where the devil have you been? If getting a car is going to turn you into an irresponsible . . . This is it, Woody. This is the last time for a trick like this. Where have you been? Mom's been wanting to call the police for the past hour."

Woody had seen his father angry often enough but never so agitated. It was strange to see him almost distraught. Woody had no idea of what his parents had gone through since he had left. They had expected him back, as he had promised, in a few minutes. He had been gone almost four hours.

"I'm sorry, Dad," Woody said. "We weren't any place. I didn't know it was so late . . ."

"You had to be some place, Woody."

"Well," Woody said, "I went over to Johnson's for gas. He gave me a free battery charge, and that took an hour. Then he said to drive around for half an hour to help set the charge. So, I did. Then I took the guys home and came home."

"That was a pretty long half hour," Ahern said, unconvinced.

"We got stalled once with vapor lock when Dick tried to drive," Woody said. "And I guess we forgot the time talking about the work we're going to do. The guys are coming up tomorrow night, and we're going to drop in a new clutch."

"I didn't think you were doing anything wrong," Ahern said. "But when you leave in your car and we don't know where you've gone, and you're gone for hours, we worry. That's one thing we'll have to have understood right now, Woody. When you go out in your car, I want to know where you're going and when you'll be back."

"Aw, Dad . . ."

"It's for your own protection," Ahern said. "When you start driving around, you're exposed to more hazards than you might realize. I don't want to frighten you, but we've had trouble in town with carloads of older boys beating up younger boys. When you're out driving around looking for excitement, that's the kind you might find. That kind of trouble will be looking for you."

"We didn't have any trouble, Dad," Woody said. "Not a bit of any kind."

"Well, I just wanted to let you know what you might run into . . . aside from the normal hazards of driving. It's unpleasant, but it's something you ought to know about."

"I'll be real careful when I'm out," Woody said. "I promise."

"Your mother made me go out and look for you," Ahern said, speaking in his crisp, no-nonsense coach's way. "We're not going to have any more of that. I am not going to be one of those parents who drives around town half the night asking every Tom, Dick, and Harry if they know where his child is."

"Dad . . ." Woody muttered uncomfortably.

"You can 'Dad' me all you want to, Woody. That's how it is."

Woody pictured his dad out looking for him, interested, anxious, worried about what might happen to his son. And he thought, suddenly, of what Dick had said at the gas station; about what the kids in junior high had said about him and his father.

"Furthermore," Ahern continued, "you had no right to drive around without the registration. You could have got in trouble over that."

"I didn't think I'd be gone so long," Woody said.

"That's not the worst of it. Did you know you weren't even insured until after I came home and called Bob Moore? What would you have done if you'd been in an accident before that?"

This really frightened Woody. "I . . . I thought we were insured."

"You *thought*. There's a financial responsibility law in this state. You either have to be insured or post a ten-thousand-dollar bond. Without registration, without insurance . . . Do you know what your fate might have been if you'd had an accident?"

Woody stood silent, with his head bowed.

"A little accident on the way to the gas station could have meant your going to reform school or jail. Did you know that?"

Woody shook his head.

"An accident in which you were in the wrong, uninsured . . . do you know what would happen? They could get a judgment against us that would cost us our home, our savings, and possibly part of my income for the rest of my life. That's what your little thoughtlessness might have done."

"I didn't want to go," Woody said in a choked voice.

"But you went."

Woody nodded miserably. "I wouldn't have if I'd known. I'd rather give up my car right now and *never* have a car than hurt you because of it, Dad. Really. I mean it." He was trying to pay back for the hurt he had inflicted when he'd quit the team.

"I know you mean it now," Ahern said, his voice softening. "We're lucky nothing bad did happen, but that has to be the last carelessness. You understand, don't you?"

"I understand, Dad."

"You're not a child anymore," Ahern said. "Your car isn't a toy. Every time you drive away, your life, the lives of your passengers, the lives of everyone you meet, are in your hands. Don't ever forget that, Woody. In particular, watch out for the little ones. They can't always remember about staying out of the street. They do get excited and run out there without looking."

Woody nodded and rubbed his eyes with his knuckles. Going out for a drive had seemed such a casual affair. He hadn't realized, hadn't really thought what going for a ride meant.

Ahern sighed. "Well, son," he said in a warm, affectionate voice, "I think you understand what I've said, and why."

Woody nodded, smiling, ashamed to give his father more than half a look.

"Now that that's over," Ahern said, walking closer to Woody's car and looking it over, "how do you like your forty-dollar special?"

"It's a terrific buy for the money, Dad," Woody said eagerly. "Except for the clutch slipping, it's in just about perfect shape. And we're going put in a new clutch tomorrow night."

"How much will that cost?"

"Ten or twelve for the parts, I think."

Ahern pursed his lips doubtfully.

"It's worth it, Dad," Woody argued. "I mean, if we let the clutch slip any worse, we'll wreck the flywheel. This way, for a few bucks, and with a little labor, we've got a clutch as good as a new one."

"That does seem to make sense," Ahern said. He grinned at Woody. "But then, so many of the things you *say* make sense."

"I was wondering, Dad," Woody said, remembering his empty gas tank, "if I could give the flywheel a break by borrowing your car after school tomorrow, to go and get the clutch parts."

"Why . . . I guess so." Ahern wasn't quite sure how Woody had maneuvered him into that position.

"Thanks a lot, Dad," Woody said.

"You sure you fellows know how to do the job?" Ahern asked.

"Nothing to it," Woody said. "The manual shows every step. All you do is disconnect the brake hoses, cables, and shocks, disconnect the shackles at the front universal joint ball, and slide the rear end back. Then we unbolt the transmission and lift it out, replace the old clutch with the new, bolt up the transmission, connect up the driveshaft and the other things we disconnected, and we're ready to roll. It's a snap. Guys in school do it in no time, they say."

Ahern laughed and surrendered. "You make it sound good, I'll say that for you. Well, coming in with me? It's past your bedtime."

"In a minute, Dad," Woody said. "I'd like one last minute to look over the car. You know how it is, the first night."

"Okay," Ahern said. "But come right in."

When Woody's father was gone, Woody approached his car and stood looking at it, lost in thought. Then he walked around it; touching it everywhere, speaking to it in an affectionate undertone as though it heard and understood and felt. He was certain that somehow this car felt toward him as he felt toward it; that it was glad to be his, happy when he drove it, and sad when some stranger took the wheel. In its own way, Woody felt, it was like him. It wasn't fancy, powerful, admired, popular, one of the crowd. It was different, with its own special personality. They belonged to each other. There could never have been another car for him or a different boy for it.

## CHAPTER 11

ONCE AGAIN, WOODY AHERN BEGAN HIS DAY at school by opening his locker and suspiciously sniffing the interior. A small smile of satisfaction touched his lips. There wasn't the faintest trace of banana odor. Graffan had taken his warning to heart. Since it was a warm day, Woody somewhat reluctantly took off his black Road Rockets jacket and hung it in the locker, noticing that he was first in the locker this morning and had his choice of hooks.

Carrying a notebook in one hand, a ballpoint in his shirt pocket, Woody strolled toward his homeroom. He was wearing dark khaki slacks and a light blue sports shirt that brought out the blue tints in his eyes. He walked with a confident but not cocky step, a contented man among men. This morning, even though he had walked to school, it didn't matter. He had a car.

Again, for a reason he couldn't fathom, it seemed important that he let Sandra Rowan know of his good fortune. He was sure, some-how, that it would make her happy.

Woody went into his homeroom and took his seat, sitting with his head up, ready to signal the moment Sandra turned to look at him. But she seemed very busy with some kind of work and never looked around. When the bell rang for them to go to their first class, she was out of the door before he was on his feet. His first class was in a different direction from hers, so he planned to tell her later. It hadn't yet dawned on him that she was trying to avoid him.

On the way to his class a couple of boys who had tried to sell him their cars caught up with him. "I hear you bought Sam Rizzell's heap," one of them said.

"Yeah. I got a pretty good deal on it. Dan Ilder located it for me."

"You've got your work cut out for you," the second said. "I had a chance to buy it before Sam did, but I bought the car I've got instead."

"Well, it's something to mess around with," Woody said. "We needed it for the club."

"You should have bought my car," the boy said. "It's good trans-portation."

Woody looked at him. "How come you want to sell? Getting a better one?" He couldn't imagine any other reason for a boy want-ing to sell his car.

"No." The boy looked unhappy. "My father works down in the cement plant, and he's been laid off . . . we don't know for how long. With the insurance and everything, we can't afford it. My job money's needed at home."

"That's tough," Woody said. "Maybe you could put it on blocks until things get better."

"I guess you wouldn't know how it is," the boy said, "your father having a steady job like teaching. We need what the car is worth to eat on." He didn't say it bitterly but as information.

"That's tough," Woody said again. Yet what he thought was that if a fellow couldn't afford a car, that's the way he had to take it. On the other hand, if a fellow like himself could, there was no reason why he shouldn't have one.

"I'll ask around," Woody said. "Maybe I'll hear of somebody that could pay a decent price."

"Thanks." The boy looked at Woody, his expression friendly. "I still tell you . . . you'd have been better off buying my car. You'll put as much in yours before you're through, and it won't be half the car."

For a moment, Woody was affronted by this derogatory remark about Sidekick, and then he figured that the boy was feeling bad and that he could afford to be big about it.

"Well," Woody said, "we'll see. Maybe I'll surprise you."

He motioned in farewell and went into his first class. There, as soon as he was settled, he began figuring what he would need to buy later that afternoon.

It seemed natural for Woody, whispering back and forth with those around him about who wanted to borrow paper or ask what the assignment was or what day it happened to be, to mention that he had bought a car. It seemed the gentlemanly thing not to keep the news to himself. And he was shocked, when the period was over, to overhear two boys discussing him in the hall.

"Did you hear that Ahern bragging about his car?"

"Yeah. You'd think that junker was the world's greatest automobile."

"And bragging about all the things he's gonna do. You'd think he was the first guy that ever worked on a car."

"Do you think he knows anything about cars?"

"Him? Don't make me laugh."

"He's always talking about cars in class."

"Yeah, *talking*. I can talk about cars, too. So can you. Anybody can *talk* about cars."

The boys drifted away. Woody looked after them and shook his head, pitying them. They didn't understand at all. He hadn't been bragging. Just telling. And there was nothing wrong with telling. He knew the two boys, knew they didn't drive, and he thought he understood. It was natural for them to be jealous and envious of his good fortune. He'd felt the same way about other lucky boys in the past. Someday, when he saw them walking, he'd give them a ride in Sidekick. And when they saw how he'd restored the old car to better than perfection, they'd eat their words.

Woody knew which way Sandra would be walking to her next class, and he hurried to intercept her. He hoped *she* wouldn't think he was bragging when he told her about his car. But he didn't expect she would. She'd be interested. And that would make her interested in him. He saw her walking down the hall ahead of him, her graceful, slightly swaying motion reminding him of a slim, supple tree in the wind. He ran to catch up with her. "I've been trying to talk to you since yesterday," Woody said, slowing his pace to hers. "You're a hard one to catch."

She looked at him with suspicion in her dark brown eyes. Was this another trick? He had seen her stick out her tongue at him.

"What did you want to see me about?" she asked coolly. She tried to be extra dignified to make up for the horrid face she had made at him.

"I wanted to tell you," he said, "I bought a car yesterday." He looked at her and beamed.

"Oh?"

It was so impersonal it chilled him.

"I'm not trying to brag about it," he said. "I thought you might like to know."

"Why?"

He was stumped and looked at her painfully. "I don't know. I just thought . . ." He wasn't sure what he thought. "I thought you might like to ride in it sometime. It's not much of a car, so don't get your hopes up for anything fancy. It's a very old car and kind of noisy and doesn't look like much. Of course, when the club gets through with it . . ."

"A car doesn't have to be new," Sandra said. "Just so it's clean."

"Clean," Woody repeated hollowly. He had a vision of Sidekick's smeared gray and black exterior, of the old plush seats stained with grease and oil, the dusty, dirty carpets, the musty smells, the faded patches.

"Clean . . ." He licked his lips. "It will be clean," he said. "Yeah."

He thought of paint, and upholstery cleaner and seat covers. Suddenly they were necessities.

Sandra turned to look at Woody, and when he looked back, there was no doubt about his interest in her, despite the way he was sputtering around.

"I . . . didn't think you'd want to talk to me," Sandra said, feeling a girl's need for a little oath of loyalty.

"Why not?" He couldn't have been more puzzled.

"After what I did yesterday."

"What you did?"

"The face I made. It wasn't very nice. But I . . ."

"Oh," Woody said grandly, much relieved. "He deserved it."

It was Sandra's turn to be puzzled. "He . . . ?"

"That Graffan," Woody went on, "he's really a creep. What was he doing . . . teasing you before I came in? I share lockers with him. He always brings bananas. He's the one." Woody meant that Graffan was the one who had made him smell of bananas the day Sandra refused the date, but she didn't know this, and decided not to find out what Woody meant. Let well enough alone!

Now it was Woody's turn again. It was his turn to invite her for a ride at a definite time, or something like that. And something like that was exactly what he had in mind until she had mentioned the necessity of a car being clean. That would take time. They reached the door of their classroom, and Woody sighed heavily, smiling at Sandra. "Would you care for a ride in my car? I mean, when it's cleaned up. We're on it right now, and you know what a mess mechanical work is." He shook his head and chuckled uneasily.

"I think that would be very nice," Sandra said. "Whenever you're ready."

"Fine. It's a da— . . . fine, fine. I'll let you know first thing."

Woody turned and staggered toward his seat, exhausted by what he had been through. Now, he realized, there were complications. He'd intended on driving to school as soon the clutch was in. But if he drove to school, he'd have to ask Sandra to ride, and she wouldn't ride in it if it was dirty. So, he really couldn't drive to school until it was all fixed up inside. Now why, Woody asked himself, had he rushed around and got himself entangled with a girl? Look what it had done. He'd been getting along just fine, and now he couldn't drive his car to school. And after all the years he had waited. What a silly thing for him to do . . . to get involved with a girl when he had a car to worry about!

Pondering his problem, Woody came up with what seemed to be the answer. The big spring dance was taking place in five weeks. He'd ask Sandra to go with him, and if she agreed, he'd try to have his car in shape by that time. In the meantime, he wouldn't be under pressure to give her a ride and could more or less forget about her. That seemed the answer, all right.

— — —

"Darrell," Mrs. Ahern asked her husband, "do you know a girl named Sandra Rowan?"

Ahern thought for a moment, sifting names and faces in his mind, not sure which year this name and face belonged to.

"I think," Mrs. Ahern said, "she's in Woody's class."

"I remember her," Ahern said. "Why?"

"What's she like?"

"Oh, she's a pleasant little girl. She's bright, pretty, rather shy, well-liked . . . why?"

"I was cleaning out Woody's pockets before putting his clothes in the laundry, and I found a note he'd sent her. And her answer."

"Well, imagine that," Ahern teased a little. "I'm sure you didn't read the note, did you?"

"I didn't mean to, but I couldn't help it. I don't think I'm a hovering mother, but if Woody is getting interested in a girl, it's only common sense to find out something about her."

"Was the note that serious?"

"No, but it was a beginning."

"You don't mind if he has a girl, do you?"

"Of course not. The right girl could be a good influence on him. But Woody's so young, and so inexperienced in knowing what people are like. It would be just like him to fall for some girl who . . ."

". . . isn't good enough for him?" Ahern finished her sentence with a chuckle.

"You know better than that. But it's the innocent girls who are most attracted to boys with bad reputations, and I thought it might work the same way for an innocent boy."

"Woody might be attracted to a girl like that," Ahern said, "but I doubt she'd waste much time on him. He's still one of the little boys in high school. I doubt very much that Sandra Rowan will lead Woody astray. *I'll* stick to worrying about him and his car," Ahern said soberly. "I was so sure he wouldn't be able to find a car that would run, and he's found one he can drive home. That complicates matters."

"There might be some hope," Mrs. Ahern said. "You know how good Woody is at taking things apart and how bad he is about putting them back together again. I have a feeling that once he starts working on his car, it will never be in one piece again."

"He's starting tonight," Ahern said. "They're going to put in a new clutch."

"Is that difficult?"

"They practically have to take the car apart to get at it."

"Well, then." Mrs. Ahern brightened. "Now I know I can forget about the car and do all my worrying about the girl."

— — —

As soon as the last bell rang, Woody flew toward his locker to get his club jacket. He had a lot of important business on hand. First, he had to find Sandra and line her up for the spring dance. Then, he had to rush home to get his dad's car and be off to buy the clutch parts.

He pulled open the locker door and reached in for his jacket, only to recoil with a look of horror. A powerful odor of meat and garlic had hit him full in the face. Woody yanked his precious jacket and held it about a foot from his nose. It reeked. "Move, Ahern," an irritating voice said behind him. "I need to get in my locker."

Woody whirled to face Graffan. The tall boy stood with his head hanging, his long black hair falling over one eye. Woody held up his jacket, too angry to speak clearly. He shook the jacket in Graffan's face. "You . . . what the . . . I'm gonna . . ."

"You were always griping about the bananas, so I quit bringing them," Graffan said in an infuriatingly innocent voice. "You didn't tell me I couldn't bring salami. You should have told me, Woody."

"You think you're wise," Woody gritted. "If I wasn't in a hurry . . ."

Graffan smirked, gloating over his victory. "You mean if you had the guts, don't you?" Suddenly, Woody grabbed Graffan's shirt with his left hand and pulled back his right.

"I'll report you!" Graffan squawked. "You're not allowed to hit a guy with glasses! You hit me and I'll have the police on you."

"I'm not going to hit you where it will hurt your glasses, Graffan," Woody said in a soft, calm voice. "I just want you to know I don't like salami, either. *That* salami!" Woody stepped in close to Graffan and hit him a hard, short punch in the pit of the stomach. Graffan doubled over with a hoarse bellow and sank to the floor. "Don't make a production out of it, Graffan," Woody said. "I know I can't hit that hard." He swung around and trotted away.

He had intended meeting Sandra inside the school, but the salami smell on his jacket had him worried. It was *worse* than bananas. He went outside and waited for her. When she came along, he fell in step with her, rather far to one side, slightly behind her, and on the lee side of the wind.

"Hi," Woody said.

"Hi." The look of pleasure on her face when she saw him gave him courage.

"I meant to ask you, Sandra," Woody said carefully as they strolled along the tree-lined walk. "Do you have a date for the dance yet?"

Sandra turned and gave him a cool look of censure.

"Doesn't that come under the heading of my business?"

"I just wondered," Woody said, flustered at the ice in her voice. He didn't see anything wrong about asking that question. Sandra slowed, waiting for him to come a little closer, but he kept his distance. She didn't know what was wrong with him. She wondered if he was ashamed to be seen with her and was trying to pretend they weren't together. It would be just like a boy.

"Have you asked any other girls?" Sandra asked, taking a step toward Woody.

He retreated a step, maneuvering to stay on the downwind side of her. "No. You see, I answered your question." He wished he had left the jacket in the locker.

"I only asked you because you asked me. To show you what it was like."

"Well . . ." Woody had a harassed expression on his face. "Well, I wanted to ask you."

"And . . . ?"

"And what?" Woody was really bewildered.

"You said you *wanted* to ask me. When was that?"

She was teasing him, twisting away from him, making him come after her with his hat in his hand, figuratively speaking, so he wouldn't think she could be taken for granted. Woody hated these evasive, teasing tactics . . . and he enjoyed them. That is, he would have enjoyed them if he hadn't been so self-conscious about the odor on his jacket. He was frantic to have her accept before she caught a whiff of him and changed her mind.

"I mean I wanted to ask you now," Woody said, looking at her with imploring eyes.

"Hmmm." She didn't know why he seemed so upset over merely asking for a date. It thrilled her to think that it was the effect she had on him. Not many boys had given her the opportunity to experience the power of being a desirable woman. She wanted to prolong it.

"You know," she said, looking away, "the spring dance isn't quite like any other dance."

"Yeah," Woody said, not really caring to discuss the matter. "I know."

"Usually," Sandra said, "it's the dance where steadies go. Or if you go with someone, people think it's a sign you're going to go steady."

"I know that," Woody said ungraciously, unnerved by his attempts to keep out of smelling distance. "Look, do you want to go with me, or don't you?"

"That's a fine way to ask," Sandra said frostily.

"I'm sorry . . . I . . . It's just that I've got a lot of important things to do this afternoon, and . . ."

"Oh?" Her eyes flashed with sudden anger.

"Oh, damn it!" Woody said desperately. "I didn't mean it that way."

"Don't swear at me, Woody Ahern," Sandra said indignantly. "I don't take that from anyone."

"I wasn't saying it to *you*," Woody said tiredly. "It was Graffan. Him and his d— . . . He had salami sandwiches in the locker and my club jacket is all smelled up. I . . . If you smell anything, it's Graffan."

"Oh, that *is* annoying," Sandra said, anxious for a chance to be sympathetic and understanding. "I didn't notice it, but I guess you're closer to it. I have the same trouble."

"You have?" Woody beamed.

"Yes. My locker mate uses the most awful cheap perfumes, and they smell up my clothes, too. Here . . ." She stepped close to Woody and held up her arm. "You smell it on my new spring coat?"

Woody bent his head to sniff at the arm of her coat. It was the closest he had ever stood to a girl on purpose since he'd become a big boy. He sniffed dutifully at the coat, but what he was most aware of was that their faces were now only a few inches apart. To Woody, the faint odor of perfume on her sleeve was heady stuff. He stared into Sandra's brown eyes, so very close to his, and at her smooth skin, her delicate nose, and pleasant, soft lips. His knees began to shake.

"Isn't it awful?" Sandra asked, dropping her arm.

Woody continued to stare at her, slightly dazed, his head reeling from the perfume and the closeness. "Yeah," Woody said. "But salami is worse."

"Oh," Sandra said, "I don't mind it."

"Is it okay for the spring dance, then?" Woody asked. "I'll have my car really fixed up and cleaned up by that time. So, I could call for you and take you home myself."

Sandra studied Woody's face as he stared intently at the sidewalk and waited for her answer. She liked him, and she knew her parents would approve of him and of his parents. Well, she liked him *in spite* of *that*. For a moment she wished that he was older, and smoother, and more able to take command in a definite, sure, masculine way. But then, she thought, if he was like that he wouldn't be interested in her. Anyway, he was only a tenth grader. By the time they were juniors and seniors, he would be older, and maybe smoother, and . . . maybe . . . still like her.

"What do you like to do?" Sandra asked suddenly.

Woody lifted his head. "You mean like the way I like to work on my car?"

"Yes."

"I like to work on my car."

"What else?" She looked brightly curious.

"Oh," Woody said, "I like to swim when it's hot and mess around and ride around and go fishing . . ."

"That's interesting," Sandra said. "We like the same things. My father used to take me fishing with him all the time when I was younger. I'm pretty good at it."

"That sure is interesting," Woody said. "I mean, about us having the same interests. I like to read a lot and listen to the radio. I don't care too much for TV . . . just a few special programs."

"That's just the way I am. Isn't that funny?"

"It sure is a coincidence," Woody admitted.

"It sure is."

They both shook their heads in wonder.

"I bet if we compared," Woody said, "we'd find that we liked a lot of the same things and didn't like a lot of the same things."

"I'm sure of it."

Woody laughed awkwardly. "Well, I suppose that's what makes some people friends and some people not friends."

"That sounds logical."

Slowly, they had begun walking again. Woody noticed that they were heading toward Sandra's home . . . and he had important clutch business elsewhere. "Uh . . . what do you say, Sandra?"

"About what?"

"The spring dance."

"You asked me to go with you."

"I know."

"And I said I would."

Woody blinked. She *had*? "When?" he asked stolidly.

"*When!* All the time! Do I have to put it in writing and have it *notarized?*"

"I guess I'm pretty dumb when it comes to girls," Woody said. "But it sure would help a guy if you just said yes or no sometimes."

Sandra laughed, pleased with the way things had gone. She guessed Woody would walk her home now, and perhaps stop in for a minute and meet her mother, and they might play a few records and get to know each other a little better. But she didn't know how Woody's mind worked, or about the clutch parts, and how he felt about his car. She didn't know that while he liked her *very* much, his heart belonged to an ancient, creaking vehicle called Sidekick.

Woody came to a stop. At last it was settled. He had a date for the spring dance. "Well," he said abruptly, looking at his watch, "I have to be going. The club is putting a new clutch in the car tonight, and I've got to get the parts. See you around, Sandra."

He gave her a big smile and a friendly wave, and then he was moving away in the opposite direction at a walk. Going somewhere *important*, obviously. Going to do something *much* more important than being with a girl.

It was a good thing Woody didn't look back. Because Sandra, left high and dry without a warning, her pleasant plans for the afternoon rudely shattered, reacted according to sudden impulse. She made a horrid, insulting, irritated face at Woody's back, and again stuck out her tongue at him.

— — —

Woody had walked about two blocks when a car pulled up alongside him. The driver, Albert Johnson, was a junior and also one of the boys who had tried to sell his car to Woody.

"Want a ride?" Johnson called.

For a moment, Woody couldn't believe his good fortune. No one had ever stopped for him before. He got in Albert's car eagerly.

"How's your heap?" Albert asked. He had heard about it, too.

"Needs a lot of work," Woody said.

"Don't they all," Albert said. "All the time."

"I guess so," Woody agreed.

It was odd, how much he felt at home with Albert. And he knew why and why Albert had stopped for him. Even though he was on foot, he owned a car, and that made him one of the fellows. Now he was where he belonged—among the boys who owned and worked on cars. It was just that simple.

Albert dropped him off at home and left with a friendly wave. Woody waved back. It sure was wonderful to be one of the boys with cars. They had something in common, even though most of them, like Albert, were older than he was. It made him their equal, even in their eyes. In the one day he had owned a car, he felt that he had grown up years' worth of ordinary life and experience. Things sure changed when a guy owned a car.

# CHAPTER 12

AFTER DINNER, WITHOUT SAYING A WORD, Woody sprang a little surprise on his parents without seeming to do so on purpose. He went into his room, and when he came out, he walked into the dining room and paused so they could get a good look at him.

"Well, look at that," Ahern exclaimed, an affectionate smile on his face. "It *looks* like a real mechanic. What do you suppose it is?"

Cheryl laughed and clapped her hands. "It makes you look like a monkey!" she yelled at Woody. He pretended to be angry, but he felt too pleased for anger.

"Now I can stop worrying about your good clothes," Mrs. Ahern said. "Just be sure you don't sit on the living room furniture with those on." Woody endured it all, self-conscious and proud. He was wearing one of his afternoon purchases, a suit of dark green mechanic's coveralls, huge and baggy, buttoned up to the neck.

"They'll fit a little better after they're washed and shrink down," Woody said. "But they're just what I need for all that dirty work under the car." He put an old khaki cap on his head. "This old fishing cap ought to keep the grease out of my hair." The very talk about work and grease made him glow with pleasure.

"You certainly look the part of the master mechanic," Ahern said. "Are you all set for work?"

"Almost." Woody nudged his nose with his knuckle. "I've got the parts I need, but I have to ask you a favor, Dad."

"Shoot."

"Well, I hate to dismantle the car out in the driveway in case it might rain or something. It would be a lot safer, and we'd have a better light, if I could clear out the other side of the garage and use it."

"For how long?"

"Until we get the clutch in. Tonight, and maybe, if we have any trouble, tomorrow night."

"It would be simpler if I let you use my side of the garage for a night or two," Ahern said, getting his car keys. "You can move mine out and yours in."

"Be careful, Dad," Mrs. Ahern warned good-naturedly. "Remember the basement."

"It won't take us long," Woody promised. "The guys will be over in a little while. Want to see the stuff I bought today, Dad?"

"I'll be out when I've finished my coffee," Ahern said. Woody ran out.

Mrs. Ahern looked at her husband and shook her head. "*Now* he's got the garage. I suppose we're forbidden to use that, too, as long as he's in there."

"Well," Ahern said tolerantly, "they do have to be inside. And for a night or two . . ."

"Want to bet?" Mrs. Ahern asked sardonically.

"It's outside again in two nights, finished or not," Ahern said emphatically. "Believe me." But he looked worried.

Woody backed his father's car out of the garage and got in his own to drive it into the garage. Annoyingly, it wouldn't start. He gave up when the battery began to sound weak. The guys could push it inside when they came. Meanwhile, he sorted over the parts he had bought that afternoon, checking them against the factory manual. There didn't seem to be any reason why the job wouldn't be a breeze.

Jim Bob and Sonny showed up in a couple of minutes, dressed in old clothes and ready to work. A few minutes after that, they were surprised to see the Pooch drive up. Dick Slater got out of the car, wearing faded denims and a navy flying jacket. He talked to the Pooch for a moment, and the Pooch drove away. Dick sauntered toward the garage, smoking a cigarette.

"For a minute," Jim Bob said to Dick, "I thought you were bringing the Pooch with you."

"Let's not start in with him," Woody said. "If he starts coming around, we'll never get rid of him."

"He's getting to be quite a buddy of yours, ain't he, Dick?" Sonny asked.

"He's a jerk," Dick said.

"Why do you run around with him?"

Dick looked at Sonny and laughed sarcastically. "That doesn't mean anything. You're a jerk, Redhead, and I hang around with you."

The boys began to find places where they could lean comfortably against Sidekick. "Come on, guys," Woody said impatiently, "let's roll the car in and get to work. We've got a clutch to change."

Dick squinted at Woody. "What are you supposed to be in that outfit? You look like a hot dog that got into a baloney skin by mistake."

"Joke," Woody said. "Now let's push it in."

The boys got around Sidekick and pushed the car into the garage. Woody put blocks in front of and behind the front wheels, to wedge them securely. Then he got a jack out of his father's car and began to jack up the rear end of his car. The others stood by and watched interestedly.

"This is really it," Sonny Mack said proudly. "We're working on a car at last. Just like the other guys in school who have clubs."

"You mean *I'm* working on a car," Woody panted.

"What can we do, Woody?" Jim Bob asked. "Only one guy can work the jack at a time."

"I'll tell you what you can do. As soon as I get the car up high enough, slide those concrete blocks under the frame. And somebody else do it on the other side. Not too far forward."

Jim Bob and Sonny took positions with the concrete blocks. Dick watched, his hands in his pockets. When Woody gave the signal, the two younger boys tried to slide the blocks in place. Woody crouched down near the jack and directed them. "Back a little, Jim Bob . . . *this* way . . . more . . . more!"

"They're hard to push," Jim Bob complained. "They're heavy."

"Get down on the floor and push them," Woody said roughly. "You don't have any leverage, trying to move them squatting down like that."

Jim Bob looked at the grimy floor and gingerly lay down on it on his stomach. "It's cold," he said.

"It won't kill you. Now you, Sonny . . . lie down so you can see what you're doing. There . . . that's the way. Now I'll let the car down on the blocks."

Woody let the car down and removed the jack. The two younger boys joined him, brushing off their clothes.

"We're going to need coveralls, too, if we're going to do much of that," Jim Bob said. There was a note of satisfaction in his voice. He had just performed some real work around a car, and it filled him with a sense of accomplishment.

Sonny Mack felt a similar pleasure at having dirtied hands at automotive labor, and he was anxious to plunge ahead. "Gimme a wrench there, Woody old pal," Sonny said, rubbing his hands together zestfully. "Old Redhead is rarin' to go."

"I just thought of something," Jim Bob said in his childish voice. "This is a regular meeting night. Shouldn't we have a regular meeting, with the regular roll call and everything?"

"We don't have time for that stuff now," Woody said, critically examining the results of their recent labor. "What's the point of playing, when we can be working?"

Dick snapped away the remains of his cigarette. "What do you want me to do, Woody?" Even he, at the moment, was willing to work.

"I thought Sonny and Jim Bob could start unbolting the shackles and stuff at the rear end," Woody said. "I'll get under the transmission, and you can work on it from inside the car."

"Boy," Sonny said happily. "We're really going. Imagine us, pulling a transmission and putting in a clutch."

"I'll get the wrenches," Woody said. "If we work fast, we can do the job and road test tonight."

Woody's father came into the garage. "How are you boys coming along?"

"Swell, Mr. Ahern!"

"We're really zingin'!"

The boys shouted their replies in loud, enthusiastic voices. Now that they were working men in working clothes, they didn't feel the reserve around Ahern they had felt when they were only wishing for a car. Ahern smiled. It was a pleasant scene he saw, the boys in old clothes, around an old car, with signs of work in progress. It was the very picture Sid Wheeler had painted for him. It was good to look at.

Woody approached his father, looking proud and purposeful in his green coveralls and khaki cap. "We've made a real good start, Dad." Woody was anxious to show his father how well he had done that afternoon, and how professionally he had planned the work. "Let me show you the clutch assembly I bought. Right over there."

"That looks awfully new for junkyard pickings," Ahern said.

"That's not junkyard stuff," Woody said. "You don't gain anything buying this stuff used. It's all rebuilt. Ought to last a hundred thousand miles. And for the few dollars more it cost . . ."

"How much was it?"

"Altogether," Woody said, "and that means everything that goes in, it was about eighteen dollars. That's dirt cheap for as much as I got. And it's the only major purchase I had to make."

"It's enough," Ahern said. He bent down to see what the boys had accomplished under the car and then said, suddenly and emphatically, "Oh no, Woody. Absolutely not."

"What's wrong?" Woody asked, hunching down beside his father.

"You'll have to put your car on something safer than concrete blocks. That's definite."

"They're all right, Dad," Woody said reassuringly. "All the guys . . ."

"Never mind about the guys," Ahern said, straightening up. "I don't want to be a killjoy, but concrete blocks aren't safe. There's a story in the paper almost every day about someone who was crushed to death by a car they had up on concrete blocks, chunks of wood, or an ordinary jack. Why, those blocks could split apart or collapse at any moment."

"What are we supposed to do? The car has to be up."

"The only safe way is to use jack stands. You ought to know that."

"I know," Woody said, his face a picture of dismay. "But they cost ten bucks a pair."

"I'm afraid that's ten you'll have to spend. So far, you've only spent about half your life savings on your car. Another ten won't break you, and it might save your life."

"It'll just about break me," Woody muttered.

"What?"

"I had to buy some other things, too," Woody said defensively. "You can't rebuild a car with your bare hands."

"What things?" Ahern asked suspiciously.

"Basic tools and stuff," Woody said. "I needed the wrenches I didn't have, and the man at the store said I'd be lost without a trouble light and a creeper. I got a real good buy on some seat covers, and I needed some spray paint and masking tape. I mean, a car has to be clean enough so you don't get your good clothes dirty. And I needed a new set of shocks for the rear end, for safety . . ."

Ahern leaned against the front fender of Woody's car. "Woody," he said slowly, "how much did you spend this afternoon? I mean for everything."

Woody frowned and twisted up his face as though he were figuring things out for the first time. "It seems to me, Dad," he said in his most businesslike tone, "and this includes *everything*, mind you, like my coveralls, and creep-in oil, and gaskets and stuff . . . it seems to me that I spent . . ." Woody's voice faltered a little, "about sixty dollars."

"You didn't!"

"Gosh, Dad, I didn't buy anything I didn't need right away. I was careful."

"For a forty-dollar car," Ahern said, not knowing whether to laugh or be angry. He gestured helplessly. "Wrenches I can understand, Woody. And the coveralls, *and* the creeper, *and* the trouble light. But why the fancy seat covers and paint and that other stuff *now*?"

Woody could have explained easily enough. He could have said he'd bought the stuff because Sandra Rowan wouldn't ride in a dirty car, and that was why it was essential now. But he didn't explain. Not that way.

"I knew I was going to need the stuff," Woody said, "and I got real bargains. Some of those things, like the creeper and the covers, I got for less than half price. That's a pretty big bargain to pass up. And the man said . . ."

"Oh, never mind what the man said," Ahern interrupted impatiently. "All I know is what you said. You said you wanted a forty-dollar car to practice on with a wrench and a book. Now you've gone out and spent practically every cent you earned and saved. And for what? For an old, broken down, dirty, ugly, miserable wreck of a machine that wouldn't be worth forty dollars if you put two hundred dollars worth of new parts on it. And that is a fact!"

"I just bought what I had to have!" Woody cried in his own defense. He was outraged. The attack on his car was like a direct attack on himself.

"I ought to make you take every bit of it back," Ahern said.

"It says on the bill all sales are final," Woody muttered.

"I'm not impressed by what it says on the bill," Ahern snapped. "I'll take the stuff back if you won't."

Woody saw an opportunity to prove that he was reasonable, trustworthy, and sensible. "Maybe what I could do," he said, "is take back the stuff I don't need right this minute, trade it for jack stands, and take what's left over in cash."

"That sounds more like it." Ahern was anxious to meet Woody at least halfway. Woody was a boy who needed careful encouragement in the manly art of backing down. "That sounds fine." Father and son smiled at each other, happy that they had found a way to get on the same side.

"I'll do it first thing tomorrow afternoon," Woody said. "I think I can get along without the seat covers and the interior paint and stuff like that." And he could. Sandra would have to wait a while for her ride, but it was more important to have a creeper and a trouble light and plenty of tools on hand. It was more immediately important to have good shocks on the car than a girl inside it.

"That sounds very reasonable," Ahern said. "You'll only be delayed a day. Meanwhile, I'm sure there's plenty of other work that has to be done and can be done from topside."

"We'll find something," Woody said.

"I'm sure you will. Good luck with your labors." Ahern took a last look at the car, raised his eyebrows a bit, and went into the house.

The members of the Road Rockets Auto Club gathered gloomily at the rear of their club car.

"That was a short job," Sonny Mack said resentfully, scratching his head with the end of a wrench.

"Maybe we could have our regular meeting," Jim Bob suggested. "We could talk about our plans for rebuilding, and we could meet inside the car." He wet his finger with his tongue and tried to remove a spot from his clean, carefully ironed work shirt.

"I don't want to talk about rebuilding," Woody said, taking off his cap and shoving it in a back pocket. "I want to work."

"What could we do that your father wouldn't kick about?" Sonny asked. "Clean and gap the plugs, or something like that?"

"Naw," Woody said. "I'm not in the mood for piddling around with it. I was set to do some real work. Well, let's jack it up and get it off the blocks."

Woody jacked up the car. The two younger boys slid the blocks aside, and Woody let the car down on its old bald tires. The night's work was done.

"I've got an idea," Dick said restlessly. "Since we can't do any work, let's crank up the old mill and cruise around a little. See what the rest of the world is doing."

Sonny and Jim Bob were all for it, but Woody wanted to work on the car and do something to improve it.

"We could look in on the drags again," Sonny said.

"Maybe choose somebody or find a carload of girls."

"Or run into those guys who want to beat us up," Jim Bob said, putting a damper on that idea.

Woody shook his head. "We're apt to ruin the flywheel and everything if we run hard before we've got a new clutch in. Let's not act like a bunch of crazy kids."

"Well," Sonny said, "I've got a better idea. I made up some club cards today in school. Why don't we put on our club jackets and drive around and help people in trouble? That's one of our club aims, isn't it? Just like working on a car."

"I'm for that," Jim Bob agreed. "We'll be working tomorrow night, so let's do the helpful car project tonight. What say, Woody?"

"It's a wonderful idea," Woody said. "Only I used up my two bucks' worth of gas last night. The tank is empty, and I don't get paid until tomorrow. Of course," he added, "there's no law that says I have to buy all the gas. I'll take you guys around a little if you can pop for a little fuel."

Dick snorted. "Big deal."

Jim Bob and Sonny exchanged glances. They had never thought about contributing gas money. After all, it was Woody's car, and they were just going along for the ride.

"I can put in half a buck," Woody said. "Anybody match me?"

"I can," Jim Bob said.

"All I've got is thirty cents," Sonny mourned, hoping he would be exempt from the draft.

"I'll take it," Woody said. "Dick . . . ?" Instead of the argument he expected, Woody was amazed to see Dick take a dollar from his pocket and offer it. "I got a buck," Dick said. "Fifty for tonight, and fifty for last night."

"Now," Sonny Mack said hollowly, "I've seen *everything*. What happened? Are you sick or did you inherit an oil well?"

Woody counted the money. "Looks as if we're in business," he said. "I'll tell my folks we're going."

Woody went inside the house and approached his father, explaining why they wanted to got out.

"That sounds like a noble project," Ahern said. "Just don't be too late, and stay out of trouble. And if you happen to break down and can't get started, call me."

Woody returned to the garage, the boys pushed Sidekick out into the street, and Woody started on the downhill slope.

Sonny scrambled into the back and plopped down heavily,

laughing between heavy breaths. "Maybe the first people in distress we ought to help are ourselves," he panted. "I can't take these hand starts."

"Probably the points," Woody said. "I was planning to put in a new set."

"That's work on this car," Jim Bob said. "You have to disconnect the fan, loosen the generator, and . . ."

"That's the idea of this outfit, isn't it?" Woody demanded. "Work?"

"I wasn't complaining," Jim Bob said, his feelings hurt. "I was just saying."

Woody gassed up at the service station, then drove to the edge of the street and stopped. "Which way?" he asked the club in general.

"Which way to what?" Dick answered.

"Which way do we go to find people in trouble who need our help?"

Dick was about to reply sarcastically when he saw that Woody was grinning. "I don't know," Dick said. "I had the map, but I must have lost it."

"Well, we'll just cruise around kind of easy," Woody said, driving on to the street. He relaxed and leaned back, forgetting about his loose seat, and almost fell over backward. "Gotta fix that seat first thing," Woody grunted, pulling himself forward.

He drove down some of the major streets in town, with everyone in the car looking out hopefully for some sign of a motorist in distress. But all the cars on these streets were running smoothly (more than could be said for Sidekick) or were parked.

Woody drove around town for about twenty minutes with no luck. The boys were terribly disappointed. In all their former club sessions, when they had planned and dreamed of the day they would be driving around doing good, they had somehow assumed that the streets would always be lined with motorists in need of assistance. They had seen themselves busy changing tires for helpless old ladies, starting stalled engines, making minor, quick repairs that amazed and pleased various drivers in distress, and generally making the world a better place to motor in. So, it was disheartening to drive around and around and around, bursting with the desire to do good, and find nothing to do. They were willing, they had emergency tools in their car, and they were, they believed, able. Yet no one needed them. It was quite a letdown.

"You wait until we're in a hurry sometime," Woody said. "There'll be millions of them needing help."

"That's just the way it will be," Sonny agreed solemnly.

"You always find good fishing when you want to swim," Jim Bob added philosophically. "Oh well, it's fun just to ride around, anyway. I'm satisfied."

"Maybe," Woody said thoughtfully, downshifting and taking a corner in second gear, "we've been looking in the wrong place. You usually see more people in trouble out of town than in it. We could try up Buffalo Road and back on Valley Drive."

"Only one trouble with that," Dick said. "There'd be plenty of cars parked along the road, but you wouldn't know if they were broken down or neckers."

"We could ask," Sonny suggested. "Who knows? Maybe they're necking because they're broken down. You know, it would be something to do while waiting for help."

"We'll try some of the back roads," Woody said. "If people are in trouble, they'll be out working or trying to flag us down."

Again, their hopes rose as Woody drove out of town and along some of the more deserted nearby roads. They rattled and bumped over rough gravel surfaces and raised dust on the dirt roads.

"We shouldn't get too far away," Jim Bob said anxiously, looking at the dark, empty fields outside his window. "We could break down too, you know."

"If we can help others we can help ourselves too," Woody said, annoyed at Jim Bob's doubts. He had faith in his car's ability to run forever, as long as there was gas in the tank and oil in the crankcase.

They bumped and groaned along without talking, listening to the loud exhaust, grunting a little as Woody hit chuckholes and they were shaken up.

"What this car needs more than anything else," Dick said, "is a radio. This is getting dull."

"I don't know," Woody said, slowing a little as a rabbit ran across the road in the dim glow of his headlights. "I feel pretty good." Out here, in the country and in the dark, it was easier to express himself and not feel he was sounding corny.

"It's a pretty good feeling, going along like this," Woody went on. "I mean, knowing that we're out to help somebody that might be in trouble . . . maybe somebody around the next turn, who's stuck and feels isolated and out of reach. And then we come along, and they're saved. I don't know about you, but I feel pretty good about it."

Woody's words meant nothing to Dick, but they impressed the younger boys. What he had done was to give them something they sorely needed to combat what had been a frustrating evening—a sense of worth, of dignity, and of meaning as human beings. There was no other word for it. Considering themselves as Woody had described them, they felt noble.

Woody drove on for several more minutes, an eye on his gas gauge. He didn't want to empty his tank every time he went out. "We'll head back toward town at the next crossing," he informed his passengers. "Looks as if it just isn't our night."

They sighed, gave up on the idea of helping anyone, and resigned themselves to enjoying the ride and reassuring each other about how nice it was to have a car for the club at last and about all the wonderful changes they would make on the car. As of old, when they had inhabited their basement headquarters, they talked knowingly and easily of custom body work and engine modifications and argued about which carburetor set-up was best, or if a magneto was superior to the best battery ignition system for street use.

"Look ahead!" Woody shouted. "Somebody in trouble!" Jim Bob and Sonny cheered and stamped their feet, then leaned forward to look through the windshield.

"It's two men changing a tire," Woody said. "I think there are a couple of ladies in the car."

"See?" Sonny shrieked in Woody's ear. "Just like I said! Broken-down neckers!"

"Grab the tire tools," Woody ordered tersely. "We're about to go into our first action." Sonny got hold of a jack, Jim Bob took the handle, and Dick got a lug wrench. As they approached the car, they could see, in their headlights, two middle-aged men examining a rear wheel and two women as old as their mothers sitting in the car.

The moment he had seen the car in trouble, Woody had stepped on the gas. Now he brought his car to a sliding stop. A second later, the club members were outside, yelling happily and waving the tools they carried, each racing to be first to reach the crippled car and give aid.

They had almost reached the car when the two men stood up, one holding a lug wrench, the other a jack handle. They yelled something the boys couldn't hear, and then, to the boys' horror, the men raised their weapons high and charged, swinging the wrench and jack handle, and yelling threats and curses. There was no doubt that they were advancing to maim or kill.

The boys skidded to a stop, trying to scream their peaceful intentions, but the men were in no condition to make out what the boys' shrill cries meant.

Jim Bob and Sonny fled at once, shrieking for help. Woody stood his ground for a moment, with Dick at his side. "We want to help you!" Woody screamed. "Please listen!"

The men came at him, their faces distorted with rage. For a moment Woody was too frozen by horror to move. He heard Dick cry, "Go, Woody!" and then he was aware that he had dropped whatever he had been carrying and that he was running for his life. He ran down the road, past his car, with Dick beside him. The men came after them, only a few feet behind, running swiftly. Woody knew that they would smash him with their iron weapons if they caught him, and he ran as fast as the terror and shock in his body could force him on.

Woody heard the men behind him shouting hateful curses, and a moment later a jack handle flew past between Dick and himself, skidding in the dirt ahead of them. A second later, something struck Woody a stunning blow on the left side of his head. He cried aloud, stumbled, and fell on the road, sliding on the dirt and stones. The object that had hit him fell just beyond him—a heavy iron lug wrench.

As Woody fell, he knew a dazed terror. Now they would get him. *Now they would kill him!* He tried to get to his feet, sobbing with fear and pain, but his feet collapsed under him, and his head throbbed.

There were, suddenly, feet by his head, and he cringed, expecting a kick. But above the feet he heard a familiar voice shouting its own curses and threats. Dick stood over him, feet braced. In one hand he held the lug wrench that had hit Woody, and in the other the jack handle the men had thrown. With their weapons in his hands, he screamed wild curses and threats at the two men, daring them to come close, crying he would smash in their heads, smash in their faces, kill them, kill them, *kill them!*

Woody got to his hands and knees, shaking his head. Suddenly something struck him in the side, and he cried out.

"The dirty-crazy rat guts are throwing stones," Dick sobbed angrily. "I'll kill them!"

Woody could hear the stones striking the ground around them. He heard one hit Dick and heard Dick's angry gasp of pain. Then Dick was pawing at the road for stones, and flinging them back, throwing wildly, trying to destroy with every stone.

Woody got to his feet, feeling a terrible pain on the left side of his head. He put his hand there but was too frightened and stunned to know what he felt. He heard himself crying, "Do I have an ear, Dick? Do I have an ear?"

He felt Dick's hand grasp his arm. "Can you run, Woody? Can you run?"

"I think there's blood in my eye," Woody gasped. "Lead me." He grabbed Dick's jacket and followed as Dick ran.

Then Dick slowed and stopped. "We're safe now," he panted. He began to curse horribly, and, now that the danger was over, he suddenly broke into tears and began to throw up in the road.

Dick's reaction was violent, but brief. He regained control of himself and looked at Woody, trying to see what damage had been done. "You're bleeding a little," Dick said, "but it doesn't look too bad. It must have just skinned you."

"It's sure sore," Woody said. "But I guess I'm all right. I still can't figure out what happened, or why."

They jumped nervously at a noise beside the road. A moment later Jim Bob and Sonny crept out of the bushes, glassy-eyed and trembling. They made small, frightened noises when they saw the blood on Woody's face.

"All right now," Woody said, his voice shaky. "Everybody calm down. We're all right now. Dick . . . I guess I've got you to thank for getting me out of it. So thanks. It was gutty of you to stand by me. I won't forget it."

"Aw, I didn't know what I was doing," Dick said. "I was trying to run, but I was too scared to move." But he was pleased. Truthfully, he didn't know why he had stopped to defend Woody. It hadn't been a planned or conscious thing. All he knew was that he had seen his friend go down, and he couldn't run another step after that.

The men had gone back to their car and were making repairs with the tools the boys had dropped. The boys stayed where they were, far away, and waited until it was safe to return to their car.

They talked a little, but they were shaken and upset. They were no strangers to violence. All of them had seen fights and had been in fights, but they had never encountered anything like this. The adult world, the vague adult world which they waited to enter, and which, though around them, was really remote from their realities—the reasonable, controlled, restrictive, protective adult world—had suddenly gone mad and turned on them with flaming eyes. The world of their fathers and mothers had tried to destroy them. They would never again, for the rest of their lives, be wholly free of the fear of human beings.

The other car drove away. When the road was dark and quiet again, the boys walked slowly toward their own car, ready to flee at the slightest sound. When they reached their car, Woody walked around, looking at the ground. He came back to the others. "I guess they took our tools," he said. "The thieves."

"We've got theirs," Dick said. "We're even."

The moon was up; the road and the countryside lay quiet and deserted in the cold light. Every shadow seemed to hold menace. The boys shivered and got into their car, anxious to get away. Sitting there, it was a trap.

The starter groaned dismally, but the motor didn't catch. Again and again, his hands trembling, Woody tried to start the car. It was hopeless. They sat in the car in an agony of apprehension and helplessness.

"Never again for me, boy," Sonny said in a cracked, bitter voice. "I see anybody in trouble along the road, they can *die* for all I care." He was almost bawling.

Jim Bob, huddled in one corner of the back seat, lifted his face toward the roof of the car. "I don't even know what it was all about," he whispered. "Why did they want to hurt us?" He shuddered as he saw the men come at him again, their faces contorted, their arms raised, and he felt like closing his eyes and screaming. No one had ever wanted to hurt him before. Everyone had always liked him and been kind to him. Especially adults and people bigger than himself. He had always looked to them for kindness and protection. He had never before looked into the face of hatred. He had never suspected that the big bodies of adults contained such wild fury. He turned his face against the greasy back of the seat, his eyes closed tight, his teeth clenched.

Dick lit a cigarette and smoked with quick, nervous puffs. He had learned his lesson. The only reason he had come along on this trip was to make up a little for the night before, when he'd stolen gas and stripped cars with Pooch. He had never really stolen before, although he'd always swiped little things. And, having stolen, he felt it would balance the score if he went along with the club and helped someone in distress. But he had learned his lesson. The adult world didn't need any favors or any consideration from him. All you got trying to be nice was a kick in the teeth or a wrench thrown against your head. From now on, he wasn't having any mercy on anybody. From now on, he'd forget he ever had a conscience. He'd get paid back for what had happened. He'd make it back at night, with Pooch. They'd strike back. They'd strip cars and take whatever they wanted. From now on, there were no holds barred. After tonight, he didn't owe anybody anything. Whatever he wanted, he would take.

Thinly, in the night, they heard the sound of a police siren. It came closer, and soon they saw headlights and the revolving red light on top of the prowl car. Woody opened his door and stumbled out. "I'll flag them down," he said. "They'll help us. We'll tell them what happened. Maybe they'll catch those . . . people . . ."

Woody went around to the front of his car and moved his arm up and down. The police car swung around so its lights were full on Woody and his car. Two policemen got out and advanced.

"You fellows in there . . . outside!" One of the policemen motioned with his flashlight at the three boys in the car. His voice was hostile, his manner grim. The other policeman looked at

Woody, saying nothing. When the four boys were lined up beside their car, the two policemen looked at each other.

"Do you think *this* could be the outfit?" one of them asked, his light on Jim Bob's terrified face.

"You can't tell by looks," the other one said.

"Who are you people?" the first policeman asked. "What are you doing out here?"

"We're the Road Rockets," Woody said. He nudged Sonny and asked for a card, which he handed to the policeman. "We were looking for people to help. We saw this car with a flat tire, and we stopped to help. Then the men chased us with tools and threw them at us. I got hit." Woody pointed to the bloody place on his head.

The policeman examined the card Woody had given him and shook his head. "We got a report from some people that they were attacked by a gang of young hoods. Said they ran up yelling and screaming and shaking weapons."

"If that was us," Woody said, "we were racing to see who could get to help them first. We had tools with us. I don't know . . . I guess they didn't understand . . ."

The policeman advanced and looked at Woody's head. "Looks like you've just been scraped," he said, his voice more kindly. "Who are you kids, anyway?"

They identified themselves. The policeman who had examined Woody made a clucking sound in his throat.

"Your father was my coach the year you were born," he said to Woody. "What do you think he'll say about this?"

Woody shook his head silently.

The policeman looked at their car, shaking his head in disapproval. He opened the door and looked inside, flashing his light around. "Where'd you get all this stuff back here?" he asked suspiciously.

"It's all ours," Woody said. "It's club stuff. We can prove it."

"Uh-huh." The policeman got behind the wheel, almost toppling over as the seat sagged back with him. He shook his head again and examined the registration. Then he switched on the lights, beeped the horn, and tried the clutch and brake. He got out and approached Woody. "You know you're almost out of brakes, don't you?"

"We're planning to put on new ones," Woody said.

"Your lights are too dim to be safe, and you only have one tail-light," the other policeman said. "No license plate light. Did you know that?"

"I just bought the car yesterday," Woody said. "We're just starting to fix it up."

"Well, you take the car home, and don't drive it again until those things I mentioned are fixed. Understand? The next time it will cost you. It might even mean a weekend in jail. Understand that?"

"Yes, sir," Woody said, feeling terribly tired.

"You kids ought to know better than to cruise around at night in an old wreck like that," the policeman said. "Especially if you're a car club. All you can expect from this night cruising is trouble. You're lucky those people didn't catch up with you. They were so scared they might have killed you. Can you make it home yourself now?"

"I think so," Woody said. "If we could get it started."

The policeman sighed. "We've got a jumper cable. We'll start you." He got a jumper cable from the police car and attached it to the police car battery and to Woody's. Then he signaled for Woody to engage his starter. Woody did, and in a moment Sidekick roared into noisy life. The policeman came around to Woody's window, listening. "Are you running without a muffler?" he demanded.

"It's got one," Woody said. "The fellow who sold it to me put it on. I think it's a motorcycle muffler."

"It's illegal, whatever it is. You put the right muffler on that before you drive again. Plus the other stuff. Understand?"

Woody nodded wearily.

"All right. Now you go home and get taken care of. And stay off the streets at night if you don't have any business on them. You'll stay out of trouble and give us a break too. Now go on . . ."

Woody drove away. The police car followed behind him until he was safely in town, and then it turned off.

"How do you like that?" Dick asked the others angrily. "First, we get jumped for nothing, and what happens? Do the cops care what happened to us? They don't care. They pick on *us*. The fuzz." Dick muttered. "That's the kind justice you get from the fuzz."

"You can say that again," Woody added resentfully.

"Know what I just did?" Sonny cried wrathfully from the back seat. "I tore up all those courtesy cards I made and threw them out of the window."

"You're not quitting the club, are you?" Woody asked over his shoulder.

"That part of it I am." Sonny said it with such quivering emphasis the others had to laugh. "From now on, let's just be a car club that fixes up cars and has fun. Let the people who get stuck call a tow truck."

The boys chuckled at that too, and their spirits kept rising, and soon they were talking in high, excited voices about their experience. Now that they were safe, they were able to shed their conscious fears, and what had been a nightmare now seemed more like a thrilling adventure.

Woody stopped to let Sonny and Jim Bob out. "I was just thinking," Woody said. "Let's not tell anybody what happened tonight. If it got out, our folks might get scared and not let us ride around anymore."

"That's for sure," Jim Bob said.

"You guys will be over tomorrow night, won't you? To put the clutch in?"

"You bet," Sonny said. "The usual time."

"Right," Jim Bob added. "You couldn't keep me away."

And, to show he was brave and determined and capable, he spat on the sidewalk.

Woody drove toward Dick's house. "You'll be there too, won't you?" he asked.

"Ain't I always?"

"Yeah," Woody said, his mind at rest

"I wish I knew who those people were," Dick said. "I'd sure fix them."

"How?"

Dick grinned crookedly in the darkness. "I got my methods."

"Best thing to do is forget it," Woody said. "Boy, things sure have been happening since I got this car."

Woody let Dick off and drove away. Dick stayed outside on the sidewalk, watching him go. Almost the moment Woody was out of sight, another car drove up slowly, and Pooch's anxious face looked out. "I thought you was never coming back," he said. "I got more orders. You want to go along?"

Dick breathed in deeply. Here was a chance for a little revenge . . . if not against the people who had attacked him, against somebody just like them. "Yeah, I'll go. We're partners, ain't we? Shove over and let me drive."

# CHAPTER 13

W<small>OODY CONSIDERED STOPPING SOMEWHERE</small> to clean up before going home, but after thinking it over he decided not to. It would look too suspicious. When he reached home, and Sidekick was safely parked in the driveway, Woody went into the house and halted just inside the back door. "I'm home," he called out loudly and cheerfully.

His mother's voice answered from the living room. "That's good."

Woody called back, "Don't be scared when I walk in, Mom. I got a little scratch on my face, and it bled."

"Come in and let me look at it."

Having prepared her, Woody went into the living room. His mother took one look at him and gasped. "Good heavens, Woody! What happened?"

"It wasn't much," Woody said. He grinned at her and his father and Cheryl, who looked at him speechlessly. He didn't know how he looked . . . his clothes smeared with dirt, his face covered with dirt and blood, and a huge purple bruise over his left temple.

"Wasn't much," Mrs. Ahern repeated, going quickly to look at him. "How did you do it?"

"I guess I got careless," Woody said. "I had the hood up, and forgot it had to be propped. When I let go, it banged me on the head."

"But your clothes . . ." His mother looked anguished.

"That's from crawling around to look under the car," Woody said.

"Oh, that car!" his mother exclaimed. "That *car*! Come into the bathroom and let me clean you up. That's an awful lump on your head."

"It's not much," Woody said. He wondered why his father hadn't said anything but didn't dare look at him. Now, too, he was aware of a splitting headache.

"Take it easy with me, Mom," Woody said. "It's kind of sore."

"Are you sure you weren't fighting?"

"Why would I fight? I told you."

In the bathroom she cleaned his face tenderly, trying not to hurt him. He winced and groaned and complained at her slightest touch. "If you ask me," she said, "I think you ought to see the doctor."

"I don't need a doctor," Woody grumbled.

His father spoke from the bathroom door, quietly but with authority. "We'll run over to see Doctor Framme as soon as you dry your face."

"Aw, Dad . . . why make such a fuss over a scratch?"

"It's a head injury," Ahern said in a matter-of-fact tone. "And all head injuries ought to be checked. That is something I know about."

Woody knew from his father's tone that he would have to obey. Grumbling, he complied, delaying only long enough, at his mother's insistence, to put on clean slacks and a clean shirt.

Woody's father didn't ask any questions as they drove to the doctor. Woody was content to lean back and let his father drive.

His head throbbed painfully, and there was a sore place by his ribs where the stone had hit.

Dr. Framme's offices were attached to his home. He ushered them into an examining room and examined Woody's head under a strong light. Dr. Framme was a young, stocky man, with strong, steady hands.

"How did it happen, Woody?"

Woody was about to tell the hood-falling version of his accident, but his father spoke first. "He was hit accidentally with something about as solid as a lug wrench. That's why I brought him over."

Woody avoided looking at his father. His heart pounded painfully. How much did his father know? How had he found out?

"Not very much 'give' in that," Dr. Framme said genially. He proceeded with the examination, checking Woody's eyes, his reflexes, his sense of balance, and even the strength of his grip in either hand. "Have you felt sleepy since you were hit?" he asked casually.

"No," Woody said. "Just sore."

"As hard as your head seems to be," Dr. Framme said, "I think that wrench might need me more than you do." He turned to Woody's father. "He checks out perfectly. Not the slightest sign of injury to the brain." Woody's heart skipped a beat at that. "I'll put a dressing on it and give him something to ease the headache, and I think he'll be all right. He might stop in for a minute tomorrow, and the next day, just to be on the safe side."

Again, on the ride home, Woody was silent, but worried. The dressing on his head made him feel lopsided. Finally, his father said, "Want to tell me about it?"

Woody looked at his father. "How did you know it wasn't the hood, Dad?"

"The police called. Luckily, I answered. The policeman was one of my old pupils."

"That's what he said. Does Mom know?"

"I haven't told her yet. It's not that I want to keep things from her, but it would hit her pretty hard. I mean, the idea of anyone chasing her son and trying to beat him with a weapon."

"Yeah," Woody said, feeling very manly, and very close to his father. "Mom does take things to heart, kind of."

"Don't think," Ahern said quietly, "that I didn't."

"It was crazy, Dad," Woody said in a strained voice, suddenly close to tears. "We went out to look for people who needed help. We saw this car, and stopped, and ran over to help. And then, all of a sudden, these two men came at us with wrenches. We ran, and they chased *us*. They threw the wrenches at *us*, and one hit me. Then they threw stones." Woody paused, too choked with emotion to continue at once. "And all we wanted to do was help them. They must have been drunk or crazy to do a thing like that."

"Or frightened," Woody's father said.

"Of *us*?"

"They didn't know who you were."

Woody was confused. Was his father sticking up for the people who had attacked him? How could that be?

"I'm sure you know this, Woody," Ahern said. "We've been having a lot of trouble lately with gangs of young hoodlums who've been stopping cars, smashing them up, and beating up the people inside. Actually, when you boys went out driving, I wanted to warn you to be careful of people like that. But I didn't, because I didn't want to frighten you. I guess I didn't know how to say it without running the risk of making you feel I thought you were a little kid."

"I've read about those guys in the paper," Woody said. "And heard about them at school." He remembered the carload of cruel-looking young men who had tried to provoke trouble on Main Street.

"The people didn't know who you were," Ahern said. "All they saw was a group of teenagers in black jackets running toward them at top speed, yelling and waving clubs of some kind. For all they knew, you were the hoodlums they'd heard about."

"We were just racing to see who'd reach them first," Woody sighed.

"I want to tell you something that I'm ashamed has to be said," Ahern said. "To the people who don't know you, you're a teenager, and your friends are teenagers. And practically everything you hear, or see, or read about teenagers portrays them as vicious, conscience-less hoodlums. There are just enough young people like that to taint every child. The result is, people are afraid of strange teenagers.

"I'm ashamed I have to say this, Woody, but I have to, for your own protection. If you are out with a group as you were tonight, and you want to approach strange adults, don't all of you go forward at once, and don't run. One of you approach them slowly—I don't know, maybe with your hands in the air—to show you mean no harm and need not be feared. That's a terrible thing for a man to have to tell his son. But you've found out what can happen if you aren't careful."

"I see what you mean, Dad," Woody said. "I can see why we scared them."

"I know," Ahern said angrily. "But it makes me sick! I don't know what it is, but there must be something wrong with a society that's afraid of its own children."

"On top of that," Woody said, "the cops picked on us because we were teenagers. First, they searched the car as if we were thieves. Then they told me they'd put me in jail if I didn't fix my lights and brakes and muffler."

"I wouldn't call that picking on you," Ahern said. "All they did was demand that you obey the laws the rest of us do. What did you want them to do, ignore your violations because you're young? The reason they picked on you wasn't because you're a teenager. They were simply treating you as they would any adult."

"My head hurts," Woody complained suddenly. "I've got an awful headache."

Ahern gave him a knowing, tolerant look. "Okay, Woody. I'll quit."

They were silent until they reached home and Ahern swung into the driveway. He drove past Woody's car and into the garage.

"Dad . . ."

"What?"

"Do we have to tell Mom what happened?"

"We should. She has a right to know."

"What if she wants to take my car away from me?"

"She won't," Ahern said. "We've talked about that. Our taking your car away won't cure what ails you."

"I didn't know anything ailed me," Woody said in a stiff, insulted tone.

They walked out of the garage. Woody stood by while his father closed the door. "What ails you," Ahern said, "is the ancient and honorable disease of growing up. In your case, you believe that owning a car is proof that you're a man."

Woody watched his father check the doors, shaking them to make sure they were securely closed. There was something old and fussy about the way he did it. The moonlight glinted on his high forehead and light, scanty hair. Woody despaired of ever making that man understand what the car meant in his life; what it had done for him, and how it had changed his standing with other boys . . . and at least one girl.

"If we made you give up the car without a really good reason— such as your being a reckless or dangerous driver—you'd think we were denying you the chance to be a man. That would only aggravate the disease."

Ahern walked over to Woody's car and looked at it closely, touching it lightly with his hand. "You have to find out for yourself that ownership of anything, in itself, means nothing so far as your *self* is concerned. Any fool of legal age with enough money can buy anything he wants. That doesn't make him less a fool. All it does is make him a fool with possessions. You don't have to be wise or mature to want things or own things. Right now, you're convinced the only way to prove you're a man is to own a car. Believe me, the way you might have to prove your manhood is by giving it up . . . all by yourself."

Woody shook his head helplessly. His father just didn't understand what a car meant to a boy in this day and age. It *was* the difference between being a boy and a man. And it *was* worth every effort, every labor, every sacrifice that had to be made in its behalf. But there was no way he could make his father know that.

Woody noticed his father looking at him closely, his expression serious and undecided. "You think I don't understand, don't you?" he asked in a friendly, quiet voice. "You think I don't want you to have a car."

Ahern drew back and turned to look at the car again. "Do you know how much I want you to have this car? After everything I've said about it?"

Woody shrugged, lost in trying to follow what his father was getting at.

Ahern approached Woody and looked down searchingly into his upturned face. "Something happened to you tonight, Woody," Ahern said in a gentle voice. "Because of it, you and I, for the first time in our lives, share a common, terrifying feeling. We both know what it means to be boys who are under attack and who fear for their lives."

Woody swallowed but said nothing. Ahern looked at Woody's car again.

"Let's sit in your car a moment," he said, smiling a little. "I don't want to lecture you, but I need to talk to you. Will you sit with me a minute? I think that's the best place."

Woody nodded dumbly and moved toward the car. His father got in the passenger side, and Woody slid under the wheel. His father leaned back, stretching his long legs under the dash. "Roomy, these old cars," he said. "Feels like old times."

"That's why I like older cars," Woody said. "They don't build them this comfortable anymore." He waited for his father to go on, to explain.

"The boy you are, and the boy I was, have something in common," Ahern began, staring at the cracked face of the clock set in the dashboard. "I think they ought to meet. When I reached my seventeenth birthday, the way I tried to prove I was a man was to enlist, and to fight in the war. The war was three weeks old then.

"I was still seventeen years old when I went overseas as an infantryman. I was a small-town boy who had never been away from home before. When I left, I carried an automatic rifle. I was the BAR man in our squad. I was pretty husky. I guess they gave me the job because they thought I was strong enough to carry it.

"I was still seventeen years old when I went into my first action . . . that is, when I went where people would try to kill me, and I would try to kill them. I don't know how to explain what it was like to be under fire. Perhaps, after what happened to you tonight, I don't have to. Only my fear lasted more than a few minutes. And for the first time in my life, I saw friends killed . . . from out of nowhere. That's the way the bullets and the fragments come . . . from out of nowhere. You crouch, you hide, you're insane with terror, and you are killed or crippled by pieces of metal that come unseen from out of nowhere. That's what makes it so horrible sometimes. You almost pray to see the enemy, to reassure yourself that you are fighting against other men . . ."

Ahern stopped and cleared his throat.

Woody gripped the steering wheel and looked through the windshield, trying to imagine his father at the age of seventeen in battle. He couldn't. "It must have been pretty terrible," he said lamely.

"Perhaps no worse than what you went through for a little while tonight. I don't know how to measure things like that."

Ahern leaned back, looking at the headliner in the car. "We moved up," he continued. "Finally, my squad deployed along the edge of a clearing just inside the woods, where we'd be hidden. We were lying there, resting, wondering what to do next. At that moment, I was more tired than frightened. Fatigue is a luxury in combat. You only indulge the feeling when you're reasonably safe.

"We were lying there, and someone on our left began firing. We looked into the clearing, and then, just to our left, a squad of enemy soldiers jumped to their feet and began running toward a sheltered spot to our right. They shouldn't have done that. They should have crept and crawled. But I suppose they were too frightened for that. Maybe one man panicked, and the others were sucked in by his panic. They rose like a covey of quail, suddenly, and they were in flight. I don't think I was even consciously aware of what I was doing. I reacted like a soldier. I opened fire with my automatic rifle, and, bunched the way they were, they all went down."

Ahern's voice had, in the telling, become level and emotionless. It was almost as though he were reading the words.

"A little later we were able to advance, and I stopped to look at the men I had killed. Until that moment, it hadn't been like killing anyone. It had just been . . . shooting. I looked at them. They were the enemy. Eight dead men. I say 'men,' but I don't think more than two or three of them were older than I was. They might have been fresh from the recruit depot . . . maybe that was why they panicked.

"At the time, I don't know what I felt. I didn't think of them as being young, because they were as old as I was. I didn't feel proud, and I didn't feel guilty. These are feelings that you have in normal times and in normal situations. I don't even know if I thought of them as human beings. If I felt anything, it was relief. That's what the enemy dead represented . . . relief. If they were dead, they couldn't shoot anymore. Each one that died meant one less that might kill me. I think that's all they meant to me then.

"But when I went to war, Woody, I didn't go to kill, but to save. I knew what it was all about when I was seventeen. I knew the war had to be fought to save democracy. I knew I was fighting for the freedom of everyone on earth. And I knew . . . even then I thought about it . . . that I was fighting to keep the world free for my children, if I were to survive, return, marry, and have children. As it turned out, for you and Cheryl."

Ahern's voice lightened. "I was still seventeen when I was hit, hospitalized, and discharged from service. I went back to school, met your mother, and married her when I was nineteen and still a student." Ahern laughed softly. "Someday, you ought to read the papers and magazines of those times. How they carried on about crazy teenagers rushing into wartime marriages. How they raved! Thousands and thousands of those marriages didn't work out. They were hysterical romances, based more on fear and uncertainty than love. With the whole world slowly destroying itself, young people were frantic. Their feelings could best be described in those two lines of the Housman poem: 'I shall have lived a little while, before I die forever.' Mom and I were two of those crazy teenagers. Only our marriage lasted. And many, many more of those marriages lasted. Their offspring are your classmates."

Woody stirred and touched the bandage on his head. "Do you want to go in?" Ahern asked. "Do you feel bad?"

"I'm all right," Woody said. "I mean, it's only a bruise, not a real *wound*."

"Don't envy me my scars," Ahern said. "There's nothing glamorous about them. All they represent is where I got hit."

Woody bowed his head, his chin on his chest. "I guess I must seem like an awful little kid to you," he said, "after what you went through when you were a boy."

"No," Woody's father said. "I didn't tell you this to make you feel inferior, or grateful, but to help you understand. I did what the boys of my day had to do, that's all. Just as you are doing, or will do, what the boys of your generation have to. If you had been alive then, and my age, you would have done the same thing. If I were a sixteen-year-old boy today, I'd be crazy about old cars, too . . . perhaps this one. It isn't the boys who change from one generation to the next, it's the world. And the kind of world you live in determines largely what you do—or think you have to do—to be a man."

Woody's father turned toward him, tucking his left leg under him and extending his arm along the seat, his fingers near Woody's shoulder.

"On the surface," Ahern continued, "your generation seems to live in an easier world than mine. But mine seemed easier than my father's, and his seemed easier than his father's. But don't let the outer trappings fool you. It's no easier for a boy to become a man now than it ever was. And it never will be easier, no matter what kind of society you live in. When you're young, it's your fate to lie awake at night wondering what's going to become of you, and who you're going to become, and what, and where you'll fit in with the rest of the world, and whom you're going to marry. These problems are the same, good times or bad, war or peace. And you have to work things out for yourself according to who you are, and what the world you live in is like."

"I've thought about those things," Woody admitted. "And worried about them, as you said. I didn't know everybody else did."

Ahern extended his arm and patted Woody on the shoulder. "It's a free world we've given you," he said, "but not an easier or a safer one. The peacetime automobile has killed more of our young people than all the enemy guns in all the wars we've ever fought. Every time you go out on the road in your car—no matter how routine the trip—you face more hazards, and probably have more narrow escapes from disaster, than most wartime patrols on most of their missions."

"I'll be careful," Woody promised, soberly aware of his own courage in wanting to drive his car.

"I'm sure you will be. But that's only half of it."

Woody looked at his father with questioning eyes.

"I know that you, and the people whose opinions you value,

regard ownership of a car as a sign of manhood. Since that's the way you feel, I'll expect you to carry the entire burden of the car on your own shoulders. Otherwise, it's a sham."

"That's the way I want it," Woody said.

"All right," Woody's father said. "I hope you can keep your car and that you can keep it running. It will probably make your life much more pleasant. But, since it means so much to you to have a car, it will mean a greater loss if you have to give it up. Do you see what I mean? It wouldn't mean just giving up a car. It would be like giving up your manhood. That's where I think you're making a mistake . . . in allowing the car to represent you. I want it to belong to you, not you to it . . . You look cold, son. Shall we go inside?"

They got out of Woody's car and met in front of it.

"Does Mom know about . . . the war?" Woody asked.

"A little. Not as much as you do. You're the only one, other than the men in my squad, who knows."

"I won't tell anyone," Woody said solemnly, impressed by the confidence. It made him feel he was older and more mature. There was also a feeling of pleasure in that he shared a secret with his father that no one else in the family knew. One part of his father belonged to him alone.

"I'll get around to telling Mom you boys were chased," Ahern said as they reached the back door. "I'll tell her you were bruised when you ran away and fell down. I won't make it sound too bad. And I'll leave out the part about the lug wrench."

"That'll help a lot," Woody said. "She probably wouldn't be able to take a thing like that as calmly as men have to." He reached up and touched his bruised head, close kin to his father's wounds. They walked into the house together.

# CHAPTER 14

Woody Ahern awoke with the frantic, sinking feeling that he was late for a race.

Usually, when Woody awoke, it took him several sleepy minutes to figure out what and who he was, to realize it was morning, and to concede that it was his duty to get out of bed after a while . . .

This morning his eyes flew open as though they were operated by springs. And he was aware, even before his eyes were in proper focus, of all the important jobs he had to do that day and how little time there was in a day to do them all.

First, there was school to sit through. When school was over, he would run to get his dad's car, hurry home with it, take the parts he didn't need back to the dealer, exchange them for parts he needed, and hurry home with the car. Then he had to rush to the dairy to work, he had to see Dr. Framme, and he had to race home for dinner. Then he would be ready to put on his coveralls and get to work installing a new clutch with the assistance of the club members. What a day it was going to be!

Woody scrambled out of bed and said, "Oof!" as the sudden movement made his head ache and spin. But he didn't have time to play at being hurt. He grabbed a towel and washcloth and a small leather case that held his toothbrush and special brand of toothpaste, his comb, hair dressing, and special bar of medicated anti-acne soap. So armed, he went to the bathroom.

The dressing was still in place over Woody's bruise and still clean. But the swollen place was very tender, and every time he touched his face or had to move his facial muscles, it hurt. It was difficult for him to be both fast and careful as he scrubbed his face with the special soap, brushed his teeth for two or three minutes, then combed his hair. He looked at himself searchingly in the mirror. His concern was not the bruise on his head, but the hint of one or two blemishes threatening to break out on his chin and nose. Carefully, he daubed the spots with a touch of medicated cream and hoped for the best.

He dressed quickly, choosing the first combination of slacks and shirt that seemed to blend, neglecting his usual morning gripe to his mother that his favorite shirt or favorite slacks were always *being* washed and ironed, but never *getting* washed and ironed. Then he was ready for breakfast.

Woody's mother was so unused to such speed on Woody's part that she didn't have his breakfast ready yet. He sat at the table and drummed impatiently with his fingers, feeling the pressure of all he had to do that day.

"How's your head, Woody?"

"A little sore, Dad." Woody watched his father's hand reach for a coffee cup. The forefinger curled around the cup's handle . . . just as, Woody thought suddenly, it had curled around the trigger of the automatic rifle. He watched the finger tighten as his father lifted the cup and was almost surprised not to hear the explosion of gunfire.

Woody's mother brought his breakfast and examined him with a critical look of concern. "You look a bit pale," she said. "Are you sure you're well enough to go to school?"

"Sure, I'm all right," Woody said. Then, thinking ahead, beyond school, he said quickly, "I was wondering, though. My head does ache a lot. I mean, it might be hard for me to have to do a lot of reading and studying with a sore head. Maybe I ought to stay home this morning and see how I feel."

"What do you think, Darrell?" Mrs. Ahern asked.

"Woody's the best judge of how he feels."

"I feel being in school wouldn't help my headache any," Woody said. "Maybe I ought to take it easy for half a day. I could rest, and maybe take an easy drive over to the parts store to make the exchange, and do a few quiet things on the car to get it ready . . . and rest a lot, taking it easy . . ."

"We'll try school," Ahern said. "It might be difficult to explain why a boy who's too sick to be in school is well enough to drive around town. Besides, you can take it easy in school for one more morning."

His father's tone was pleasant, but Woody knew it was the final word. He gave up his hope of cutting school to get a head start on his errands.

When Woody reached school, everybody he met had to ask him about his head. He gave them the falling-hood version, and there were a good many chuckles about the hazards of working on a car. But before very long one of the other boys in the club—Woody didn't know which one—couldn't keep the truth to himself and had to relate what had happened to a friend. The story spread through the school like a prairie fire, and Woody was besieged again, this time for all the true and gory details.

He didn't know how many times he was cornered by groups of boys who had to hear it all. Some of them, he was sure, came to listen three or four times. But again and again Woody found himself the center of a gang of boys who used his experience as a platform from which to launch into accounts of their own adventures. And these were not little boys. These were the boys he had always wanted to mix with and associate with. Mostly, they were the older boys with cars, most of whom had, because of car ownership, found themselves in some kind of jam at one time or another.

It was a great day for Woody, aware of how intently they listened to his description of what had happened, noticing the equality the experience had won him, and even the respect the boys seemed to show. Somehow, more than ever, he was one of them now.

It was such a full day of talk, of telling, of hearing other similar experiences, of describing his plans for the car, of getting masses of conflicting advice on how to rebuild, that the day was over before Woody could settle down to face it. He realized only during the last hour that he hadn't yet talked to Sandra, and now she was in a different classroom. There had been a crowd of boys every free minute, asking and telling, and talking cars and adventures. He wanted to see her, but he had so little time to get everything done.

When school was over, however, he stole a jittery moment to find Sandra and explain how busy he was. He was so concerned with his own problems that he failed to notice the coolness in her manner.

"Boy," he exclaimed with a great sigh as he joined her and walked along by her side. "What a day! I've been trying to see you all day to tell you what happened last night."

"I've heard all about it," Sandra said. "Two or three times."

"The guys wouldn't let me go," Woody said, looking at his watch. "They had to hear all about it."

"I noticed the girls crowding around you too," Sandra said. "I can see why you found it difficult to find me."

"You should have crowded around with the others," Woody said. "Boy, it was something. I nearly got killed. I wish I could tell you about it, but I have to run. I have to exchange some car parts, and see the doctor, and work on my job, and then work on the car. Man, am I busy!"

"Well, if you're that busy, you don't have to waste your time talking to me," Sandra said. "You can tell me all about it some day when the other girls aren't crowding around you."

"That might be a long time from now," Woody said. "It looks as though I'm going to be busy working on my car day and night for weeks to come."

This was it, Sandra thought. This was goodbye. One day of having other girls stand around oohing and aahing about his adventure, and he was through with her. Now that he thought he was a big wheel, he evidently thought he could do better in the girl department, too. It had been a very short romance. He had told her in no uncertain terms that he was going to be too busy to see her. She could take the hint. She repressed an impulse to tell him that the left side of his head wasn't the only place it was swollen. But she didn't want him to think she was hurt by being discarded so abruptly.

Sandra stopped walking. Woody halted too, looking anxiously at his watch, obviously eager to get away from her.

"I'm afraid I have to run," Sandra said, making a show of looking at her own watch. "I've been meaning to tell you . . . the spring play goes into rehearsal today, and I'll be busy every afternoon and most evenings. So, you needn't bother to call me, or anything like that. I just wouldn't have the time to spare." And that, she figured with a slight toss of her head, told *him* off.

Woody faced her with a pleased grin. She had solved his problem. Now he didn't have to worry about taking her out when he had to spend all his money on the car. "Say, that's just great, your being busy with the play," Woody said happily. "Now you won't be left high and dry while I'm busy." And before Sandra could recover from that, he went on. "It's real lucky, our both being busy at the same time. Well, I've got to get going. I've got to get those parts and get the car in shape if we're going to have decent transportation to the spring dance. And maybe," he said, looking at her with a sudden hopeful tenderness, "a good car to take you other places, too. I mean, if you still . . ." He didn't know how to say what he wanted to say, so he sighed a great sigh and said, "See you," and ran off.

Sandra watched him run off, shaking her head in a dazed, confused way. That boy! First, he acted as though he liked her. The moment she responded he turned his back on her. Just as she was ready to call it quits, he was back, acting interested and showing affection. And the minute he had a date with her, he forgot all about her and ran off again. *Didn't he know anything about going with a girl?*

Sandra walked out of the school building. She saw Woody trotting toward the field where the junior high kids practiced baseball. She could see him trying to run easily so he wouldn't jar his head. Seeing him run, dogged and purposeful, she understood him for the very first time. Suddenly, it came to her. That was really it. He didn't know anything about going with a girl! The explanation was so simple that she laughed—touched, exasperated, and relieved all at the same time. Here she had been attributing all kinds of insidious motives to his behavior, envisioning him as a scheming boy who had been trying to trick her. And all the while the only thing wrong with him was that he didn't know how to be a boyfriend. Why, she had known him since they started school together. She knew he had never dated and never had a girlfriend. No wonder he was so clumsy and understood so little.

By his very words, all his effort and work was to get his car ready for their big date. That meant he was interested in her, despite all the girls who had hung around him all day. And the only reason he was always flying off to work on his car instead of being with her was so that the car would be good enough for her. He didn't know that the little things were more important to girls than the big ones . . . that just going to a dance in a car didn't mean anything. Girls went to lots of dances with boys because they were asked, not because it meant anything. What really mattered were the little everyday things that a girl did with a boy she really liked—such as exchanging confidences, listening to records together, and just being together and talking, without having to be entertained or going somewhere. What was important— romantic—was having a friendly minute or two every day . . . not being like strangers for weeks and then getting mushy on a date and then not talking to each other for weeks after that. It was being a good . . . well, even a *dear* . . . friend that was important. And Woody didn't know that. He didn't know anything about girls. He acted as though he wanted to be her boyfriend. Well, she wanted him to be, but not in the crazy, haphazard way he was going about it. If he was going to be her boyfriend, he would have to learn how to be a good one. And the only way he would find out how to behave with a girl, and do the things that would make him liked, was for her to teach him.

There was only one problem. She didn't know any more about boys than he knew about girls. How was it done?

Woody trotted steadily toward the junior high practice field, harassed by the swift passage of time. He was late. He should have been on his way to the parts store by now. He remembered, as he ran, that Dick might be waiting for him at the high school for their walk to work. Woody slowed his pace, undecided. Then he decided he didn't have time to go back. Dick would guess that he had gone on ahead. He'd be that smart. Woody picked up his pace but felt guilty. He didn't like to run out on a friend like that, even if it wasn't a big deal.

Woody was just turning in at the practice field when a car honked behind him and swept past. He looked over his shoulder and saw Dick at the wheel of the Pooch's car, with the Pooch riding passenger. The car roared off in second gear, weaving from side to side, leaving Woody in its wake of dust and oil fumes.

Woody waved, glad that Dick had a ride to the dairy. It never occurred to him that Dick might have driven off without looking for him at school.

His father's car was parked in the teachers' lot, not far from the entrance to the practice field. Woody got out his keys, unlocked the car, and got in. He was in a hurry for more reasons than one. He had always avoided coming to this place. When possible, he always approached or left the high school in a way that would take him far from the field. In winter he preferred to walk home, no matter how cold it was, rather than meet his father here and ride.

As Woody got behind the wheel of the car and rolled down the window, he felt the old urge to get away as soon as possible and be off the hated ground. But as he was about to start the car he stayed his hand and listened, hearing the sounds of the boys at practice, and the strong, deep voice of his father directing them.

Suddenly, without consciously thinking of it, Woody opened the door and got out of the car. Slowly, despite the pressure of time, he approached the field, keeping behind a large tree that stood at the edge of the field. When he reached the tree he stopped, and then, not knowing exactly why, he looked around the tree and watched his father work with (the thought of the phrase set Woody's teeth on edge) "his boys."

For a moment, he thought there had been a mistake. There was his father, dressed in baseball pants, a sweatshirt, and baseball cap, with a whistle dangling from a cord around his neck. He was holding a bat, showing a group of thirty or forty boys how to grip the bat and swing it parallel to the ground. That part made sense to Woody. But the boys!

Always, in his mind, he saw himself in the middle of a thick jam of boys, all bigger, stronger, louder, and more capable than himself. Always he had retained this picture, of himself being hemmed in, hidden from the view of the coach, his father, by the bigger boys . . . the better boys.

But the picture faded. It had to fade. Woody stared at the boys around his father. Why, they weren't big at all. They were little kids, that was all. Just little kids! His father towered above them, and he, if he walked out there, would tower above the mob of little kids. He would be able to see his father, and his father would be able to see him, even if he stood in the middle of the pack.

Woody stepped around in front of the tree. For the first time since he had quit the junior high teams, he was setting foot on the junior high field. He advanced slowly, his knees shaky, his heart beating rapidly. He stood on the outer fringes of the squad while his father demonstrated the proper way to swing, and he was pleased and proud at the way the little kids listened to and watched and admired his father, and at the way his father told the little kids what to do.

Ahern, looking at his squad for possible questions, saw Woody standing at the rear, his face pale and solemn. He smiled at Woody over the heads of the junior high boys. "Do you need me for anything, Woody?" he called. All the boys turned to look at Woody.

Woody wet his lips, aware of his size, aware that, except for a few exceptionally large boys, these were all little kids. "I just wanted to tell you I was taking the car, Dad. Do you want me to pick you up later?"

"No, you get your business taken care of," Ahern said. "I'll ride home with Mr. Elrick. He's working with the track team."

"Okay, Dad." For the first time, Woody was aware that out here his voice was deep. "I've been watching your practice, Dad," Woody said, and added words he never thought he could say aloud. "Your boys look pretty good for this early in the season."

The meaning of Woody's words was not lost on Ahern. He smiled slowly and nodded. "We're coming along. Our boys might come up with a good team if they work hard."

Once, "our boys" would have meant Ahern and his team. Now, Woody knew, his father meant "yours and mine." And for the first time in Woody's life, that was how it seemed to him.

Woody drove home and threw the part he had to exchange in the trunk of his father's car. He drove to the parts store as fast as he dared without risking a ticket. By now he should have been at the dairy. Where had the time gone? He arrived at the store in a nervous sweat and carried the parts inside. To his dismay there were several customers ahead of him, and only one slow man to wait on them. Woody squirmed and bit his lips and almost burst with impatience as the clerk took forever to hunt for nozzles and bushings, checked specification numbers in catalogues, discussed possible substitutions, looked up prices, and wrote out sales slips. When he did bring out an auto part for some mechanic who was leaning against the counter, there was always a technical discussion between that mechanic and some other mechanic waiting his turn, and the clerk *had* to listen and join in, smoking cigarettes and telling stories, and getting slower every minute.

It seemed to Woody that the clerk, seeing him there with all the stuff he was bringing back, was trying to avoid him. But at last, there were no other customers ahead of Woody, and he was able to explain his situation.

To Woody's surprise, the clerk offered no objections. He got out the jack stands, the brake linings and fluid, and the electrical parts to fix the taillights. By the time Woody had exchanged the things he didn't need for the things he did, he needed another dollar in cash. And that took the emergency dollar he always kept folded in his wallet and pretended wasn't there.

His business over, Woody drove home, parked the car, and hurried to the dairy. He was an hour and a half late, and still hadn't seen the doctor.

Woody looked into Dick's egg-candling corner on the way in, but it was dark and deserted, and the radio was silent. Dick had quit work about a third of the way through a case of eggs. This wasn't unusual if he was ahead on his work. Woody went to his own area, changed into his white bib overalls and rubber boots, and began his

wet, steamy job. He worked as fast as he could, constantly looking at the big clock on the wall to see if he was picking up any lost
time. Although he worked at top speed, he didn't skip over any of
his work or do it less thoroughly. He knew how important it was
that the vats be spotless before they were sterilized, and even in his
hurry he was careful to do the job right.

Rushing, he was soon soaked with water from his rinse hose and
suds bucket. He attacked the inner walls of the vats with his brush,
scrubbing furiously and splashing soapy water in every direction. It
hurt his head to work that way, but he ignored the pain.

He was hanging over the rim of the small vat, his toes barely
touching the dairy floor on the outside, his hands just reaching
the bottom of the vat, when a hand thumped against his back. He
grabbed the rinse hose, ready to give Dick a burst of water in the
face as he straightened up. It was the way he sometimes put out the
lighted cigarette in Dick's mouth, to repay Dick for dropping a rot
down his overalls once in a while.

Fortunately, Woody checked before he acted, and avoided turning the hose on his employer.

"What are you doing?" Mr. Stonelee asked. "Trying to set a new
world record? I didn't know you could move so fast."

"Got a lot of work lined up on my car tonight," Woody said.
"We're installing a clutch. I want to get an early start." He looked
at the wall clock. "I guess I won't, though. I got a late start here."

"I know. For a while I thought you weren't coming in, either.
You seen Dick?"

"Not since right after school," Woody said. "He was headed this
way."

"I guess he never got here." Mr. Stonelee looked annoyed. "The
least he could have done was finish that case and put it in the cooler.
Can you do it for me, Woody? When you're through here?"

Woody looked distressed. He usually did help out when Dick
didn't show, but *tonight* . . . he was late already, and he wasn't very fast

at candling. It would take him forty minutes to finish the case. He wanted to beg off, but he didn't see how he could. Mr. Stonelee always depended on him, and he couldn't turn him down now. Not when he needed his salary so much. And he could use the candling money, too.

"I'll do it," Woody said, looking at the clock again.

"I knew I could count on you," Mr. Stonelee said, looking relieved. "You know, if Dick doesn't do any better than this, I'll have to fire him. If you know any good, steady boy who wants that job, bring him around. It should be good for ten or twelve dollars a week, the way business is picking up." Woody hesitated. He didn't want Mr. Stonelee to think he was after Dick's job, because he'd rather be broke than undercut a friend. But if Mr. Stonelee was going to fire Dick, and was looking for another boy . . .

"I think Dick will be back on the job," Woody said. "He wasn't feeling very good today."

"He's been getting more unreliable all the time," Mr. Stonelee said. "I'm really looking for another boy."

"Well," Woody said, wiping his hands on his white overalls, "if you hire another boy, how about me?"

Mr. Stonelee shook his head. "I've never had a clean-up boy like you, Woody. It's easier to find a boy to candle eggs properly than do your job the way you do it."

"What I meant was," Woody said, "my taking both jobs. I could candle eggs the days I didn't clean, or nights. I don't want to sound greedy, but you know how it is when you're building up a car. I need every cent I can get for parts and stuff. It sure takes the money."

Mr. Stonelee grinned. "It sure does. Well, if you need the money, I'd just as soon you have the job. I'll give Dick another chance. If he lets me down again, it's your job."

"I'll tell him that," Woody said. "Maybe he'll settle down and work."

Woody went back to his scrubbing with conflicting feelings. He wanted Dick to keep his job, but he also wanted the ten or twelve dollars a week it represented. That was much more than he made on clean-up, and it was an easier job. With the two jobs, he'd be earning almost twenty dollars a week, and it would be a cinch to support his car on that, no matter what he did to improve it—new paint, new engine, or new anything. And there would be money left over for dates, too. What more could he ask?

As soon as he was through cleaning, Woody sat down in his wet clothes to candle the eggs. He did them carefully, sorting the good eggs according to size and weight. Since he wasn't too familiar with the job, it was an hour before he was through and had everything put away. Then he headed homeward, beginning to feel weary from the fast pace of the day, the extra work, and the long time between meals.

He dragged into the house late, explained why he was late, and waited impatiently for his mother to warm his supper. When it came, he wolfed it down.

"You'll choke or get sick, eating like that," Woody's mother said.

He pointed to his watch. "We should have been at that clutch an hour ago. We want to get it done tonight. The guys been here?"

"They've been in the garage for ages. They'll wait for you a little longer. So, eat slowly."

Woody nodded, gulped down a few more bites of food, and then, his hunger pangs eased for the moment, dashed into his room. He climbed into his mechanic's coveralls, put on his cap, and came out again to get an extra bite or two of food while standing up. His mother scolded him for gulping his food, for not sitting at the table, for grabbing food in his hands, and for eating with his hat on. Woody nodded in agreement to everything she said, listening to nothing, and then ran out to get at the really important work of the day. The time to install the clutch had arrived at last!

# CHAPTER 15

WHEN WOODY WENT OUT TO HIS CAR, Sidekick was alone in the driveway. There was no sign of the club members. Woody was disappointed. Somehow, he had expected to find the other three busily at work, the driveway ringing to the sound of happy chatter and banging tools. For a moment, he thought the boys were gone, but a blue cloud of cigarette smoke drifted out of the left front window, and suddenly Woody knew where they were and what they were doing.

Woody approached the car and looked in. Dick was lying on the front seat, his head under the wheel and his feet on the upholstery. Sonny and Jim Bob were side by side in the back seat, reclining almost on their shoulders as they lay back and supported their feet on the front seat backrests. They were all smoking, and the inside of the car was a thick haze.

"Don't you guys work too hard, now," Woody said sarcastically, leaning in the front window. "You might strain something."

"Oh, hello there, Woodrow," Dick said lazily, puffing smoke at Woody through the steering wheel. "You're just in time to lend a hand."

"Didn't you guys do *anything*?" Woody demanded. "You've been out here for an hour. You could have had it all unbolted by now."

"We didn't want to start until you came," Jim Bob said. He was wearing a blue chambray work shirt, denims, and shiny black boots. "You know, it being your car and all . . . we didn't want to mess with it when you were gone."

"I can see how worried you are about my car," Woody said, "putting your feet all over the upholstery and throwing ashes and cigarette butts all around the interior."

"In this car," Dick said, "that comes under the heading of improvements."

"I've got some news for you, buddy," Woody said, opening the door. "The old man is going to can you if you miss any more eggs. He told me so today. One more strike and you're out."

Dick tilted his head back, looking at Woody from an upside-down position. "He can't fire me. I've already quit."

"Didn't you tell him?"

Dick chuckled. "I figured even a guy as dumb as Stonelee would get the idea all by himself when I didn't show up for a couple of weeks. He caught on real fast."

"What happened? Another job?"

"You might call it that," Dick said. "Another source of income, anyway. So, I don't need Stonelee and his lousy two-cents-a-dozen candling money."

"I do," Woody said.

Dick struggled to a sitting position. "*You* do," he said with a twisted smile. "You're a real friend, aren't you? You sure moved in on me."

"No, I didn't. You said yourself you quit. He had to have somebody to take your job. He hired me because I wanted it if you didn't. I need every dime I can make. You know that."

"Okay, okay," Dick said. "It's your job now. So let's forget it." But he looked angry and bitter. He had quit the job without a word to his employer, yet he was offended because Woody had taken it. Mainly his anger was because Stonelee hadn't been left in a jam; because Dick knew he wouldn't be missed at all.

"Now that we've settled that," Woody said, "how about a little work now that I'm here? We've got to get going."

The boys got out of the car reluctantly, stretching and yawning while Woody backed his father's car out of the garage.

"All right," Woody called impatiently when he was on the ground again. "Let's go, guys. Let's push Sidekick inside."

"Listen to the boss man," Sonny grumbled to Jim Bob. "All he needs is a whip."

As soon as the car was inside and blocked, Woody got the jack and raised the rear end. Jim Bob and Sonny took their places on each side of the car and set the jack stands according to Woody's directions.

"All right," Woody said, pleased with the way things had gone so far. "Now let's get to work. Sonny, you and Jim Bob start at the rear end, unbolting the shackles and disconnecting the brake lines. Dick, you get at the transmission from inside the car, and I'll slide under it and start unbolting there. We ought to have the job done in thirty minutes."

Woody went around to the front of the car and came back pushing the creeper along the floor and carrying the trouble light.

"Look at him!" Sonny cried as Woody lay on his back on the creeper and prepared to push himself under the car.

"What about me?" Woody asked, switching on the trouble light.

"We gotta lay on the cold dirty floor. You got a creeper to move around on."

"I need the creeper up here," Woody said. "There's a lot of moving around. You can lie in one place and do your work."

"And a light of his own," Dick said. "Nice that *somebody* can see."

"What do you have to see?" Woody asked. "You haven't had your hands out of your pockets since you got here. What do you plan to do?"

"I'll sit in the car and read the manual," Dick said, "and answer your technical questions."

There was a sudden, anguished cry from Sonny. "Darn old rusty bolts back here," he complained loudly. "I got a whole mess of rust in my eye." He slid out from under the car, holding one hand over his right eye.

"Go in the house," Woody said. "Ask my mother to wash the eye for you. You'll get it infected, rubbing it."

Sonny went into the house whining about his hurt eye and the rusted bolts.

"Woody . . ."

"Yeah, Jim Bob?"

There was a note of defeat in Jim Bob's voice. "I can't get anywhere with my side."

"What's the trouble?"

"Well, I got the mud and rust cleared away, but the bolts are rusted on. And the wrench won't take hold. It looks like somebody wore the corners off the nuts, so the wrench slips."

"Don't let it throw you," Woody said. "You have to expect things like that with an old car. I bought some creep-in oil in case we had this trouble. I'll get it for you. Soak 'em good, and give the oil a couple of minutes to work. They'll come right off."

Woody switched off his trouble light, rolled out from under his car, got the creep-in oil, and handed it to Jim Bob. While Jim Bob used it, Woody stretched to ease his back. Dick yawned loudly. Sonny came back from the house, his eye red and weepy.

"This is going to be some job," Sonny complained. "It'll take a month just to get it unbolted."

"Come on, you guys," Jim Bob called plaintively. "I'm doing all the work myself. How about a hand?"

Woody hunched down. "How's the oil working?"

"It isn't," Jim Bob said unhappily. "The only thing I did was get my shirt all spotted with oil and grease."

"I'm not getting under there again unless I've got goggles on," Sonny stated. "I ain't gonna lose no eyes just to mess with this old junker."

Jim Bob pulled himself out from under the car. "I can't do anything under there," he said. "We'll have to cut the bolts."

Woody pushed his cap back on his head. "Boy," he said in great disgust, "what a car club! What a bunch of master mechanics. Can't even remove a couple of shackle bolts." He looked at the sad, pouting faces of Sonny and Jim Bob, and knew what the trouble was. They were kids, playing at being mechanics. They weren't much bigger than his dad's junior high boys. They weren't real men like the car owners, or the other real mechanics he ought to have working with him. They were just kids. All they wanted to do was sit in the car or ride around. And these were the helpers he had to depend on to rebuild Sidekick. It wouldn't work. Somehow, he'd have to get in with a better club, with other boys who owned cars and knew how to work.

"Well," Woody said gruffly, "I'll take a look at those bolts. I wish I had Dan Ilder and his gang working with me. We'd have had it finished by now."

"I don't want to seem like a wet blanket," Dick said as Woody lay on the floor and looked under the car, "but what's the point of unbolting the transmission if there's nothing underneath to hold it? It's got to be lifted to line up with the driveshaft, doesn't it?"

Woody pulled himself out from under the car and lay on his back in the open, his face thoughtful. "I wonder how I forgot about that?" he said. "We can't do a thing unless we've got some support. What we need is a hydraulic jack under there, so we can raise and lower by fractions of an inch."

"It would be a cinch with a hydraulic jack," Dick said disinterestedly.

"I can get one," Woody said, getting to his feet. "You guys go ahead with the unbolting, and I'll run up to the service station and borrow Lou's."

"Borrow some bolt cutters, too," Sonny added glumly. "Just in case we can't get the nuts unstuck."

"And get me a better wrench," Jim Bob said. "This little crescent doesn't have the power."

As Woody headed for his father's car, Dick called after him, "I'll settle for a Coke, Woody. With plenty of ice."

The moment Woody was gone, Jim Bob and Sonny got inside the car to rest. Dick wandered out to the end of the driveway and looked at the sky. He was bored with what they were trying to do. More than that, he knew there was no place for him in what was going to happen here. He had sensed that when he had quit his job at the dairy. That was the first step in cutting himself off from being Woody's close friend. And it had to be.

Dick turned to look at the clumsy rear of Woody's car, hoisted awkwardly in the air on the jack stands. The car was doing it. The car they had talked about, dreamed about, and planned for together. And as long as it had been talk, and dreams, it had been all right. They could be friends.

But he knew Woody. Woody owned a car. And Woody would make it run. He would have a girl to ride in it. He was already becoming one of the "ins" at school. He was a property owner, a boyfriend, and there was a place for him in the school community. He would belong.

As long as he and Woody had been on the outside looking in, he could be Woody's friend. Now Woody would move inside, but he would go alone. He liked it where he was, on the outside. And yet, as he looked at Woody's car, and felt contempt for Woody's affection for it and all it stood for, he was also jealous of Woody.

The sound of a familiar motor came to Dick's ear. He turned his back on Woody's car, smiled, and reached for a cigarette. A car cruised slowly around the corner and eased to a stop. A familiar, anxious, questioning face looked out.

Dick's blood pulsed with new pleasure. He was outside, but he wasn't alone, wasn't helpless, wasn't a victim of anything. He had freedom, and he had power, and he had a follower. He opened the car door. "Move over, Pooch," he said. "I'll drive." And he drove away.

Jim Bob and Sonny sat in the back of Woody's car and smoked. For a while they said nothing, then Jim Bob asked cautiously, "How do you like this rebuilding? It's kind of fun, isn't it?"

Sonny pursed his lips and blew out a thin stream of smoke. "Kind of, I suppose." He ran his fingers back through his bristly red hair. "It would be more fun if this wasn't such a filthy old wreck."

Jim Bob nodded. Somehow, when he had imagined working on cars, he had always imagined the kind of cars he saw in the auto magazines, where everything was new and chromed and spotless, and there wasn't any rust or grime to cope with.

"When I get a car," Jim Bob said, "I'm not going to buy any old junker like this. I'll get me a real show car that will be some fun to work on."

"Yeah," Sonny agreed. "You take a heap like this, and what do you have to show for your work? A heap. You gonna buy a car?"

"My mom says I can have one when I'm sixteen," Jim Bob said. "You know, to make up for my father being gone most of the time. She's going to buy it for me. I can get anything I want, probably."

"Get something sharp," Sonny said. "Then you and me can promote us some women."

"It shouldn't be hard," Jim Bob said. "Not when they see what I'll be driving."

"Boy," Sonny said, wrinkling his nose, "this sure is a wreck inside and out. It's no fun working on an old wreck."

"Not for me," Jim Bob said.

"And that Woody," Sonny said. "Griping because we're in his club instead of guys like Dan Ilder. You heard that, didn't you? He sure thinks he's something, just because he got stuck with this old junker."

"He sure acts like he's too good for us," Jim Bob said. "Bossing us around like we were little kids." Jim Bob sighed. "Remember the swell meetings we used to have, before Woody got his car? It was fun in the basement, talking about cars. And getting hot dogs and Cokes."

"Yeah," Sonny said dreamily. "Them was the good old days, all right."

Jim Bob kicked the back of the front seat. "Then this old car had to come along and spoil the fun."

"I'll bet you something," Sonny said. "I'll bet the two rides we had are all we'll ever get. What'll happen is that we'll do all the work and rebuild the car, then Woody will be taking his girl for rides when it's all fixed up. And you know where that will leave us, don't you?"

"You're right about that," Jim Bob said solemnly. "That's just the way it will happen. A fine car club we are. All we'll have is dirty work and no rides around. There'll be plenty of riding around when I get my car. Mom says I can have a credit card at the gas station. I won't be two-bitting *my* friends for gas money."

"When's your sixteenth birthday?" Sonny asked brightly, a smile of delicious anticipation spreading across his face.

— — —

Woody swung his father's car into the driveway and hopped out. "I've got the stuff!" he yelled, hauling the hydraulic jack out of the trunk with a loud, pleased grunt. "Where are you guys?" He rolled the jack into the garage just as Sonny and Jim Bob climbed out of his car. "Did you get those shackles unbolted and brake lines off?" Woody asked briskly. The two boys exchanged glances.

"We tried," Sonny said, "but they wouldn't move. The nuts are too rounded off for the wrench to get a bite."

"I brought these bolt cutters," Woody said, taking the tool from his coverall pocket and handing it to Sonny. "See what you can do."

Sonny took the bolt cutters and slid under the rear of the car. "There's no place to grab hold with them," he said.

"There has to be," Woody answered. "Come on, try a little. You guys quit at the first trouble you find."

Woody slid the hydraulic jack under the transmission and pumped it. He got down on his stomach to check the position, then raised the jack a little more.

"Now we've got it," Woody said. "That takes the strain off. And we can adjust it just the way we need it. How you coming, Sonny?"

"I'm making a little progress," Sonny lied. "My eye bothers me. Lend me the trouble light a minute, so I can see this thing."

Woody slid the trouble light back to Sonny.

"Woody," Sonny said, "there's something leaking on the rear wheel."

"That's the brake fluid," Woody said. "That came out when you disconnected the line."

"I didn't disconnect the line," Sonny said.

"Neither did I," Jim Bob said. "Boy, it's cold in here. I'm getting a chill."

Woody got on his creeper and pushed himself under the car to examine the rear wheel. He tried to make a joke out of his discovery. "What do you know," he said. "I thought my brakes were weak because the linings were bad. The trouble was right here all the time. I've got a leaky wheel cylinder. If I had known that earlier, I could have bought a repair kit this afternoon and saved the money I spent on new linings."

"They might be bad, too," Sonny said.

"No," Woody said authoritatively, "it was this wheel cylinder."

"But your brakes squeal," Sonny persisted. "That means worn-out linings."

"Doesn't have to," Woody said, riding Sonny down with his tone. "Could be a bad adjustment, that's all."

Sonny didn't answer. He didn't feel like being told he was wrong every time he opened his mouth. If Woody knew so much, let him fix it.

Just then Woody's father came into the garage. "Telephone for you, Woody. It's Mr. Stonelee."

"I'll be right there," Woody said, getting out from under the car and standing up. Suddenly he felt very weary. He had been on the run all day, under pressure and nervous tension, and it was catching up with him. His head was hurting more, too, but he didn't say anything about it. He didn't want to complain to the others and spoil their fun working on the car. Only now did he realize they were a man short. "Where's Dick?" he asked.

"He disappeared," Sonny said. "We thought we heard a car, but we're not sure."

"He probably went for that Coke, or some butts," Woody said. "If he comes back while I'm on the phone, start him on the transmission. You guys can keep on doing what you're doing until I get back to check."

"That means nothing," Sonny whispered in Jim Bob's ear, and they both laughed silently.

Woody went into the house with his father. "It's probably about tomorrow's work," Woody said. "I'm going to candle eggs the days I don't clean vats. Dick quit to work on some other kind of job."

"Mr. Stonelee sounded a little upset," Ahern said.

"I don't know why he should be. Everything's in order up there."

Woody picked up the phone. "Hello . . . Mr. Stonelee? This is Woody."

Stonelee's voice sounded abrupt and annoyed. "I thought you were going to finish the eggs, Woody."

Woody looked puzzled. "I did, Mr. Stonelee. I finished the case and put it in the cooler."

"Why didn't you do the other two cases?"

Woody's jaw dropped. "Other . . . two? I didn't see . . ."

"They were right there, Woody. Under the one you finished."

"I guess I didn't notice them," Woody said. "I was only thinking about the one case. I'll do those others first thing tomorrow after school."

"That's too late. I need them done tonight." Woody looked helplessly at the phone. "Gee, I'm kind of busy right now . . . we just got started on my car . . ."

"I'm sorry, Woody. I know it's rough on you. But if you want the candling job, you'll have to do it when I need the eggs. It's that kind of a job."

"Okay, Mr. Stonelee," Woody said. "I'll be right up to take care of them."

"Good." Stonelee's voice was cheerful again. "I knew I could count on you, Woody. You're a dependable boy."

Woody put down the phone. "I have to go to the dairy and candle two cases of eggs," he said dejectedly. "May I use your car, Dad? I feel a little tired to walk."

"You look too tired to work," Woody's mother said emphatically. "Where you ought to be right now is in bed. You're pale as a ghost and your eyes look terrible."

"I've got to go, Mom," Woody said desperately. "I need the job. It won't take me long."

"You look ill to me," his mother said. "What did Dr. Framme say about your head today?"

Woody stared at her. "I forgot to go," he said.

"Oh, Woody."

"I'm all right," Woody said. "I'll go see him tomorrow. After all, it was only a bump from the hood, and that's hardly more than tin. I'll be back soon."

Woody went out to the garage and told Sonny and Jim Bob the news. "If you guys want to keep on working," Woody said, "you don't have to quit because I'm not here. You can do as much and have as much fun by yourselves. And when I get back I'll pitch in, too. Maybe we can take a run in Dad's car to a drive-in for some chow. I'll see you soon."

Woody drove to the dairy and took his place in the little egg-candling room. For a few minutes it was restful just to sit and perform the tedious little motions of candling and weighing. But he was tired, and he soon found it difficult to keep his eyes open, or to know what he saw when he peered at an egg against the light. He was clumsy, too, dropping eggs when he went to weigh them or to put them in the case. By the time he had done fifteen dozen eggs, his head ached, his eyes ached, his neck was stiff, and his back felt as though it would break. But he kept on doggedly, sitting there in his bulky coveralls, with the dressing (by now soiled) on his bruised head. He sustained himself by thinking that his work was for Sidekick; that every dozen eggs he candled meant he was two cents closer to buying a wheel cylinder, or plugs, or gas; that every case was sixty cents closer, and that the two cases he had before him represented a dollar twenty cents for parts that Sidekick needed . . . He reached for another egg.

Tired and sleepy and worn out as he was to begin with, it took Woody two hours to candle and put away the two cases of eggs. He dragged himself out of the dairy feeling that every bone and muscle in his body was battered, bent, or bruised. He breathed in the fresh night air to revive himself and wondered how Sonny and Jim Bob were doing on the club's car. Thinking of them, he went back into the dairy, and into the cooler. When he came out again, he carried a present of ice cream bars, orange drink, and chocolate milk. When he got home they could have a little refreshment break, then maybe do a little more work.

Woody drove home with his gifts, but when he got there the garage lights were off and there was no sign of Sonny or Jim Bob. Woody climbed wearily out of the car, and the minute his feet hit the ground the garage lights went on. He smiled. Sonny and Jim Bob were there! They must have turned off the lights for a joke when they heard him coming. He lifted out his load of ice cream and cold drinks from the dairy and went inside.

He was met not by his friends, but his father. "I'm glad you're back, Woody," Ahern said. "Lou Johnson has been calling all night. He says he lent you his hydraulic jack for a couple of minutes, not a couple of hours. He needs it and wants it back right away. I couldn't take it while you had my car, and he's alone in the station."

"I . . . I *need* the jack," Woody said thickly. "I can't take it back. I need it to hold up the transmission while we work."

"Woody, it's Lou's jack. And *he* needs it."

It was the last straw. "That's *his* tough luck!" Woody cried defiantly.

Ahern was about to be harsh with Woody for that remark when he noticed how weary and distraught the boy looked. It was the kind of bone-weariness and tension and frustrated anger he had once known himself on long, weary, seemingly pointless marches, or after long days in danger.

"It's after eleven, Woody," Ahern said gently. He put his hand on Woody's shoulder. Woody didn't move away. "I'll take the things back to Lou Johnson. You go in and hit the sack. You look beat."

"I am," Woody said. Now he understood why Sonny and Jim Bob were gone. After eleven . . . where had the hours gone? They'd have more time tomorrow.

"You know, Woody," Ahern said, "if your new job means late hours like this on school nights, you'll have to quit."

Woody shook his head. "I need the money," he said, looking at his car, seeing how much had to be done.

"Even so, I won't let you ruin your health for any reason."

"This was special. Emergency." Woody yawned noisily. As far as he could tell, not much had been done to the car, but he was too tired to look. He would look tomorrow, when he had more time and wasn't so tired . . . and after he had borrowed his father's car to go get the wheel cylinder. And tomorrow night, it would be different. They'd all get busy real early, and it wouldn't take them an hour to pull the transmission and put in a new clutch.

# CHAPTER 16

THE NEXT DAY AT SCHOOL was a letdown for Woody. For an entire day, he and his car had been the center of attention. Somehow, he expected the same situation to exist on the second day. But scarcely anyone asked him about his head or his adventure, and those who asked did it casually, sometimes walking away before he had time to answer. He went around feeling rejected and disappointed.

Woody tried his best to maintain his status with the car-owning boys. Whenever he had a chance, he cornered one or more of them, filled them in on his car and his plans for it, and tried to get their advice about how to proceed with his work. Much to his surprise, some of them didn't seem at all interested in his project, and some knew less about working on a car than he did.

In particular, Woody tried to talk to boys who belonged to good car clubs, hoping they might see him as a potential member and his car as a worthy candidate for a club project. It wasn't that he wanted to get rid of Sonny and Jim Bob exactly, but they were kids, and they had already shown they weren't much help working on a car. What he needed, he realized, was to associate with the older boys who knew how to work on cars and enjoyed doing it. There wasn't much point in talking over his problems with boys who didn't own cars. Even if they were interested, they couldn't really understand the problems the way other owners could.

But even the car-club boys didn't react with very much interest or enthusiasm, and none of them got the bright idea that he was needed in their clubs. Somehow, every time Woody began talking about his car, the other boys wound up talking about their cars, and he wound up listening to their plans and problems. And when he heard them talking about the late model engines they had already installed, about the intricate combinations of engines and transmissions they had worked out, of their experiments with dual-coil systems versus magnetos, or their actual results with dual four-barrel carbs against a three two-barrel set-up, he and his old car and his clutch job seemed very small and insignificant potatoes indeed.

In his effort to make friends with the boys he felt he belonged with, and to win their attention and respect, Woody grew reckless. Instead of confining himself to his immediate problems, which he saw were elementary and dull, he talked more about his future plans. He hoped the boys would be more interested when he mentioned what he called his plans to install the hottest Pontiac engine option linked to a LaSalle floor-shift transmission, with a motorcycle type gearshift assembly. He tried so hard to sound impressive that he didn't know where to stop and acted as though he were actually considering changes that the other boys knew ran into thousands of dollars. And, knowing he was talking dreams, they lost interest in him and his car. They could tell by the way he talked that he was stuck and was looking for free mechanics. And they had problems of their own.

Woody didn't know this. To him, they were boys who had everything they wanted. He had never noticed that some of them could only afford to drive their cars one or two days a week, and that they walked or shared rides the rest of the time. He had never really been aware how often many of the boys went carless because they were without four tires that would hold air, or had a dead battery, or a toothless transmission, or valve trouble, or (as he had) a shot clutch, or a dozen other difficulties that grounded their cars. And he didn't know how long they had to save up before they could afford to fix their cars and still have something left for gas.

At school, there were always enough boys whose cars ran from day to day to make it look as though all the cars were running all the time. And Woody, envying the boys their cars, had never taken the time to notice how often how many cars were not in evidence. It had never occurred to him that once a boy had a car that ran, it would ever cease running, or that he would ever be without the money to run it.

And so, still assuming that all the boys with cars drove them all the time, without any cares or troubles, Woody wandered all over school talking about his problems as though he was the only one who had any and hoping to make the boys like him by bragging about his future plans. He had no idea of the effect he was creating as, at one and the same time, he seemed to beg free help because he had troubles, then bragged about how much better his car would be than anyone else's. By the end of the day, the word had gone around to every boy with a car to steer clear of Woody or get trapped.

Woody didn't know this. All he knew was that he felt let down after the excitement of the previous day, and that he still had a long way to go before he could claim true equality with the other boys. It would come, he guessed, when he actually drove his car. Meanwhile, he tried not to be too disappointed that they hadn't rushed to ask him in. After all, he thought, he had talked to all the boys who mattered, and had shared some confidences and experiences and ideas with them. That was more than he had ever done before, and it was a good start. So he thought.

The last school bell started Woody running again. This day, there would be time to work!

He took his father's car again from the teachers' parking lot but didn't stop to visit. He drove straight to the parts store to buy his wheel cylinder. Then he drove to Lou Johnson's again to borrow the hydraulic jack, the bolt cutters, a couple of wrenches in sizes he didn't have on hand, a hub puller, and brake pliers.

This time, Lou seemed to have forgotten the generous offer he had once made to Woody about borrowing tools. When Woody mentioned what he wanted to borrow for a little while, Lou did not respond with a smile and a hearty okay. He, too, seemed to have lost his enthusiasm for Woody's project.

"I don't see how I can let you have those things, Woody," Lou said. "I've got some jobs coming up later today and tonight that I'll need the jack and the brake tools for. And those wrenches you want are sizes I use every five minutes. I don't see how I could help you without going out of business myself."

"I don't know what to do, then," Woody said. "I was counting on them." Lou Johnson went out to pump gas for a customer, and when that job was over he found some other work to do, and then had another gas customer. Woody waited for him to come back and discuss which tools he could lend, but Lou seemed to have forgotten him. Woody looked at his watch and grimaced. Losing time again!

Then Lou came toward him. Woody decided to ask for the jack for a specific time when Lou wouldn't be using it, and to guarantee he'd have it back in whatever time Lou needed it. That seemed fair enough.

"You want some gas, Woody?" Lou asked.

"No. I . . ."

"I wonder if you'd mind moving your car, then. You've got my second pump blocked, and I need it."

"Sure," Woody said. "I'll move it."

He went out and drove the car away from the pump to one side of the station. He stopped, intending to shut off the engine and go back and wait until Lou could talk to him about the tools. He looked back and saw Lou watching him. "So long, Woody," Lou called. Then he turned his back to check the oil in the car he was servicing.

Woody put his father's car in gear and drove away.

Boy, Lou Johnson had sure given him the brush! Just wait until he had his car running. It would be a long time before Johnson got any of *his* business. If he was going to be one-way about lending a few measly tools for a few measly minutes, he'd better not count on getting any business from Woody Ahern!

Now Woody didn't know quite what to do. He drove around for a while, then remembered he was supposed to see Dr. Framme. He drove to Framme's office. The doctor's parking lot was jammed with cars. Woody shrugged and drove away.

Since he didn't know where he could get a hydraulic jack, Woody found himself faced with a change of plans. It was true the clutch slipped, but it would move the car. Perhaps the best thing to do was work on the brakes first. It really didn't matter, since both jobs had to be done, and the brakes had to be fixed before he could drive. All he needed were a hub puller, brake pliers, and a pint of brake fluid. And, since the last of the money he had saved was in his pocket, he could buy the tools he needed and have money left over.

Woody turned the car and drove back across town to the parts store, where he bought the hub puller, brake pliers, and brake fluid. The store was having a sale on chrome tailpipe extensions, so he bought two of those; one for the tailpipe on the car and one for the second pipe he intended putting on when he installed headers. He also bought some friction tape, a can of liquid steel, a spark plug wrench, and a set of feeler gauges, all of which he would need as the work progressed. He didn't feel too bad about spending practically all his money, since his two jobs at the dairy would be paying him almost twenty dollars a week. He even priced hydraulic jacks, with an eye to having his own when he needed it. That, however, would take some saving.

When he left the parts store, Woody drove past Dr. Framme's office again. There was still a crowd, so Woody drove home and unloaded his purchases. He thought he would work alone on the car until supper time, but when he went in the house to change into his coveralls, the rest of the family was at the table and the meal was being served. It was that late!

"I'm sorry I'm late," Woody apologized. "But I've been to Dr. Framme's a couple of times, and his place was so jammed I couldn't get in."

"And were there," Ahern asked, "any places with lesser jams where you *could* get in?"

"Oh, I did run over to the parts store for a wheel cylinder. We're going to fix the brakes tonight. That has to be done before I can drive."

"What happened to the clutch?"

Woody sat down at his place at the table. "I thought it would be better to have all the critical items taken care of first. Your life can depend on your brakes."

"That's true enough," Ahern said. "Do you know how to change wheel cylinders?"

"Oh, sure," Woody said. "There's nothing to it."

"One of those twenty-minute jobs, like pulling the transmission?"

Woody's face reddened resentfully. "That's all it would take if I didn't have to candle eggs at the same time, and we had a jack."

Woody's mother sat down at the table. "I have a request to make. Could we possibly eat dinner without talking about cars and parts and tools? It gives me the feeling I'm having a picnic in a garage."

Cheryl looked at Woody hopefully from her end of the table. "Could I help you work on your car, Woody?"

"Cheryl! Didn't you hear what I just asked?"

Ahern put his napkin on the table and looked at his watch. "I hate to eat and run," he said, "but I'm due at a meeting. I'm on the committee to arrange sodding the new Little League baseball field."

"The trick in this house," Mrs. Ahern said, "is to name the committee that you're *not* on."

Ahern grinned. "They always need somebody connected with the schools to make the meetings respectable. And since I'm both a classroom teacher and a coach, I'm a natural target for almost anything. Leave the car for me tomorrow, Woody," Ahern said. "I have to drive boys."

"Okay, Dad," Woody said.

Ahern left but was back in two minutes. "Woody," he said in the precise, deliberate tone he used when he was annoyed. "How many trips did you make to Dr. Framme's office?"

"Two," Woody said.

"The Dr. Framme who lives in this city? There was half a tank of gas in the car when I parked it at school. It now reads empty."

Woody looked at his father questioningly. So, the tank was empty. So, it had to be filled. What was he supposed to do about it? Invent a way to run a car without gas?

"Well, Woody?"

"I went and got the wheel cylinder," Woody said. "And I had to see Mr. Johnson. That's about all the driving I did."

Ahern returned to the table and sat down, running his hand over his balding head with a weary gesture. "Look, Woody," he said, trying to sound as reasonable as he felt, "don't run me into the ground. Just because I let you have the car when you asked for it yesterday doesn't mean you're to take it whenever you want to, and without asking. I needed the car today."

"I had to get the stuff and go to the doctor," Woody said. "I thought it would be okay."

"You know, Woody," Ahern continued, "when you wanted a car, you painted a glowing picture of how much better off we'd be. I would be able to have my car all the time, and you would run errands in yours, take Cheryl places, and just make life easier for everyone. What has happened since you got your car is that you've got mine, too. In effect, you have two cars, and I don't have any."

"I'm going to do those things," Woody said, as though trying to explain to a child. "How can I run errands in my car before it runs? As soon as I get my car running, I'll do all those things."

Ahern shook his head. "That's not good enough. I mean, you can't use that as an excuse to take over my car. You're still welcome to use the car when you ask for it for a specific reason. But when you start driving forty or fifty miles a day on behalf of your car, I expect you to pay that expense. That's part of your car's cost. You can't let your car sit in the garage and drive mine all over at my expense, and then pretend you're paying your own car costs. Do you understand what I mean?"

"I can't support your car and mine," Woody protested.

"I can't support two cars either," Ahern said, "no matter how the cost is camouflaged. From now on, I want you to ask me before you take my car. I'll allow you what I think is reasonable mileage, but beyond that it becomes your cost."

"Boy," Woody exclaimed bitterly, "talk about tightwads!"

"Watch your language to your father," Mrs. Ahern commanded Woody indignantly.

"Let him blow off steam," Ahern said mildly. "I think Woody and I understand each other. Don't we . . . son?"

To Mrs. Ahern's surprise, Woody spoke in a restrained, reasonable manner. "Do you think it would be possible," Woody asked, "that I could have your car one afternoon a week, or maybe Saturday morning, to do what I have to do? Get all my shopping done for parts and things? That might take some cruising around to the salvage yards, too."

"I think we can work something out," Ahern said.

"With my two jobs," Woody said, "I could pay you so much a mile for the use of your car . . . I mean, enough to cover gas, oil, wear and tear, and all that."

"You don't have to go that far," Ahern said.

"I want to, Dad. I want to pay my way."

"I know you do, Woody. I know you mean every word of it, and I appreciate it. But all I want you to do is buy whatever gas you use over and above what I think is a reasonable allowance as a member of this family."

Woody leaned back in his chair. "Okay, Dad," he said cheerfully. "You work it out, and I'll go along with it. You're the boss." Saying that, Woody gave his mother a "take *that*" look and resumed eating.

Immediately after dinner, Woody put on his bulky dark green coveralls and his grease-stained khaki cap. "If anybody wants me," he said to his mother as he came out of his room, "I'll be working in the garage with the guys." He looked around with cheerful confidence. "Do you suppose you could rustle up some grub a little later on, Mom? For me and the guys?"

Mrs. Ahern gave him an amused look. "Maybe I'd better ask the *boss* first."

"Oh, Mom," Woody grumbled. "Don't start that."

"All right, oh great green monster," she said. "I'll be a rustler for you, as usual. Hot dogs and Cokes. Just help me in one way. When I bring the food, it's my signal that I want the boys to go home. So, you help get them started after they've eaten . . . unless you'd rather have me yell that it's your bedtime."

"I'll do what I can. You realize, we might not be able to quit any old time. Some jobs have to be finished once you start them."

"Don't start any job you can't finish before nine thirty."

Woody sighed. She just didn't understand mechanical work, and there was no use trying to explain.

"Woody," Cheryl asked as he started for the garage, "can I help, too?"

Woody grunted something discourteous, then, not wanting any more trouble, he lightened his tone and said, "Not right now. Maybe later," and went into the garage.

None of the club members were in sight. Woody looked inside his car, but it was empty. He looked at his watch and frowned. They'd never get anything done if they didn't get an early start. He decided to get things ready. He had brought his radio out to the garage, so he hooked that up and turned it on. In a moment, the harsh sound of music bounced back and forth between the concrete walls and the floor of the garage. Although Woody listened to the radio whenever he was around it, he never really heard it. He knew whether it was off or on, but once it was on, he tucked the incessant sound into a pocket of his brain, comforted by but inattentive to it.

With lights and music on, Woody went back to the offending rear wheel and laid out the tools and parts as carefully as a country doctor preparing for kitchen-table surgery. The very feel of the new and special tools he had bought gave him pleasure, even if he did no more than pick them up from one place and put them down in another. It made him feel like a real mechanic just to arrange the tools, unpack the parts, and know there was a job to be done.

Woody was tempted to begin pulling the wheel, but he didn't. He didn't think it was fair to start alone and deprive the others of their chance to help on this necessary piece of work. They would all want to work and to learn. That was the whole idea of the club. For a moment he regretted that he wasn't waiting for Dan Ilder and the Three Musketeers, but the feeling passed. If they came, they would do the work, and he would have to watch. This way, with his own gang, they would have the fun of doing everything.

Woody rolled his creeper to the rear of the car, lay down on it, and, with his trouble light, examined the place where the brake fluid had leaked out. He was sure he knew how to go about pulling the wheel, disconnecting the brake springs, and removing the old cylinder. Just to make sure, however, and avoid any argument from Dick, Woody moved his arms and legs as though he were swimming on his back and rode the creeper to a low bench near the front fender. He reached up and got his illustrated manual on how to work on Fords the vintage of his, and "swam" back to the rear wheel, under the car. Here he hooked his trouble light to the underside of the car and began to study.

Woody read the entire procedure step by step, making sure he understood everything. Then he read the directions for changing brake drums and the right way to bleed his brake lines. And, while he was at it, he reviewed the material he had often read before about brake troubleshooting and adjusting.

Woody lay on his back on the creeper, the trouble light hanging inches above his head from where it was hooked over a brake cable. He held the book upright on his chest with his right hand, turning the pages with his fingers and, if need be, with his nose. His left arm remained curled under his head, to help cushion it. His feet, crossed at the ankles, stuck out under the rear bumper of the car. Lying like this under his car, studying, dressed and prepared for action, he knew a feeling of wonderful inner peace and contentment.

Woody finished reading about brakes and closed the book, staring up at the mud-caked underside of his car with the rusty brake cables, rusty springs, and rusty driveshaft. He blinked his eyes, surprised by the discovery he had just made. Sidekick didn't have any rear shock absorbers at all. Not of any kind! No wonder it rode like a lumber wagon and tried to do the hula on acceleration or quick stops. He'd have to get shocks. There was no high-speed stability without good rear shocks. Wait until the guys . . .

Woody looked at his watch, unwilling to believe what it showed. Last night the boys had arrived before seven. It was now three minutes to eight.

Woody pushed out from under the car and stood up. He walked down the driveway, listening, his eyes cloudy with disappointment. He stood there awhile, his hands in the pockets of his bulky, baggy coveralls, his cap pushed back on his head, his shoulders bent forward. Finally, he turned and shuffled back to the garage and into the house.

"Mom!"

"What is it, Woody?"

"Any of the guys call?"

"No. There hasn't been a call from anyone since you went out."

"Are you sure? Were you here all the time?"

"I'm sure."

"Would you do me a favor?"

"What?"

He raised his voice so there would be no mistaking the message he was sending into the living room. "Call the guys and find out when they're coming over. I would, but I'm in my greasy clothes and I don't want to walk on the carpet with these shoes."

"Since you're so thoughtful, I'll do it."

"Thanks."

Cheryl's voice cried out from the other room, "Shut up, Woody! I can't hear my TV show!"

"It's no good anyway!" Woody yelled.

"Why don't you learn to read!" Cheryl yelled back, but he was already on his way out. He went through the garage and into the driveway again, still hopeful. When the guys came, he thought, and they did the work on the brakes, it would be a big lift. Once they'd done one job, the others would be easier. Before they knew it the car would be a jewel, painted in gleaming white, with crimson trim, chrome spinner hubs, and all the rest. He and his buddies would show those other guys how to restore a car. They'd have it running like an expensive watch. No swaps and no conversions, but the original equipment brought to perfection. That was the ideal way.

"Woody . . . are you out here?" His mother stood by the garage door.

"Right here," Woody said. "What'd you find out?"

"Mrs. Slater said Dick went somewhere with a boy called Pooch. Is that right?"

"Yeah."

"The other mothers said Sonny and Jim Bob went to the movies together."

"Oh . . . yeah," Woody said. "Sure. I forgot all about that. This wasn't the night they were supposed to come over at all. How about that? I clean forgot." He stood with his back to his mother. "I'll work a little while by myself," he said. And although he tried hard to sound casual, and he might have fooled a stranger, his mother wasn't fooled.

She wanted to speak a comforting word, to let him know she understood how it felt to be abandoned and to wait in vain. But she knew, from his tone and from his back being turned toward her, that he didn't want her to know his real feelings.

She took one last look at the shapeless mass the coveralls made of his body, at the stiff set of his neck and head.

She felt sorry for him, but she also felt disappointed and discouraged. She had known there would be struggle and heartache and frustration in his life, but she had hoped it would be over a more noble or worthy cause than this. To see him suffer because of an old car almost made a mockery out of his human sensitivity. What a waste of unhappiness!

And yet, it was because she loved him that she allowed him to retain his pride before her. She pretended to be fooled by his casual words. She called out, in a cheerful, neutral, unsuspecting voice, "All right, dear. Don't work too late." Then she went into the house.

When he was safely alone again, Woody went back into the garage. His car waited for him in the harsh light. It looked, on the jack stands, like a weary old elephant vainly trying to raise its tired old rump high in the air and stand on its front legs.

"Boy," Woody said to his car, resting his hand affectionately on its side, "it looks like we're alone in this. But we'll show them, won't we? We'll show them what we can do."

Woody walked around his car, examining every precious detail of its scaly, rough old hide. "I'm going to give you new brakes," Woody told his car, "and anything else you need. When you're in shape I'll start in on your looks. You'll be the best-looking, best-running car in town when I'm through with you. How about that, eh?"

Woody examined the dents and ripples in the car's skin, the dashboard and its instruments, the dusty, grease-stained upholstery, the cracked window glass, the loose front seat, the bare metal floorboards. He struggled with the hood and raised it alone, propped it up, and studied the engine. Everything was covered with a thick layer of hardened grease, oil, and dirt.

"I'll make you fly, old boy," Woody promised the rusty, dirty old flathead engine. "I'll make you sing." He patted the car again, and told it what he thought of Dick, Jim Bob, and Sonny. "We don't need those creeps," Woody said, "do we?"

He was sure his car heard and understood. He was almost surprised that it didn't talk back. "I'll take care of you," Woody promised. "Nothing's going to be too good for you."

He tugged purposefully at his cap. It was better this way, with just himself and Sidekick. Nobody would be sitting inside, abusing the car, insulting it, and doing more damage than good. It would be all his own now. "The first thing I'm going to do," Woody confided to his car, "is fix the brake on that rear wheel. You just be patient, and I'll have it done in a little while."

Woody went to the wheel he had to work on and examined the tools and parts he had laid out when he was waiting for the others to come. He could begin now. Any time. And he would.

The garage seemed big and cold and empty. The sound of his radio seemed to emphasize the emptiness and lack of people. There should have been voices and guys moving around . . . Woody opened a door of the car and put the car in gear, to keep the rear wheel from turning while he worked on it. The first step. Now, to the wheel.

He went, instead of to the wheel, out to the driveway again, and stood for a while longer with his hands in his coverall pockets, hoping that his mother had heard wrong, or that the other mothers didn't know what they were talking about. After a while, he returned to his car. He got a lug wrench and tried to loosen the lugs so he could remove the wheel. They, too, were rusted on so tightly it was as though they had been welded on. Woody grasped the ends of the wrench and tried his best to rock a lug loose. He grew red in the face as he threw all his weight on the wrench again and again. The old car swayed and shook, but there was no give. Woody tried again, kicking down on the wrench handle, and spun the wrench off the wheel against his shin. He swore and danced around on one foot, holding his sore shin with a hand that was raw from wrestling with the wrench. He bent down and picked up the wrench.

"You're sure not trying very hard to help!" he said angrily to the wheel. He found a hammer, fitted the wrench to a lug, and pounded the end of the wrench handle. All that this did was bounce the hammer dangerously near his nose and sting the hand that held the lug wrench in place.

Sweating, frustrated, his anger mounting, Woody straightened up to rest. He remembered his creep-in oil and got that, soaking the lugs. While he waited for the oil to work, he leaned against the garage wall, strangely restless and resentful. There wasn't any reason for him to be doing this alone. The guys ought to be on hand to help. They'd talked so big about rebuilding . . . Woody took off his cap and rubbed his forehead with his arm. Right now, they were at the movies, or riding around, and he was all by himself, with all the work to do alone, and none of the right tools with which to do it.

Woody stared at the oil-streaked wheel. Nobody wanted to lend him any tools. Nobody wanted to give him any help. Nobody cared whether he had a car or not. And it *wasn't* any fun to work alone. It just . . . wasn't.

He thought of all the boys with cars who might have helped him, who knew how to help, and who could make the job a lot of fun. But where were all the others? Why didn't they want to join him? In all the magazines he and his own club had read, there had been dozens and dozens of pictures of happy car club members posing proudly with cars they had worked on together and rebuilt. That was the way it was supposed to be, the way he had counted on. That was the way it was with all the other guys. What had gone sour with him and his car? Why, of all the guys in the world who had a car to work on, did he have to be the only one who had to work alone?

Woody slid downward against the wall until he was in a sitting position, his arms wrapped around his knees. He thought of the plans he had made, the work he had done, the money he had spent. And now, here he was . . . alone.

The back door of the garage opened. Woody looked up, gloomy and resentful. He saw Cheryl, dressed in some of his old, outgrown denims, her hair tucked up under one of his old caps. She came forward hesitantly, smiling shyly, hopefully, and proudly. "Woody . . . is now the 'later'? Can I help you work on your car?"

Woody stared at her, crushed by the enormity, the indignity of the situation. It was the last straw. If he had needed anything to convince him of what an outcast he was, this was it . . . to find that the only person in the world who was willing to work with him was his eight-year-old sister!

"You get out of here, Cheryl!" Woody yelled in a sudden fury, his face turning purple. "Get out!" He reached for the lug wrench and brandished it over his head. "You get out before I bash you!"

Cheryl cried out in fear and ran into the house, screaming tearfully for her mother. Woody threw down the lug wrench, his body trembling, his eyes burning with tears. He brushed his eyes roughly with his sleeve and leaned back against the garage wall, stretching his feet out before him. All the money he had spent . . . all the hard-earned money. He stared dully at the ancient car that seemed to be waiting uncomfortably to be put out of its misery. All the work that had to be done . . . Woody's heart sank as he faced his grand project alone. And for the first time he wondered, ever so slightly but ever so painfully, about the wisdom of his purchase.

The low moment passed. Woody accepted the facts. And, true to his nature, he pressed on. He got the lug wrench and tried again. This time he made progress. And after much straining and pounding, he had removed all the lug nuts and the wheel itself. At once his spirits lifted. Even working by himself, there was hope. And the victory, if won all by himself, would be that much sweeter and greater when it came. Removal of the back wheel represented the first real piece of work that had been done since he had bought the car. And knowing he could complete the job at hand gave Woody an entirely different outlook and feeling. The loneliness was gone, the dejection was gone, the doubt was gone. He would work alone, happily, as he had worked alone so many hours when he was building his models. His low moment had marked the end of an attitude and a belief. Until that moment, he had been thinking about the car like a little kid, in terms of his car club, and modifying, and playing elaborate games with auto tools. All that was gone now. Now, he looked at his car with a mature eye, for a mature purpose. He needed transportation, and by himself he would transform his car into a safe, dependable means of transportation. Actually, he was glad the car club days were over. They had been getting to be a bore and a pain in the neck. From now on this was going to be his own personal car, and he would use it for his own personal needs. The day of the toy was over.

Feeling older, settled, more competent and mature, Woody went into the house, kicking off his shoes before he walked on the clean floors. "Where's Cheryl?" he asked his mother.

"In her room, crying. She said you threatened to hit her with a wrench. Don't take your feelings out on her, Woody. She only wanted to help."

"I was raving around because I'd just banged my shins," Woody said. "If she wants to, I'd like to have her come out and help me."

"I'll ask her," Mrs. Ahern said, just as though Woody was in the habit of seeking Cheryl's company. She went into Cheryl's room, and a few minutes later came back with Cheryl in tow. Cheryl's face was still wet with tears, but she tried to smile.

"Would you like to help me put on a new wheel cylinder?" Woody asked in a polite, formal manner.

Cheryl nodded solemnly, now embarrassed because she had been crying.

"Come on, then," Woody said. "I'll tell you what to do."

The sunshine broke through in Cheryl. "I'm going to work on Woody's car!" she sang. "Can I wrench something, Woody?"

"You be careful," Mrs. Ahern cautioned Woody. "I don't want her to get hurt. Don't let her do anything dangerous."

"I won't," Woody said. "You don't have to worry." He won Cheryl completely with his next sentence.

"After all, she isn't a tiny little kid anymore."

It was amazing to Woody, who had asked Cheryl to help him only because he wanted to prove he was grown-up and kind, how much difference it made to have even her around. The moment he had someone to talk to, and listen to, and share his problem with, the garage didn't seem cold and lonely anymore, and the work became more interesting.

First, while Cheryl hunched near him with shining eyes and eager, interested face, Woody explained what the job was going to entail, and why it had to be done. Cheryl kept nodding and looking, trying her best to make sense of everything he said. And Woody felt wonderfully expansive being able to lecture about car repairs and sound like an expert.

"Now what I want you to do, Sis," Woody explained, "is hold the trouble light on the place I'm working. I'll tell you if I need it moved up or down, or left or right . . . you do know left from right, don't you?"

"I knew that *years* ago."

"Well, I didn't know. I don't know much about what you do know, I guess. Anyway, the other thing I want you to do is hand me the tools I need when I need them."

"The way the nurse does for the doctor!" Cheryl cried.

Woody grinned. "Kind of. These are brake pliers. Those are regular pliers. You know what screwdrivers and wrenches look like. When I want a wrench, I'll tell you what size. You'll find it right here, on this spot. You know numbers, don't you?"

"Sure I do!"

"Good. Now get back a little while I use this hub puller to remove the hub and drum assembly."

Woody reached for the hub puller.

"Let me hand it to you, Woody."

"It's right under my hand, Cheryl."

"I know. But I want to do my job."

Woody laughed. "All right. Hand it to me." He liked having it handed to him, being waited on. And as the work progressed, he enjoyed more and more giving an order and just having to hold out his hand. To have an assistant who obeyed orders, believed implicitly in his knowledge, and didn't try to argue with him made him seem more professional.

Lying under the car, Woody examined the entire brake area. "Shoes are worn out, cylinder boots are shot . . . no wonder I didn't have brakes. Even the fittings leak . . . want to see?"

"In a minute."

Woody rolled out on the creeper to look at Cheryl. She was trying to get something out of her eye. The hand she was doing it with had some skin scraped off.

"How long has that been in your eye?" Woody asked.

"Since the last time I looked under."

"And you didn't say a word," Woody said, feeling a real respect and admiration for Cheryl. "When that happened to Sonny, he yelled and bawled like a little baby. And you skinned your knuckles too . . . why, you're a lot better help and braver than those stupid crybabies. You're all right, Cheryl."

"Can I help you a lot, Woody?"

"Sure you can," Woody said impulsively. "From now on, you're my official assistant."

"My eye is clear now," Cheryl said, smiling brightly. "What can I hand you now?"

Woody heard his father drive up and get out of the car. Ahern came into the garage, silently watching as Cheryl handed Woody a screwdriver. "I'm helping Woody," Cheryl said proudly.

"I can see that," Ahern said. "How's it coming, Woody?"

"I've got the old shoes and cylinder off, and the new brake shoes on. I'll have the new cylinder kit hooked up in a little while."

"You're kidding," Ahern said.

"Really, Dad. It wasn't so tough. As I told you . . . if you can read and use a wrench, you can work on an old car."

Ahern went into the house. "What's been going on around here in my absence?" he asked his wife. "Witchcraft? You know what I just saw in the garage, I suppose. Where are the other boys?"

"They didn't come," Mrs. Ahern said. "It was awful. If you could have seen him waiting . . . he was so disappointed and unhappy."

"I'm not surprised," Ahern said. "I knew they'd get sick of it sooner or later. But I am surprised that it happened so soon. And Cheryl . . . that I find hard to believe."

"He came in and asked for her."

Ahern chuckled. "I didn't think he could get that lonesome in one evening. However, I'm not complaining. As far as I can remember, that's the first time they've done anything together for . . . five or six years, wouldn't you say?"

"At least. If that car makes our children friends, it's worth its weight in gold. I was about ready to give up hope."

"Let's not expect too much," Ahern said. "You know Woody. He could be breathing fire at her at a moment's notice. But it's a start."

They heard Woody's footsteps in the back entry.

"Mom . . . ?"

"Yes?"

"I'm bringing Cheryl in."

"You're what?" Mrs. Ahern drew in her breath sharply as Woody walked into the living room carrying Cheryl in front of him, chest high, across his two arms. Mrs. Ahern jumped to her feet. "Woody . . . what happened!"

A slow grin spread across Woody's smeared, grimy face. "She fell asleep."

— — —

Woody spun the rear wheel with his hand. "There she is, Dad. Good as new. I can't adjust the brake any further until the master cylinder is filled. But there's no use doing that until I check all the other wheel cylinders. I don't want to buy brake fluid four or five times. Will you help me bleed the lines when it's time? I need you to work the brake pedal while I'm at the wheels."

"Be glad to," Ahern said, "if your club members aren't around."

Woody snorted. "There isn't any more club," he said. "The guys didn't show up tonight."

"Maybe they will tomorrow night."

"No," Woody said. "They just chickened out. I can tell. They talked big before we had a car, but they sure chickened out fast when it came to real work."

"It is more fun to talk about cars than work on them," Ahern said.

"Not the way they used to talk." Woody's mouth twisted into an expression of smiling contempt. "Remember how they begged me to get a car? How much they said they loved to work on cars? They practically talked me into shooting over a hundred bucks on an old car, and then they walk out and leave me holding the bag. That's pretty tricky."

"Oh, you put up some pretty good arguments of your own," Ahern said. "I don't think they meant to deceive you. They just found out that it isn't much fun to work on somebody else's car, that's all."

"It wasn't just my car," Woody said. "It was the club's car."

"Sure it was," Ahern drawled. "Everybody with an equal voice, equal rights to drive, an equal chance to use the car . . ."

"Even so," Woody said stubbornly, "if a guy really likes working on cars, it doesn't matter whom the car belongs to. I'd be glad to help any of the guys at school work on their cars any time . . . just as soon as I've got my own car in shape." Woody looked fondly at Sidekick. "And I'll have it in shape before you know it. I should have the brakes and lights fixed in less than a week, and then I'll give you back your garage."

"How about the clutch?" Ahern asked. "I thought that was first on your list."

"I'll tackle that when I find some guys to help me. It's no one-man job."

"Maybe I can help you," Ahern suggested.

"I mean," Woody said, without the slightest intention of insulting his father, "guys who know what they're doing."

"Oh," Ahern said, repressing a laugh. "I see."

"Guys," Woody said, unable to keep a ring of pride out of his voice as he looked at the wheel he had fixed all by himself, "who have studied about cars, and have some experience working on them. You know . . . guys like me."

# CHAPTER 17

SITTING ON HIS HEELS, Woody grasped the left front tire with both hands and worked the wheel off the axle. He rolled the wheel to a leaning position against the side of his car, bending low to examine the condition of the tire's tread and carcass.

The tire, like the three others on his car, didn't have any tread. It was, with the exception of one rough spot where the tire was worn through to the cord, perfectly bald. Woody poked the worn-through spot with his finger. The tire would have to go. It was so thin it might blow if he ran over a marshmallow.

For a moment, he pondered the possibility of finding a customer for his four bald tires. He had heard about a kid at school who had paid a premium price for bald tires at a salvage yard. The owner had convinced the kid they were racing slicks. There might, Woody thought, be another boy like that at school. It wasn't that he wanted to cheat anyone, he just needed more money so desperately. When you thought about replacing your tires, you began thinking at fifty or sixty dollars. And you didn't get very good rubber at that price. Anyway, this tire was worn through, and soft, and he didn't think you could find two guys in the same school dumb enough to buy anything automotive that was worn out.

Sighing, Woody turned his attention to the front wheel. He looked at it and yawned. Fixing the brake system on the first wheel had been fun. The second had been work, the third an uninteresting chore. Now he was ready to do the fourth and be done with it.

Woody's father came through the garage on his way to another committee meeting. He stopped for a moment. "How's the work coming?"

"Pretty good," Woody said. "When I finish this wheel, I'll have all new brakes."

"Aren't you through with that job yet? You did the first one almost three weeks ago."

"I thought I'd be done sooner too," Woody said, sitting on the floor and bending to work beyond his spread knees. "But I never get any time. Either I'm in school, or doing homework, or cleaning out vats, or candling eggs. Every time I get started, some farmer brings in a couple of cases of eggs, and I have to quit."

"Well, I'll tell you, Woody," Ahern said, jingling his car keys. "You can do your work in here during the summer. But the first time we have snow I want the garage back, no matter what you're doing, or what shape your car is in."

Woody felt that his father was teasing him and glowered. "You'll have your garage back before next winter," he said resentfully. "This is the only slow job I have to do. I'll be out of your garage in two weeks."

"That's what you said three weeks ago."

"I can't help it! I don't have any time, and I have to do all the work myself."

"What about the guys you were going to get to help you?"

Woody snorted angrily. "Those creeps all want to work on their own precious cars first. If I could take a couple of days off from school and work, I could get finished and be out of here."

"We won't even bother to discuss that idea," Ahern said drily. "I'll see you later."

"Could you help me bleed the lines when you come back?" Woody asked ungraciously.

"Depends on the time. I will if I'm not too late."

"If . . . if . . . if . . ." Woody grumbled to himself as his father went out. That was the only kind of help he ever got . . . "if." Then there were complaints because he couldn't rebuild a car in ten minutes. Why did they tell him to get a car if they weren't going to help him?

Woody fastened the hub puller in place, but instead of going ahead with the work, he lay back on the garage floor to rest for a minute, pulling his cap over his eyes to shield them from the overhead light.

He was confused. Whatever he had thought or imagined or dreamed his life would be like when he got a car, he had never figured it would be like this. Everything had happened according to plan, but the results were just the opposite of what he had expected. He had thought getting a car would open up his life, free him, and land him in the middle of a crowd with all kinds of interesting new activities. Instead, he had found himself more alone than ever, and his life had become one harassed race against time.

Each day he awoke thinking about his car, how much work had to be done, how many parts had to be bought, and how little time or money he had to meet these needs. The spring dance was coming up fast, and his car had to be in top mechanical shape and clean in appearance by that time. Otherwise, he wouldn't be able to go.

Each morning he made a resolve to work hard that day and make real progress. He went to school brooding about the needs of his property, resenting the precious time he had to give to his classes. Since somebody was always asking, with a sneaky grin, how soon he would be driving his car to school, he avoided the boys he had previously sought out. Sandra was so busy he scarcely ever saw her, but that was just as well. There was no point in asking for more complications, such as a date.

After his car was in shape he would have dates with her, but right now his car needed all his time and money.

Three days a week Woody raced to his cleaning job at the dairy. The other afternoons he went there to check about eggs. With Dick gone, work at the dairy was duller and more lonesome. Besides, the egg-candling job was driving him crazy. In the first place, he was slow. Secondly, unlike his cleaning job, which was on a regular schedule, the candling had to be done whenever the farmers brought in the eggs, and they brought them in at the oddest and most inconvenient times.

Some days he would have to candle eggs when he was through cleaning, and work until it was too late to do anything on his car. Or he would just be settling down to work on the car and Mr. Stonelee would phone to say that eggs had come in, and again his plans would be ruined.

In addition to his job, there was a minimum amount of homework he had to do in order to maintain a passing grade. And any night that was free of dairy work was certain to be one when he had to write a report or a theme.

There were a few nights, such as this one, when he was able to put on his coveralls and work on the car. Although he felt all the pressures to work fast and hard, he found it hard to get going. He had always imagined this work being done by a happy, noisy group of friends. It was hard to get started alone. He was so tired of being alone at his jobs and other work that he wanted, in his own few precious hours, to go where there were lights and people, to relax and have a little fun.

Even Cheryl didn't help him anymore. After the novelty of the first night had worn off, he had spoken sharply to her when she had dawdled and played games instead of paying attention to the work, and she had quit helping. It didn't seem as if there was anyone in the world who cared about what he was doing or cared to help him. His father was a little interested, but he was always busy, and his mother . . . if it ever got out that his *mother* had helped him work on the car, he'd have to leave town!

Woody lay on his back knowing he should be working on the wheel but reluctant to get at the job. Even a labor of love wasn't very thrilling when there was no one else to share the experience. He felt an urge to go down to the bowling alley, or the pool hall, or the movies, or the restaurant where most of the kids hung out. But his car needed him here. There was work to do.

Sighing a big sigh of self-pity, Woody sat up and gazed at the work he had to do. He didn't blame his car for the situation he was in. It was fate, which seemed to demand that he work twice as hard as anybody else in the world to get back half as much. Why, in spite of all the work he had candling eggs, and the time it took, he never seemed to make more than another five or six dollars a week.

Reluctantly, resentfully, Woody began tightening the hub puller. It wasn't as though he was asking for any special favors, he thought. All he wanted was what he deserved: his car in perfect condition, money in his pocket, and a full, interesting life. Just what everybody else seemed to have.

Woody looked up in surprise and hope as he heard a car turn into the driveway with a screech of tires and a roar of pipes. He looked out and saw Pooch's gaudy car with the twin horns, the chrome decorations, and the reflector tape. Dick got out from behind the wheel and sauntered toward Woody. The Pooch stayed in the car.

Woody bent to his work with new effort, pretending he wasn't aware he had a visitor until Dick stood next to him. Although it was a warm night, Dick still wore his navy surplus flying jacket. He sucked at a cigarette and blew smoke through his nose. "How you doing?" he asked Woody, his usual mocking smile in place on his lips.

"Just fine," Woody said. "When I finish this wheel, I'll have new brakes all the way around."

"How are the eggs?"

"Like always. They come in any old time."

Dick snorted. "Maybe I'll come around some time and throw rots for Cokes."

"Any time," Woody said. Dick looked around, threw his cigarette on the floor, and crushed it under his shoe. "You need any parts for your heap?"

"Some," Woody said. "My plugs are burned too bad to re-gap and use. The battery's split open, too. It just happened while the car was sitting here."

"They're easy parts to get," Dick said.

"Yeah, if you've got the money," Woody grunted. "It'll take me three weeks to earn that much extra."

"You're nuts if you spend good money for those parts," Dick said. "Look around you, boy. There are sixty million cars on the road, all with good batteries, plugs, and any other parts you need. It's all there waiting for you . . . for free."

Woody shook his head. "No midnight salvage for me, thanks."

"It beats slaving for old Stonelee, doesn't it? How do you think the other guys get by? They moonlight when they need something. Save your money for something else."

"No," Woody said, looking at his car. "I don't see it."

"What's the matter? You chicken?"

"No," Woody said, "it's not that." He was sure Dick would scoff at him, but he went ahead. "I've put a lot of hard work and a lot of hard-earned money in my car, and everything on it is mine. If I put any midnight salvage parts on, I wouldn't feel they belonged to me. I'd feel I had somebody else's stuff, and that would make part of my car belong to somebody else. I want it to be all mine."

"You're nuts," Dick said. "A part's a part. The car's only a machine."

"Maybe so, but that's how I feel about my machine."

"You would," Dick said in a mildly contemptuous tone. "Tell you what, Woody. I'll make a deal with you."

"What kind of a deal?"

"Well, if you're so wild to buy your parts, I'll sell 'em to you. You tell me what you need, and I'll deliver. I'll charge you two bits on the dollar of the new price. And some of the stuff might even be new."

"Where are you going to get the stuff?"

"What do you care?" Dick asked. "Do you ask the store where it got the stuff you buy? You're buying from me. You're paying me. Where I got the stuff is my problem, not yours. You're clean. Nobody could touch you. Why pay twenty bucks for a battery and plugs? I'll supply you for three or four bucks. I'm giving you a break. We charge other guys anywhere from thirty-five to fifty percent. But you're a special friend."

Woody was silent. Dick's offer was tempting, there were no two ways about that. If he dealt with Dick, his money would go five or six times as far. He'd be able to afford a lot of things, and right away. In time for the spring dance, certainly. The way it was, he was losing ground every day. There was always some unexpected expense to wreck his budget and his plans. And yet . . .

"I appreciate your offer," Woody said, "but I don't want any part of it."

"For crying out loud . . . why not?"

"I told you how I felt about . . . stolen parts."

"*You'd* be buying them, wouldn't you?"

"Sure," Woody said.

"Well, nobody would know they'd been swiped."

"I'd know," Woody said. "And I'd feel the same way about having them on my car."

"You've got it all wrong," Dick said. "Look, it's not like swiping money, or stealing anything like that. So you swipe a few parts off a car . . . so what? The car is insured. The insurance company doesn't miss the few bucks it has to pay, the guy gets some brand new parts, you get the parts you need, I make a few bucks, and everybody's happy and nobody's hurt."

"You pay for it when you go to buy insurance," Woody said. "They raise the rates to cover a lot of losses."

"How much?" Dick demanded. "So they raise your insurance five bucks a year. So, you save a couple of hundred buying through me. How can you lose?"

Woody knew Dick was wrong, but he didn't know how to argue with him. There was no way to steal anything and convince oneself it wasn't stealing. Yet he didn't know how to argue that with Dick. Not the way Dick had things worked out in his mind.

Dick squatted down beside Woody, thinking that Woody was pondering his offer. He lowered his voice. "You know," he said almost wistfully, "if you'd come in with me, we could really wheel and deal. Look it here." Dick reached into his jacket pocket and took out a small roll of bills. "They're all fives and tens, Woody, and that's just this week's take alone. If you threw in with me, we could double it, easy. We could go places."

"Sure," Woody said. "And I know where."

"Not a chance of getting caught," Dick said. "Look, if a stupid moron like Pooch can do it and not get caught, what would a couple of smart operators have to worry about? I tell you, Woody, the sky is the limit. What you can't sell to the guys at school you can always unload at a couple of used parts stores around town. Man, you could get rid of this heap and get yourself a real rod, and there'd be plenty of green stuff left over. Why kill yourself at the dairy for a few bucks when there's plenty of easy money just waiting for you to pick it up?"

Woody was silent, shocked by what had happened to Dick, once such a good friend. Dick's entire manner had changed, so that there was something furtive and ratlike about him. He had always been difficult to get along with, but a lot of the things he had done had been to tease and discomfit. Now there was a real sneakiness about him, a real hardness and cynicism. Unknowingly, he kept looking over his shoulder every few moments, as though afraid he would be seen or heard. Woody had a vision of Dick and the Pooch creeping around in the darkness, stripping cars, and the picture made him shudder. It was so . . . unclean and, somehow, so sad.

"We could make a real team," Dick said coaxingly in Woody's ear. "I'm fed up with Pooch. I mean, he's such a moron I can't stand being around him. But a guy doesn't want to operate alone. It's no fun alone."

No, Woody thought, it wasn't any fun alone. Nothing was.

"What do you say, Woody? Want to come in with me?"

Woody looked at Dick and saw in his eyes the open, unashamed need to have his old friend back again. He understood that feeling, for it was strong and painful within himself. He too wanted his old friend back, but he knew it could not be on Dick's terms.

Remembering their walks to the dairy, their talks and the throwing of eggs, the meetings of the club, Woody suddenly felt that he was somehow responsible for what had happened to Dick. If he hadn't bought the car they would still be working together at the dairy, still meeting in the back room of the basement. In a way, he thought, he had ditched Dick for the car.

Now he wanted his old friend back, but he didn't know how to argue his old friend out of being a thief. Dick was probably despised by the boys he stole for and probably he despised them. Woody didn't want his old friend, who had faced wrenches and stones to protect him, to be a thief. He wanted Dick back on honest terms.

Slowly, Woody began tightening the hub puller. "You ought to get yourself an old car," Woody said. "You could have fun working on it. I'd be glad to help you." Woody's face brightened with good thoughts. "Why don't you quit the Pooch and get your old job back at the dairy? It's pretty dull up there for one guy working alone. We could have some real good times again, throwing rots and helping each other work on our cars, the way we used to talk about doing it . . ."

"I thought you needed the egg money for your car," Dick said.

Woody shrugged. "Oh, I can use it, but I don't really need it. So, it takes me a couple of weeks longer to get the car in shape . . . what's a couple of weeks?"

Dick stared at Woody for a long moment, then he looked down and saw the roll of fives and tens in his hand. He spat on the floor and laughed. "Me go back to slaving for a big two cents a dozen? Don't be square, Woody. I'll do it the easy way." Dick stood up, looking down at Woody with his old mocking grin. "Any time you change your mind, my offer still holds. See you around." He strolled out of the garage, got into Pooch's car, and drove off with a great roar.

Woody continued working on the wheel without being aware of what he was doing. He was disturbed, almost frightened by how close he had come to ordering parts from Dick just because things were a little tight. To save a few dollars he had almost asked a friend to go out and be a thief for him, almost become a part of the thievery.

He could see how easy the whole thing could be. First you bought the stolen parts to save money. And then, because it was easy, and to save more money, you went out and swiped just the things you needed badly. And then the things you wanted. After that, it would be easy to steal a few parts you didn't need or want for a little money you needed. And before long you could be like Dick and the Pooch, in business as a thief.

Woody looked at his car with a puzzled expression on his face. What was there about a car that made a guy think like that? He loved every inch of this old car that belonged to him. But at the moment, he looked at it with a twinge of fear in his heart. He looked at the car, the parts scattered on the floor, and the tools. He thought of all the other boys who had cars and worked on them, and he thought of those who were Dick's customers; of all the cars with stolen carbs and plugs and batteries and accessories; of all the boys he knew who were, if not thieves themselves, in league with thieves.

And what of himself? He knew that Dick and Pooch were in the business of stealing. If he said nothing, wasn't he, in a way, an accomplice? But how could he bring himself to tell anyone, to be the cause of their arrest and possible imprisonment? He had tried to argue Dick away from stealing, but he had failed. And now, what was the right thing to do? He didn't want to see his friend become a criminal, but how could he stop him?

Woody began to work on the wheel once more, then stopped. Suddenly, the very sight of automotive parts, and the very thought of working on a car—even dear old Sidekick—was nauseating. He got up quickly and went outside and sat on the grass. He dug at his head with his knuckles, trying to think clearly. What was the right thing to do? The loyal thing to do? The honest thing to do? He searched in vain for the perfect answer that would provide a happy solution to all the problems, that would point the perfect way. And as he searched, he was aware that, for the first time, his worries were not about what he should do to his car, but what it might do to him.

"Woody . . . are you out here?"

His heart sank. He knew why his mother was looking for him. "It's too late to candle eggs tonight," Woody complained. "I'll do them tomorrow."

"Mr. Stonelee is just trying to help you. There are only two cases to do tonight, but five cases are coming in tomorrow. And since tomorrow is your clean-up day, you'd have seven cases to do. He thought you'd like to get these two done tonight."

"All right," Woody said wearily, so sick of the thought of eggs he felt like throwing up. "I'll go do them. If Dad makes any remarks about how slow I am on the car, tell him for me, will you? Just tell him what I'm up against."

# CHAPTER 18

"WHAT DID WOODY ORDER?" Pooch asked eagerly as Dick got back in the car.

"Nothing," Dick said shortly, starting the car and backing it out of the driveway.

"Oh well," Pooch said philosophically, "maybe some other time. Where to now, Dick?"

"I'm going home," Dick snapped. "You can go where you want to."

"But we have orders . . ."

"I'm sick and tired of orders. If those guys want parts, let them risk their own necks. I don't figure on going to jail for a lousy couple of bucks."

The Pooch looked at Dick with his woeful, doglike eyes. "What about our business?"

"You can have it all," Dick said bluntly. "I'm tired of the business and I'm tired of you."

"What'd I do?" the Pooch wailed. "Ain't we buddies no more?"

"Ahhh," Dick snarled, fumbling for a cigarette, "I'm sick of you."

"Why, Dick?" The Pooch almost sat up and begged, his large dark eyes moist with hurt and disappointment. "Why are you sick of me?"

"Because you're a nut!" Dick yelled. "You hear? You're a nut! A pooch! Arf! Arf! Arf!" Dick drove like mad, skidding around corners, passing every car he overtook without regard for safety or caution. And all the while, out of his deep, wild fury, he kept barking and snarling like a dog, deriding Pooch with his cries.

At last, he drew up in front of his own house and got out of the car. "Now beat it," he ordered the Pooch. "You hear? I don't want to see you anymore. Beat it!"

Dick turned and walked into his house while Pooch stared after him with hurt, doleful eyes. Dick felt as though he were walking out of a trap. My God, he thought, how close I was! How close I was to being another Pooch.

He knew he had cut himself away from everyone and everything. And it had seemed a bold, daring, and defiant thing to do—to be different, to be an outlaw, to be a lone wolf against the herd. But being a lone wolf had made him part Pooch. At first it had been a satisfying thing to have Pooch under his thumb, to drive Pooch's car as though it were his own. But now he revolted against the relationship. It had only seemed he was the Pooch's boss. Boiled down, it was the opposite. He ordered Pooch around, and drove Pooch's car, *but it was Pooch's car.* Even though he had seemed in charge, he was really tagging along with Pooch, just as he had tagged along with Woody. It hadn't been a real change at all.

Tonight, visiting Woody, he had seen it all, and he had seen the answer for himself, too. How content Woody had seemed there, all by himself, working on his car, how calm and contented he looked. And when his car was fixed, he would drive out, be accepted among the real guys at school, and have a girl. That was the answer, Dick thought. Not to fight, not to be an outsider, not to be alone. Woody was right. If he had a car of his own to care for and work on, he'd have a real goal in life, like Woody.

Dick went inside the house. His father was in the living room, reading the evening paper. He looked up as Dick came in and stared at his son. The senior Slater was a small, slight man with small, tight features. "Well," he exclaimed in a sour, sarcastic voice, "look who finally came home before two o'clock in the morning! What happened? Did the pool hall burn down?"

Dick sat on the edge of a chair and tried to smile pleasantly. "I just thought I'd like to be home."

His father looked at him suspiciously. "What do you want? An alibi? What kind of trouble are you in now?"

"No trouble," Dick said. "I just wanted to come home."

Dick's mother came in from the kitchen and sat down. She was a tall, thin woman with tired, humorless features. "I heard a car," she said. "Did someone bring you home?"

"Yeah. A guy I know gave me a ride."

The three were silent. Dick looked at the floor between his feet. "Dad . . ."

"What?"

"Well . . . if I had the money, and I kept the hours you wanted me to, and did work around the house . . . could I buy a car?"

"A car! That's all you need, isn't it? A car."

"But if I . . ."

"I heard you," Slater snapped. "It's all talk. The minute you got a car you'd be worse than ever. I know you, Dick. That's the way you are."

"I promise, Dad. I've saved up the money. All I want is an old car, like Woody Ahern's. Something I can work on and learn about cars on."

"That would be a sight," Slater said bitterly. "You putting something together. You know what happened to my car when I let you use it. The very first time I let you drive it. The very *first* time!"

"I'm older now, Dad. Really . . ." Dick looked to his mother for support. "I really need a car."

"Why?"

He couldn't explain. He didn't know how to tell them that a car was his only hope of salvation. That it was his only way back. That he couldn't go on tagging along behind the others forever. That he needed something of his own, to make him one with the other owners. He couldn't tell them that. "I . . . I just need it."

"There's no reason to have any argument or discussion about this," Slater said in his prim, final way. "You are not the kind of boy who can be trusted to own anything. Let me tell you something. When you were a very little boy, Mother and I bought you a lovely tricycle. We told you that you had to take care of it; that if you abused the privilege, we would take it away. You had it out one afternoon . . . *one* afternoon. When you brought it home it was a wreck. The wheels were bent, the seat torn, the paint scratched . . . Well, we took it away as we had made clear we would. The second thing we let you have, and you pulled the *same* trick, was . . ."

Dick wasn't listening. Now he remembered. He remembered the tricycle. He had started out to ride around the block. Bigger boys had taken it from him, knocked him down, and amused themselves by riding and damaging his precious new trike. When he had come home, dirty and weeping, his parents hadn't listened to a word of his heartbreaking story. They had seized the tricycle, taken it away, and whipped him for being a careless, thoughtless boy.

He remembered. He remembered how, his own trike taken from him, he had got his revenge. He had found smaller children with trikes and taken *theirs* from *them*, had knocked them down and damaged their tricycles so they would have to suffer, too.

It had always been that way. His parents had never in their lives *given* him anything to be all his. Everything had been attached to a rope in their hands. Everything had been lent, at their mercy. And everything had been jerked back, sooner or later, and denied him.

They had done it with everything. He guessed he had known they would find an excuse to take their car away from him sooner or later. In his nervousness and tension, he had taken it out and deliberately driven recklessly, wrecked the car, and got it all over with at once, to avoid the waiting and the insecure wondering.

Now he needed his own car. Not "on condition," not on the end of a string or a stick, but his very own, to be his very own from the first moment on. How he needed a car of his own!

"... and if you think, after the way you've been careless with every nice thing we've ever got for you, after the way you wrecked our car the first time ... *the very first time* we let you drive it ... if you think for one minute the way you've behaved in this house ... never listen ... never obey ... never cooperate ..."

"I'll be different if I can have a car. I promise."

"Promises are easier to make than to keep. Besides, why do I have to bribe you to be decent? Why do I have to pay in advance for your obedience? Is being a good son something you sell to a parent for a price? Let me tell you something. You want a car. You say it will make you a good boy. Well, I want to see what kind of good boy you're going to be *before* you get the car. Show me now— tonight ... begin now. Prove to me you deserve to be trusted with a car, and then we'll talk about it ... after I see the big change. Is that too much to ask?"

Slater was making a legitimate offer, but Dick didn't recognize the opportunity that was being presented. To Dick, it was the same old story again—a conditional offer, a gift tied to a string.

"Where are you going?" Slater demanded.

"Out," Dick said sullenly, opening the front door. "Just out."

"Yes," Slater said bitterly. "You're just the boy to have a car."

Dick walked toward the street, burning with anger. Why did he have to prove anything in advance if he wanted a car? Why couldn't they believe him? He would have changed, with a car. He was sure of it.

He stood irresolutely on the sidewalk, not knowing which way to turn. It was the same old story, and he felt the same old impulse to strike out and pass along his injury. A car slid out of the shadows and stopped in front of him.

"Dick . . . ?"

"What do *you* want?"

"I thought you might change your mind and want to stay in business."

Dick's lips tightened. He'd been a fool, expecting anything good to happen to him, thinking he could be like the others. He wasn't the kind to own anything, belong anywhere, or call anybody boss. He was free—tough. He would take what he wanted.

"Shove over, Pooch," Dick said roughly. "I'll drive."

Pooch didn't move. He said, in his humble, childish, yet stubborn way, "I want to drive, Dick. It's my car. I want to drive."

Dick stared at him, wanting to tell Pooch to take his car and go to the devil. But if he drove Pooch away, there was no one. And he couldn't go on being all alone. He had to have someone, and Pooch was the only one left.

"All right, Pooch," Dick said lifelessly. "Have it your own way. Drive if you want to. I don't care." He got in on the passenger side, and Pooch drove away.

"First we have to get a battery for Chuck Neal," Pooch said. "Then we have to go in the country and look in some farmers' tool sheds. Frank Clark is going to swap engines and needs a chain hoist." Pooch's grip tightened on the wheel. "I'll tell you what to do when we get there," he said. He waited a moment, then smiled contentedly when Dick made no objection.

The Pooch cut his lights and drove forward slowly by moonlight. The farmhouse ahead was dark. Pooch drove a few feet past the farmer's private lane, then carefully backed into the lane and killed his engine. Pointed out this way, they would be able to get away in a hurry when their job was over.

The two boys sat in the car and waited, listening. No dog barked. They could see the farmer's car and truck parked in the barnyard. Spring planting had begun, and there was no doubt that the tired farm family was fast asleep.

Pooch got out of the car, the siphon tube in his hand. He reached in back and carefully lifted out a five-gallon gas can. "Come on," he ordered. Dutifully, Dick got out and joined Pooch.

"Fill this with gas while I look around," Pooch whispered. "Then put it in the tank."

Dick took the gas can and siphon tube and walked down the lane with Pooch. They moved cautiously, keeping to the shadows.

"I'll go on ahead and scout the sheds," Pooch whispered. "Get the gas from the car or the truck." Dick glared at Pooch but said nothing. As though he needed this kind of advice from a moron!

Pooch went on ahead. Dick started toward the car and truck, but before he reached them, he saw a huge tractor standing in the shadows under the trees. He went to that, partly to disobey Pooch, and partly because it would save him a hundred steps carrying a heavy can of gas.

Dick had stolen gas so many times he hardly paid attention to what he was doing. He was too preoccupied with his disappointment and unhappy situation. When the can was filled, he carried it back to Pooch's car and poured the contents into the gas tank. He put the can and tube away and went back to join Pooch.

He found Pooch in the darkness of a shed, and felt a heavy electric tool shoved into his hands. "It's a grinder," Pooch whispered. "It's a cinch to sell to some guy planning body work. I found a chain hoist, too. I can make it alone. Let's go."

They went out of the shed and Dick's heart skipped a beat. There was a light on in the farmer's kitchen. Suddenly, the entire area was flooded with light as someone in the house turned on the yard lights. Dick and Pooch dropped their burdens and streaked toward their car at top speed. They were halfway down the lane when they heard a shotgun go off twice and heard pellets hitting the trees and grass behind them.

They reached the car and scrambled in wildly, thankful they had left it pointed toward the road. Pooch had left the key in the switch for added speed in getting away. As he turned the key and pushed the starter button, the shotgun boomed out again, frighteningly close, and a hail of shot clattered against the back of the car. The boys cowered, pulling their heads down into their hunched shoulders.

"Hurry!" Dick screamed.

The engine caught at once. Throttle open, pouring all the gas he could into the carbs, Pooch shifted into low gear and let the clutch pedal out. The car gave a convulsive leap forward, rear wheels spinning in the dirt. Then, just as the boys were about to breathe a sigh of relief, the engine died.

They were still crouching in the car, trying to get it started, when the farmer loomed up beside the car and ordered them out at the point of a double-barreled shotgun.

— — —

Woody was finishing the second case of eggs, yawning, red-eyed and sore-necked, when the music on the radio was interrupted to bring in a news flash.

Two boys, the announcer said, had been arrested trying to steal tools from the Wayne Tucker farm two miles south of town. They had been captured by the farmer, who had held them until the police arrived. They might have escaped, the announcer said, except for one mistake they had made. They had stolen five gallons of gasoline from a tractor and put it in their tank. Their mistake, the announcer chuckled, was that the tractor ran on diesel fuel. The police had not released the names of the two boys involved.

Woody sat hunched over, staring into space, not hearing the music that had resumed playing. They didn't have to release the names. He knew . . . he knew.

A hundred scenes flashed through his mind of times that he and Dick had been together. Walking to the dairy, sitting on the school steps watching cars, throwing rots behind the dairy, in the basement headquarters, running from the men with wrenches, eating ice cream in this tiny egg-candling room and laughing about something . . .

Now he sat in Dick's little room, working at Dick's job. He felt somehow that he had pushed Dick out of the job so he could take it over, that he had pushed Dick out of the Road Rockets, that it was his fault Dick had got in trouble, that, somehow, he had abandoned and failed the friend who had stood over him and protected him that night.

All his thoughts had been about himself and his car and his plans. He'd hardly noticed when Dick drifted off; he'd hardly cared. He had just been wrapped up in his own selfish plans. And now he sat in Dick's chair, earning Dick's money, and Dick was in jail. He had grumbled that Dick hadn't been a good friend to him. But what kind of friend had he been to Dick or Jim Bob or Sonny? What had he been to anyone besides himself?

He reached into the fresh case of eggs, selected an egg, candled it, weighed it, and put it in its proper box. Beginning with this egg, he felt, he was no longer working for himself and his own goals. Somehow, and he couldn't explain how to himself, he was working for Dick.

He worked on in the night, and from time to time a tear would drop slowly down his cheek as, for the first time in his life, he cried over the real-life misfortunes of someone other than himself.

— — —

"Woody . . . wait a minute. I want to see you."

Woody turned in the school hallway to see Dan Ilder walking rapidly in his direction. Woody beamed as Dan caught up with him. "I just got a letter from Sam," Dan said. "He's in San Diego. He says he likes the navy and wants to know how his car is doing."

For a moment Woody puffed up indignantly. What did Sam mean, *his* car? But then he thought of Sam, far from home, and how he must miss his old car—friend—and he softened.

"I've been working on it every day and night," Woody said. "Boy, it's always something. I put on new brakes and wheel cylinders, and then the master cylinder gave out. I put in a rebuilt master, and then I had to save up to get a new battery and plugs before I could try it out."

"That's the way it goes," Dan said. "She run all right now?"

"Well, not *exactly*," Woody said. "That old car seems to know when I'm a buck ahead, and then something else lets go. When I put in a new battery and plugs, the points turned out to be shot. I fixed *that* and drove around the neighborhood a little. The clutch was slipping so bad I could hardly move, and then it overheated."

"Bad radiator?"

"That'll probably be next," Woody said ruefully. "The hoses were so soft they collapsed and shut off the water, so I replaced them."

"Well, you fellows have done quite a bit of work at that," Dan said.

"We don't have a club anymore," Woody said. "I did it all myself."

"Good for you."

Dan moved off, and Woody stuck right with him, anxious to give him all the details.

"I think I'm in pretty good mechanical shape now," Woody said, "except for the clutch. I don't see how I can manage that alone."

"You can't," Dan said. "You'll need help. If I were you, I wouldn't just pull the transmission to get at the clutch. I'd pull the engine. If there's any oil leaking on the clutch from the rear main bearing, you can replace the slinger. The other way, you could replace the clutch and still have trouble."

"I'd like to do it that way," Woody said. "But what can I do alone?"

"Not much," Dan said. "Of course, with my car, we did all the heavy work in Bart Newton's garage, where we work on his racing cars. That's what it takes, really. Enough guys, and the right equipment."

"Oh," Woody said gloomily, "I suppose the best thing I can do is save my money and have it done by a regular garage."

"That's expensive," Dan said. He looked thoughtful. "I'll talk to the other guys. Maybe some Saturday we can come by and help you make the change. It wouldn't take any time at all, with all of us working."

"Do you think you could?" Woody gazed at Dan as though he were sinking in the ocean and Dan was about to throw him a life preserver.

"I'll try. Of course, we'll be busy on Bart's cars pretty soon. The racing season isn't very far off. But I'll see what I can do."

"Boy, I'd sure appreciate it."

"It's only a slim chance," Dan said. "By the way, what's the dope on the kid who was caught swiping stuff from the farm? I heard he was a buddy of yours."

"Dick's case comes up for a hearing in a week or so," Woody said. "My dad is going to appear as a character witness."

"I wish him luck," Dan said. "Even if he was stupid."

"Me too," Woody said. "About my car . . ."

"I'll see what I can do," Dan said. "See you later." He moved off, leaving Woody feeling both hopeful and thwarted. He'd wanted to get Dan's advice on the body work he'd started to do. Then too, he wanted to tell Dan that the clutch had to be fixed before the twenty-fifth, when he needed his car for his date with Sandra. The way it was now, no matter how nice he got it looking, he wouldn't be able to drive it unless the clutch was replaced.

Woody sighed. He really wasn't any closer to transportation than he'd ever been. He had long since stopped trying to count what he had spent on the car. Whatever he earned, he had to spend. There was always something that had to be bought. Still, when it was all done, he'd have something. He'd have a handsome old car that he had restored single-handed. There weren't many guys who had done that much all by themselves. He'd be a pretty big authority on rebuilding. Which reminded him . . . he had to buy a muffler, too. The police had ordered him to get rid of the motorcycle muffler and install one that was legal. He could do that while he was waiting for Dan and his gang to come and fix the clutch. It would take every dime he had, but it had to be done. So far, Woody realized, he hadn't spent a dime on extras. Everything had been an immediate, rock-bottom necessity. And that was all right with him. He had abandoned all his crazy dreams about ohv engines, racing gears, and even duals. All he wanted was clean and decent and reliable transportation, strictly stock. And that was what he would have. In time, he hoped, for the dance.

School, that day, released its people into the sparkle of a perfect spring afternoon. The sun was bright and not too hot, the grass was a thick, rich dark green, and the fruit trees were in blossom. Birds sang, the air was soft, and the outside world had never been more pleasant or inviting.

Woody hurried out of the building. First, he would check about eggs at the dairy. Then home, into his coveralls, and under the car, to start work on the muffler. He'd get the old one off, then buy and install the new one. Already, in his mind, he was under the car, shining his trouble light around, working against time.

He reached the steps that went down to the street and stopped. This was where he used to wait for Dick when they walked to work together. He looked down toward the street at the students' cars streaming away from the parking lot. He wished Dick were coming out of the building so they could sit and look at cars and talk before walking to work.

Thinking about it, Woody sat down by himself. He knew there was work to do; that his father was getting more and more impatient about the garage; that his mother was waiting for him to keep his promise and clean up some of the mess and grease that was always being tracked into the house. But he needed to rest. He needed a moment to relax.

And so, he sat in the sun, losing time, and watched the cars, trying to forget how much work he had to do, seeing himself, in his finished white car, driving with the rest of the guys. It was pleasant to dream, more pleasant than to race to the dairy and to run home, with work, work, work meeting him wherever he went.

A surprised voice behind him said, "Hello, Woody."

He turned. Sandra Rowan stood smiling down at him. She wore a bright skirt and a short-sleeved white blouse. Her books were cradled in her arms. Her radio was on top of the books. He hadn't heard it because she was listening through the little ear attachment. When Woody turned around, she unplugged the attachment from her ear and gave him her full attention. "I'm surprised to see you," she said. "You're always racing off in such a big hurry."

"I'm surprised to see you, too," Woody said. "You're always racing off to rehearsals."

"We don't have one this afternoon," Sandra said. "We were getting stale and decided to take a break. How are you coming with your car?"

"Oh, just fine," Woody said. He began a long recital of what he had done and what had to be done. He made sure to mention several times how it was taking every cent he had. "But," he ended triumphantly, "I think it will be all done in time for our . . . for the dance."

"I hope so," Sandra said. "Daddy said he wanted to see your car before he gave me permission to ride in it. He wants to make sure it's safe and that you're a safe driver."

"It's got the best brakes in town," Woody said. "Tell him that. And I've never had an accident of any kind."

"I'll tell him. But he'll still want to look it over himself."

Woody looked at her curiously. She hadn't sounded the least bit resentful. "Don't you get sore?" Woody asked. "Him not trusting your word?"

"He trusts me," Sandra said. "But when it comes to the cars I ride in, and the boys I ride with, he wants to see for himself."

"And you don't get sore?"

"Why should I? He'd be a funny kind of father if he wasn't concerned with my safety and welfare, wouldn't he?"

"I suppose so," Woody said slowly. "I never thought of it that way."

Sandra went down one step, then paused. "Are you waiting for anyone?"

"No. I was just taking a breather before going to the dairy. I want to see if they have any eggs I have to candle this afternoon."

"I thought if you weren't doing anything special," Sandra said, "you might like to hear some of my new records. We could sit on the back patio and listen. It's nice out there, and there's a place to plug in the record player."

"It sounds great," Woody said. "But I'd better check on the eggs. And then there's the muffler. I have to start on that right away."

"You could call the dairy from our house. If you don't have to work, you could listen to a couple of records. That wouldn't take long. Then you could work on the muffler."

Woody hesitated. He had so much to do, but it was such a nice day, and Sandra looked so pretty, and he was a little tired of lying on the garage floor by himself *all* the time. It wasn't that he didn't enjoy working on his car, but it wouldn't hurt once if he was a *few* minutes late.

Woody looked at his watch. "I guess I can spare a few minutes," he said. He didn't look at it again the rest of the afternoon.

They walked slowly, talking of little things, not caring what was said, really, so long as they could hear the sound of each other's voice and find, in conversation, an excuse to look in each other's face. Little by little, in this casual way, they tried to discover what the other really looked like, seen close and privately, marking down, in memory, the voice and the gestures, the little changes of expression, the quality of one another's personality. There was so much to be learned, to be found out about what the world was like when they were in it together.

The Rowan house was pleasant. Mrs. Rowan was friendly in an easy way that erased all Woody's self-consciousness about going to a girl's house with a girl. She said she was pleased to meet him and *seemed to be*. Then, very naturally, she was gone from the scene, and Sandra took over.

Woody carried the record player to the patio, proud of his strength. They hooked it up, and Woody looked over the records while Sandra went into the house. By the time he had picked some of his favorites to hear, she was back with a tray in her hands, bringing a couple of Cokes with a lot of ice and some cake. Woody didn't know why, but he got a tremendous thrill out of seeing her bring in the refreshments and serve them to him. He didn't know, of course, that she was just as pleased by the act of serving the boy she liked.

Woody took a Coke from the tray as she stood before him, and grinned at her, not knowing what else to do.

"That's real good cake," Sandra said.

Woody looked at it hungrily. Chocolate cake with thick white icing. Sandra had cut a king-size slab for him. He wanted it, but he didn't know how to tell her he was avoiding all sweets in an effort to keep his skin clear. It didn't seem the kind of thing a fellow said to a girl.

"I . . . I'm not much of a cake eater," Woody mumbled in some embarrassment. Unconsciously he touched a blemish on his forehead with his fingers.

Sandra put the tray aside. "Neither am I," she said. "Did you find a record you wanted to hear?"

Woody nodded and held up the disc he had selected as his first choice.

Sandra sat down gracefully on a flowered chaise lounge with an aluminum frame and leaned back. "This is so comfortable," she said. "You know how to work the machine, don't you?"

"I'll figure it out," Woody said. "I'm pretty good at figuring out mechanical things."

He put on the record, got it going, and, when the sound came on, adjusted the volume and balance. Then he sat down rather stiffly on a chair of bright red canvas with a white enameled frame and smiled at Sandra. She, reclining on the chaise, smiled back at him. Woody reached for his Coke and took a small sip. He leaned back in the chair, his feet planted solidly on the ground, and listened to the record. The air was filled with the smell of some kind of white-and-pink tree blossoms and the twittering of birds in the branches. The music played, the ice cubes tinkled in Woody's glass, and every time he and Sandra looked at each other at the same time, they smiled.

It was dark before Woody realized that it was time for him to go home and that he had completely forgotten to call the dairy about the possible arrival of eggs from the country. He hadn't even, he realized as he hurried home, thought about the work he had to do on Sidekick.

When Woody reached home, he started to enter the house by way of the garage. Then he stopped. Somehow, he didn't want to look at his car right now; to be reminded of all the work, all the problems, and all the troubles that it represented. The afternoon had been so easy, so relaxed, so carefree, that he was reluctant to erase it from his mind. He went around the garage instead, but despite himself he couldn't resist peeking in the garage window. He saw the dim, gray outline of his forlorn and abandoned car, and the sight of it brought back all the press of work and time. He could have had the old muffler off by this time. He could have cleaned up the garage, if nothing else. There was so much to do, and so little time in which to do it, and he had wasted an entire afternoon sitting with a girl and listening to songs he'd heard a thousand times before. Guiltily, he went into the house for his dinner, vowing to make up for lost time if he had to work until midnight.

But, of course, there was a fresh shipment of eggs at the dairy that had to be candled that night.

He did put on his coveralls after he returned from the dairy, and he was in the garage at midnight. That was where his father found him. He was under the car, the trouble light shining full in his face, fast asleep.

Encouraged by her first victory over Woody's car, Sandra met Woody after school again a few days later. He seemed delighted to see her, and they walked down the steps together, chatting away, feeling very close and friendly.

But a block away Woody stopped and said, "I guess this is where we take different trails, Sandra."

"Wouldn't you like to listen to some records again?" she asked. "You did have fun last time, didn't you?"

"Oh, it was swell," Woody assured her. "It was almost worth losing half a day's work on the car . . . what I mean is, I've just got to get cracking on that new muffler. I haven't even started on the body work, and that'll take a good week, fixing it up inside and out. But it'll be worth it. It's really going to be sharp. If I stick with it, it won't be long before we're riding all over in a sweet car, just as good as anybody else. See you. . . ."

She watched him hurry away from her to his *car.* The way he talked about that car . . . one of these days she was going to ask him something straight out. She was going to say, "Woody Ahern, answer this question: Do you want a car for yourself and your girl, or do you want a girl for your car?"

# CHAPTER 19

SATURDAY MORNING WOODY was first away from the breakfast table.

"Going somewhere?" his father asked.

"Just to the garage. I don't have a thing to do all day but work on the car."

"Do you think," Woody's mother asked hopefully, "that you could clean the garage today? If you could just get some of the grease and oil wiped up it would help. I can't keep up with all the dirt that's tracked into the house."

"I'll do that first," Woody promised.

"And remember, Woody," Ahern said, "I want my space back by the first snow."

"I'm working as fast as I can," Woody said. "How can I get anything done if I have to stand here and listen to arguments?" He stalked into his room, put on his coveralls and cap, and came out. "Will you have any time to give me a hand today, Dad?"

"I don't know when I can, Woody. We're having a track meet today. I'll be running events all day."

"And I'm going to the show," Cheryl said.

"Nobody asked you," Woody said pointedly. He went out alone.

The garage, early in the spring morning, was still cold from the night before, the light dim and gray. Woody got a broom and started sweeping with great, swinging strokes. He made little progress with the oily muck on the garage floor but did raise big clouds of dust. It was hard for him to sweep thoroughly because of the scattered tools and parts on the floor. He kicked some of these obstacles to one side as he worked close to his car. In a few minutes he was tired and sneezing violently from the dust. He threw the broom in a corner and walked outside to wait for the air to clear.

Outside it was bright and warm. He stood and let the sun shine on him, closing his eyes. Suddenly he felt restless. He wanted to do something active, in the sunlight. He had an urge to run and jump or throw something. It would be a good day to play a little golf, or to be out on the lake, fishing. It would be a good day to wear shorts and a jersey, and to be in the track meet, running . . . jumping.

The sun was hot on his dark green coveralls. He felt smothered and sweaty in them. He turned back to look inside the garage at the huge gray shape of his car. He didn't want to go into that dim, cold place. Not yet.

On impulse, Woody went back into the house. "You got a few minutes, Dad?"

"What for?"

"I thought I'd hunt up my gloves, and we could throw a few before you left and I got to work. Just for kicks."

"I can do that," Ahern said, surprised. Woody got a ball, a fielder's mitt, and a first baseman's mitt. He kept the latter for his own use. "Take it easy at first," Woody said. "I haven't caught a ball in a dog's age."

They stood in the back yard and lobbed the baseball back and forth easily, warming up. Woody had forgotten how much fun it could be to play catch with his father.

"You can open up a little, Dad," he called, pounding his glove with his left fist. "But, don't try any curves for a while. I've seen that mean break you throw."

Ahern threw harder. Woody crouched down to half a catcher's squat, taking the ball easily and firing it back with a snap of his wrist.

"Show me a little stuff," Woody called.

Ahern threw a let-up ball, and Woody, completely fooled, almost fell on his face trying to catch it. But he trapped the ball and laughed. The ball flew back and forth, with Woody handling all his father's pitches except his really fast ball.

"I've got to call it quits," Ahern said at last. "I'm due at the field."

"That was fun," Woody said, reluctantly taking off his glove and looking at his reddened palm.

"You handle the ball nicely," Ahern said. "You ought to try out for the high school team or the Babe Ruth League. The school is shy on catchers, and I think you'd be a natural for the position."

"They've got a lot of guys better than I am," Woody said.

"You could probably make the squad. And next year . . ."

"I'll see," Woody said. "If I have the time, I might take a shot at it." He took the gloves and ball back into the house, leaving his father with a small hope burning in his heart.

Having worked up a sweat, Woody was ready to tackle his automotive jobs. He had only a week to get his car in shape for the dance, and there was a lot to do. Once he had the new muffler on, he could start on the body and the interior. And if Dan came by to install the clutch, he'd be in shape. Except for the tires. He wondered if Sandra's father would check the tires.

In the garage, Woody got right to work, but he couldn't settle down to one task. He began by sanding some rough spots on the fenders, to get them in shape for the primer paint. But there was so much sanding to do, he saw that it would take all day to finish. He quit sanding and looked at the engine, just to *see* how that part of his car showed up. There wasn't much he could tell by looking. He poked around a little, tightening a few nuts, checking his electrical connections, and generally wasting time. When he tired of that, he decided on an experiment. He mixed up some black fabric dye he had bought at the dime store, poured it into a spray gun that was used to combat flies and mosquitoes, and pumped the mixture on the soft velour overhead lining in his car. He had decided that black would be the best and easiest color to cover the mousy, water stained, and mangy-looking fabric. At first, he got a good black color. But after a few minutes the soft material absorbed the dye, and the original color came back. Disgusted, he quit that hopeless task.

Finally, he got around to the muffler. He had taken the old one off, but the new one didn't seem to fit in the same place. He lay under the car, trying to use his feet as well as his hands to get the new muffler lined up. He was showered with rust and dirt as the old exhaust pipe, nothing more than a rusted shell, crumbled under his attack.

At last, arms weary and gasping for breath, he lay back with his arms extended on the floor, knowing that this simple task, too, was not going to be so simple. He would need new pipe, connections, a torch, and new hangers and brackets . . .

Woody jumped convulsively as someone stepped lightly on the fingers of his right hand. He couldn't see who it was, only that the shoe was a moccasin and that the ankle was trim. His face smeared with grease and dirt, his eyes bloody red from the rust flakes that had fallen into them, Woody pulled himself out from under the car and looked up. Sandra stood there, looking down at him with an impish grin.

"Where'd you come from?" Woody demanded, rubbing his sore eyes. He got clear of the car and stood up, looking like a smeared green bear.

"I've heard so much about this car, I thought I'd come over and see what it looked like." Sandra started a slow circle of the car, stepping lightly over the fringe of tools and parts that surrounded it. Woody followed, hardly knowing what to make of her. She wore, in addition to her featherweight moccasins, a pair of soft green tapered slacks that stopped at mid-calf, and a man-tailored blouse of a lighter shade of soft, grayed green. She had tied her golden brown hair into a kind of ponytail, and the total effect was one of slimness and lightness, of gracefulness without fragility. She had always seemed to Woody a pleasant, but not a very sparkling, girl. Now she sparkled.

"I didn't hear you come," Woody said. "Did you walk?"

"Rode," she said.

He looked toward the drive but didn't see her bicycle.

"I parked in the street," she said, noticing his look. "I didn't want to block your drive."

Woody's face creased into puzzled furrows. "You drove?"

"Yes," she said, trying to look inside Woody's car without touching it. "Does that surprise you?"

It did.

"I have my license," Sandra said. "And I get to use Dad's car most Saturday mornings. So, I thought I'd drive over and see the great work."

"It doesn't look like much yet," Woody said, "but it's got the best brakes in town." He went on to tell her of his plans.

Sandra nodded as she listened to him talk about the great, gray, grimy, sagging hull they stood beside, and it was hard for her to believe that the car he talked about was the one he had.

"Your plans sound wonderful," Sandra fibbed. "How soon do you think you'll be finished?"

Woody shook his head. "I don't know. It's slow, since I have to do all the work myself."

"Maybe I could help you," she offered. "I don't know anything about mechanics, but I am pretty good with a paint brush. I could help with the decorating."

Woody smiled in a superior fashion. "You might," he conceded, "but pin-striping is probably out of your line. It's not like doing posters, you know."

Woody looked at his car as though seeing it for the first time. And with Sandra there, making the future real, he knew he would never have his car finished in time for the dance. It would never be ready in a week. Now was the moment he had to face the cold facts.

"I was just thinking, Sandra," Woody said carefully, searching for the right words. "I'm not so sure I can go to the spring dance next week."

"What?"

She turned on him, eyes blazing, amazing him with her sudden fury. He'd never imagined she'd get so worked up about something as ordinary as a dance.

"What do you think you're doing?" Sandra demanded as Woody took a step back. "Do you realize where that leaves me? I've turned down a dozen invitations because I was going with you. Nobody's going to ask me now, a week before the dance! Why did you wait so long? Why didn't you tell me sooner? Oh . . . you . . . *idiot*!"

"I didn't know sooner," Woody said miserably. "I thought I'd have my car in shape."

"What's *that* got to do with it?"

"Everything, doesn't it?"

"Why?"

"You wouldn't go with me before because I didn't have a car of my own. So, I figured you wouldn't go anyway, if my car wasn't ready."

"Oh," Sandra said, relieved. "You really are an idiot, aren't you?"

"No, I'm not," Woody said. "I was just trying to do things the right way. I know I can't get Dad's car that night. He needs it. He can't even chauffeur us."

"Who cares about a car?" Sandra said. "If your car isn't running, and you can't get your dad's, we'll double date with someone who has a car."

"I don't know anybody like that," Woody said.

"I might. Unless this car bit is an excuse. Tell me honestly. Is it an excuse to get out of taking me? I don't want to go with you if you don't want to go with me."

"Sure, I want to go with you," Woody said, unaware how comical his earnest declaration was, coming from his sooty, red-eyed face.

"Okay, then if we can't get a ride, we can always walk," Sandra said. "It's only as far as the school."

"*Walk?*" Woody croaked.

"Why not?"

"I don't know . . . I didn't think anybody walked."

"We might start a fad," Sandra said, laughing at his expression. "Well, I have to go now. I just wanted to see your car."

Woody walked outside with her. "There's a chance," Sandra said, "that we could use Dad's car. I'll ask him."

Woody nodded unenthusiastically. After all his dreams about driving to the dance in his own car, he wasn't thrilled by the prospect of going to a dance in some stodgy old six-cylinder family sedan with his girl driving.

"There I am," Sandra said. "Across the street, in front of your house."

Woody stared, and then he almost groaned. And then, for some reason, he wanted to sit right down where he was and bawl at the top of his lungs.

Parked across the street, with the top down, was a snowy white Thunderbird convertible with a pale blue leather interior.

Woody's words came out haltingly. "That's *your* . . . car?"

"Yes. Do you like it?"

There was no answer. He shambled beside her in his baggy coveralls and dirty face, too shaken for speech.

"My dad's kind of a car nut in his own way," Sandra said, opening the door of her T-Bird. "That's why he's such a bug about the cars I ride in. He special ordered this one. It has a stick and overdrive instead of a slush pump." She closed the door. "How do you like the way I've pin-striped the dash?"

Her work was delicate, original and, even Woody could tell, really artistic. He looked at her with a painful, grease-smeared grin.

"Oh," Sandra said, starting the engine. "If we can get the car, I'll ask Daddy if you can drive. I think it looks better for the boy to drive, don't you?"

"I . . . I . . . I . . ." Woody couldn't think of any other words that could be said.

"Woody."

"Yeah?"

Sandra smiled at him with open affection. "I think it was real sweet, your trying to make your car nice in time for the dance. I know how hard you've worked on it."

"I guess I have," Woody said. "Well, it'll be there whenever I finish, I guess. If you'll even want to ride in it."

"Of course I will, if you want me to. But don't ever try to stand me up again because of your car. I go with boys I like, not cars." She smiled at him cheerfully and drove off. He stood in the street and watched her wheel the T-Bird around the corner. Now why, he wondered, had he ever believed that the only time girls got to ride in a car was when boys asked them? Because he sure had believed it.

Woody walked back toward his house. Looking at the house, he could see his father and mother and Cheryl behind the big dining-room window. They must have seen the whole thing; that a girl had come to see him and how she had come. Woody pretended not to see his family, but his walk took on a certain swagger. He supposed they'd be surprised to find out that he had a girl like Sandra interested in him, and that he was sort of interested in her. Well, even if it was a shock to them, they'd have to know sooner or later that he was getting along in years and wasn't a kid anymore.

— — —

Woody went back to work with a lighter heart. For the first time since he had bought the car, some of the pressure was off. He didn't *have* to get it done by the next week. Now he could take his time, build slowly and carefully.

He was surprised, about an hour later, to hear a car down the street in second gear, sounding like a sprint car. He was even more surprised when he heard tires drag and squeal as the car turned into his driveway.

The car stopped, emitting a thunderous roar as the driver stood on the gas pedal again and again, cracking his pipes like whips. Woody looked out and was really surprised to see the car that had come. His heart leaped. It was Dan Idler's beautiful Deuce. Dan had come after all to help him with the clutch. And he was a little surprised at the wild way Dan had come up.

Woody got up and walked to the garage door, wiping his hands on a rag, his face creased into a big smile of welcome. Then the smile froze. It was Jim Bob Alton who sat behind the wheel of the car, and Sonny Mack sat beside him.

When the boys saw Woody, they yelled, and Jim Bob revved the engine again and again. Woody writhed inwardly. Jim Bob would ruin the engine treating it like that. And what was he doing with Dan's car anyway? The car that had been Woody's idea of heaven on earth in automobiles.

"Hiya, Woody!" Jim Bob yelled. "How do you like the new heap?" He was not the quiet, childish Jim Bob of old. His eyes flashed, he grinned recklessly, and there was a challenge in every gesture.

Woody approached slowly, looking at the car. The beautiful paint job was dirty, the wheels were smeared and rubbed, and the left front fender had been bent and scratched.

"My mom bought it for me," Jim Bob said proudly, "for my six-teenth birthday. Pretty sharp, eh? You should have got it when you had the chance, Woody, instead of buying that dead dog from Sam. Boy, what you missed!"

"Man, can it go!" Sonny Mack screeched. "We outran the highway patrol twice already this morning, and Jim Bob got two tickets for dragging on Main Street. But they can't catch us in the country."

"I shift out of low gear at sixty-three, out of second at a hundred and five, and when I hit high gear . . ." Jim Bob hooted and hit his hands together in a sliding motion. "I'm long gone!"

"You're going to kill yourself," Woody said, his envy battling with his heartbreak at the fate of the little car.

"Man, you can't go slow in this wagon. It's a runner." Jim Bob grinned. "How about a drag when you get your heap put together?" He laughed delightedly at the thought.

Woody nodded, without meaning anything. Much as he hated to see the car in the hands of Jim Bob, he felt a greater resentment against Dan Ilder. He couldn't imagine how Dan could have let his precious car go to anyone, much less to somebody like Jim Bob. How could he have sold it to a . . . fool? After all the work of building it up, how could he stand to see it in the hands of a stupid kid who was mishandling it and tearing it apart? How had Dan been able to do a thing like that to his own car?

"Let's scratch off, Jim Bob," Sonny Mack cried. "We ain't giving the girls a chance to see us. You ought to see the way the little ladies look at this rod, Woody. *MmmmmmMMM!*"

"All the dates you want now, eh?" Woody asked jovially, so they wouldn't think he envied them.

A puzzled look came over Sonny's face. He scratched at his pinkish hair. "None yet," he complained to Woody. "I mean, we could get all the junior high girls we wanted to go with, but the real sharp ones are still playing hard to get. Just because they're bigger than we are." Sonny's blue eyes shone with new brightness.

"But you ought to see the way they look at our car, eh, Jim Bob? They really go for it."

"They sure do," Jim Bob said. "Well, we just wanted to say hello, Woody. And to see of you had any word about Dick."

"There's a chance he might get off on probation, since it's his first offense," Woody said. "Nobody knows what the judge will do."

"I wish the silly nut luck," Jim Bob said. "For old times' sake. See you around, Woody."

Jim Bob wound the engine tight, laughing at Woody as the ground shook under the deafening roar. Then, without looking, he backed swiftly into the street, turned so sharply that one front wheel lifted slightly, and threw the car into low gear. Then he was off, tires screaming, leaving two long strips of black rubber on the pavement. By the time he was a block and a half away, he was doing seventy.

Woody turned and went back into his garage, where he had spent so many hours of his life these recent weeks. He looked at the awkward bulk of his car and saw in his mind's eye the hundreds of hours of labor ahead, the hundreds of dollars of expense. He would live around and under that car for months to come. And when he was all done, he would have a car that wasn't a tenth as good as the one Jim Bob's mother had bought him.

His father's words came back to him. *You have to find out for yourself that ownership of anything, in itself, means nothing so far as your self is concerned. Any fool of legal age with enough money can buy anything he wants.*

"Or his mother can buy it for him," Woody said aloud, bitterly.

Yet, that didn't mean his own car was less precious to him, or that his own desire for a car was any less. He wanted his car because . . . he wanted it, regardless of what anyone else had or didn't have. Woody lay down on the creeper, to try again with the new muffler. But as he tried to fit it, he realized it would be useless to try until he replaced the old pipe with new, and he didn't have the money for new pipe. This week he had to save for the dance.

Since there wasn't any hurry about getting the car rebuilt, Woody got out from under again. It was such a nice day out, and he was feeling a little lonesome. It had been weeks and weeks since he'd had a real break. Suddenly he wanted to be where there were people, where lively things were going on. He thought of the track meet and decided to go. Maybe, while he was there, he'd see the baseball coach and find out if they needed a catcher.

Woody went into the house to clean up and change. He had put on clean khaki slacks and a bright red sports shirt when he heard the phone ring. He closed his eyes and prayed it would be one of his mother's friends calling for a chat, and then his heart sank when his mother knocked on his door and said the call was for him. He knew what it was even before Mr. Stonelee said his second word. There were eight cases of eggs that had come in unexpectedly, and since the next day was Sunday . . .

Woody spent the next seven hours in the cramped little egg-candling room, hunched over the light and the scales. When he finished, the fine spring day was over.

"There were some boys here to see you this afternoon," Woody's mother said as she served him a late supper.

"Who?" Woody supported his face with his left hand, his elbow on the table, and gnawed wearily at a piece of fried chicken held in his right hand.

"They were strangers to me. Older boys, too. They came in something that looked like a tow truck. Anyway, they seemed to know all about your car. The boy who spoke to me—I think he said his name was Dan—said it would be all right with you."

"Dan Ilder!" Woody cried regretfully. "I missed him. What would be all right with me?"

"They did something to your car. It took them a couple of hours."

Cheryl wandered in, in time to hear her mother's words. "They had the motor out of your car and *everything*, Woody."

Woody looked at the piece of chicken in his hand and remembered the relationship of chickens to eggs. He lost his appetite.

"He left you this note," Woody's mother said, handing Woody

a folded sheet of paper. He unfolded the paper and read what Dan had written in a neat, precise hand:

*Woody:*

*This is the last weekend before racing season, so it was now or never. Too bad you couldn't have been around to see a good pit crew in action. We yanked the motor and put in your clutch. Also checked your transmission. It's okay. We also adjusted your brakes and installed your muffler. Just happened to have some of the right pipe and our welding outfit on the truck. You'll need new front shocks soon and tie rods. Also, a valve and ring job. Also found a couple of weak spots in the radiator. Better get a rebuilt, or you'll have trouble this summer. Always something, isn't there? We tuned her the best we could, so she's ready to drive when you are, carefully, with the rubber you've got. Sorry you weren't here for the fun. Dan.*

*PS: We spent seven dollars and fifty cents for little parts and stuff we didn't have on the truck. No rush about paying, since we didn't ask first.*

*D.*

Woody put down the note. "It was Dan Ilder and the rest of Bart Newton's pit crew," Woody said. "They put the car together."

"That was certainly nice of them. Aren't you pleased?"

"I guess so," Woody said. "I mean . . . I'm glad it's ready to drive, but I missed all the fun. I would have given anything to work with those guys for an afternoon. To work and get done . . . they're a real racing pit crew."

Woody got up and went into the garage to see what had been done. His car looked the same, but there was an atmosphere of neatness that had been lacking, and of completion. Among other things, the boys had straightened up the garage and put his tools in one place. Woody blushed at what they must have thought of him.

He got in the car and tried the brake and clutch pedals. They felt good. Sitting there, he remembered Dan's note. Sidekick was safe to drive, except for the chancey tires. It was all right to start the engine.

Woody started the car and listened to it. It sounded pretty good to him. On impulse, he backed out of the garage. The clutch and brakes worked perfectly. He drove around the block a couple of times, trying to think of some place he'd like to go. He thought of going over to Sandra's, but his car didn't look good enough to show to strangers. It would have to be cleaned up, painted, and provided with seat covers. There was still plenty to do. As Dan had said, there was always something.

Woody drove around aimlessly for a while and then returned home, parking the car to one side of the drive. Tonight he would tell his father he was through using the garage. On second thought, he decided to drive inside. It looked like rain, and the window on his side wouldn't close . . . another "something" to be taken care of at the first opportunity.

Inside, Woody turned off the engine and sat behind the wheel for a moment. That was another project . . . to bind the wheel with foam rubber and plastic tape, as the racing drivers did. It gave you a better wheel to grip and was safer in case of collision or rollover. And the front seat still had to be fastened down.

Dan and the boys had done a lot, but there was still a great deal to be done . . . and bought. There was no end in sight to the work and the expenditures. There was always, as Dan had written, "something."

Woody got out of the car, feeling he ought to get to work, but not quite sure where to start. He was glad the car was running, but not as elated as he thought he would be. He had missed the only real work and fun. This afternoon would have been the kind he had dreamed of so many times . . . that he had lived for. But the fellows had come, and worked, and left, and if he picked up where they left off, he would do it alone.

Woody stood around a few more minutes with his hands in his pockets, then decided to go in and watch some westerns on TV. He had the strange feeling that he had been robbed.

# CHAPTER 20

SUNDAY AFTERNOON, WOODY WORKED ON HIS CAR. For the first time in weeks, he worked because he wanted to, and not because he had to, and he enjoyed every minute of it. First, he cleaned the car out thoroughly inside, then he washed it. When it was dry, he touched up some of the bad spots with some black primer paint. It dried dull and blended in with the lusterless quality of the other paint on the car.

Monday morning he drove to school.

It was pleasant going out to the garage, getting into his own car, and heading toward school. He drove slowly, enjoying the ride. On the way, Jim Bob overtook him with a roar. He heard Jim Bob downshift to second and then the little blue Deuce shot past him, burning rubber, weaving from side to side. Jim Bob blew a few blasts on his horn as he tore past, just in case Woody hadn't noticed him. Woody returned the greeting.

He didn't mind seeing Jim Bob pass him. For some reason he was calm and unenvious, although he still grieved to see the little car mistreated. But he was in his own car, and it was what he had wanted and bought, and he didn't expect miracles from it. And everybody would know, this morning, that Woody Ahern had put his car together and got it running. Well . . . had done a great deal of the work, anyway.

At school Woody looked up Dan Ilder to thank him for the work he and his friends had done.

"It wasn't anything," Dan said, "just a routine little job." And Woody could see that it wasn't, indeed, anything to Dan. Just another bit of work done for a friend. It was nothing to wave flags about or beat drums over.

"I see you sold your Deuce to Jim Bob Alton," Woody said. "I'll bet you hated to see it go."

"I was happy to see the money come in," Dan said with a grin. "I had a lot of money wrapped up in that machine, and I was afraid I'd have to take a beating. Fortunately, he came along with the asking price in his hand."

"Are you going to build another car now?"

Dan shook his head. "That's my start in college, that money. With what I earn summers, it might get me through. I've had enough of playing around with cars and putting too much time and money in them. The next four years I'll be busy with college. I'll get my fill of cars in the summer, on the racing circuit. But when you study engineering, you can't afford to waste much time or money on expensive hobbies. The competition is too tough."

Woody looked at Dan with something like horror in his eyes. "Won't you have *any* kind of car in college?"

Dan laughed and shook his head. "The school I'm going to doesn't permit undergraduates to own cars."

"I wouldn't go to a school like that," Woody said indignantly.

"I wouldn't have wanted to, either, when I was a sophomore," Dan said. "That was the year I began building my Deuce."

Mention of the car changed Woody's line of thought. "Jim Bob sure isn't taking care of your car," he said resentfully. "It'll be a wreck in a month."

"*His* car," Dan corrected gently.

"Don't you even care about it anymore?" Woody asked in a shocked voice. He didn't see how Dan could be so cold blooded about the Deuce.

Dan's face crinkled with amusement. "I sold him a car, Woody, not my girl."

"I thought you liked cars."

"I do," Dan said. "That's why I'm going to study automotive engineering. But when it comes to a choice between driving a particular car or getting an education, there's no contest. I take good care of my cars when I have them. That's just good sense. But that's it."

"And after all the money and work you put in on that car," Woody mourned.

"Because of it," Dan said. "That time and money almost cost me a college education. If Jim Bob hadn't bailed me out, I'd be in overalls next fall, instead of a classroom. Come with me . . ."

Dan led Woody to a window overlooking the school parking lot. There were eighty or ninety cars parked below. "Look them over," Dan said, "and point out the best one."

Woody looked. There were cars of every age and description, from battered old hulks to new, modified hardtops and convertibles. He looked a long time before he made his choice. There was only one car in the lot that he was drawn to and that was really different from the others.

"You picked your own," Dan said, watching Woody's eyes and sudden smile of recognition. "Why?"

"I don't know. It was the one I . . . I'm not sure why, but it was the way I felt."

"Loyalty," Dan said. "Loyalty to your own. To yourself. That car is you out there. Picking another one is like saying you'd rather be some other kid in school than yourself. If you owned any other car out there, you'd feel the same way about it. Because it was yours . . . and you. That's why I don't shed any tears over selling the Deuce. It *was* my car. Now it isn't. I suppose, racing being what it is, I'm used to seeing good cars wrecked or left behind or sold in favor of better ones."

Dan turned his back on the cars below. He leaned against the windowsill, his feet crossed at the ankles. "I put a lot of my money and a lot of my life in that Deuce," he said thoughtfully. "Almost too much. I know that car better than I know anything in this world. And I'll tell you something. That car, cruising at sixty on a still day, will get almost exactly eleven miles to a gallon of gas. But if it had to be done to save my life, that car wouldn't go another half mile unless I put another penny-and-a-half worth of gas in the tank. That's how much I mean to the car that I almost missed getting an education to build and support."

Woody continued looking out of the window at his car. He didn't try to argue. Let Dan feel any way he wanted to about the Deuce. He would feel the way *he* wanted to about Sidekick. It was strange, but for all Dan knew about cars, he certainly didn't understand much about their meaning. He was just cold blooded by nature and thought he knew it all.

"Well," Woody said as a bell rang, "thanks again for fixing up my car."

"It was nothing," Dan said. "I kind of talked you into buying the car. I wanted to help you get some good out of it. I looked over the work you did, and it wasn't bad for a beginner. If you're serious about automotive work, come and see us work in the pits this summer. You can get a lot of pointers in a hurry watching a pit crew work."

Woody beamed. "Don't you worry. I . . . we'll be there." He meant—and Dan knew he meant—himself and Sidekick.

– – –

A dream came true that afternoon. When the final bell rang, Woody led Sandra out to his car to drive her home. "I cleaned it out the best I could," Woody said anxiously. "I don't have real seat covers yet, but these big plastic bags that our clothes came back from the cleaners in work pretty good. They'll protect your clothes."

He got in behind the wheel, started up, and drove into the street. Instead of going straight to her home, he circled the block several times, the way so many of the others did, like ducks circling a pond as they gained altitude before pointing away to a distant cornfield.

This was it at last . . . riding around, following a few cars, and leading a few cars, while the carless boys stood on the sidewalk and the school steps and watched with envy and longing.

"I was just thinking," Woody said as he finally steered for Sandra's home. "We can go to the dance in my car after all, can't we?"

Sandra looked around dubiously at the interior.

"I'll put fresh plastic on the seats . . ."

"My dress will be different. Longer, with a very full skirt. It's white, too. If I brushed against something, it would be ruined."

"Don't worry . . . I'll have it clean."

Sandra said, "My father said we could use the T-Bird and that it would be all right for you to drive. Wouldn't you like that?"

"I'd rather drive my own car," Woody said stubbornly. "Unless you're ashamed to be seen in an old car like mine."

She tossed her head impatiently. "I told you once I don't date *cars*."

"Then we'll take Sidekick," Woody said firmly.

Smiling and sighing at the same time, she looked at his unyielding profile. She had been so sure he'd be thrilled by a chance to drive the T-Bird. He certainly was difficult to understand.

"All right," she said, "if you want it that way. But I'll cut off your head with a dull knife if my dress is ruined."

"I'll risk it," Woody said seriously, "because that *is* the way I want it."

And, when the night of the dance arrived, that's the way it was.

Woody sat at the dinner table chewing contentedly on food he hardly noticed. He was sitting, he felt, not at the dinner table, but on top of the world. His car ran smoothly, he had been invited to join no less than three good car clubs at school, and his first date with Sandra had turned out so well they'd gone on seeing one another. For the first time in many weeks, he was several dollars ahead of his expenses. The garage was clean, and there was no pressure on him to move out because he *was* out. There was work to be done on his car, but it could be done at his pleasure. Everything he planned had worked out just as he had dreamed it would. He had proved to everyone—including himself—that he could buy, build up, and afford his car.

"I've got some news about Dick," Ahern said as the family was eating dessert. "The judge has decided to give him a break."

"That's swell," Woody said. "I was hoping he would."

"He'll be on probation, of course, and if he gets into any more trouble, he'll have to serve out his sentence. He'll be going back to school tomorrow. Do you think the kids will give him a bad time, Woody?"

Woody shook his head. "We've had others in trouble. Nobody likes to rub it in. Mostly, we just pretend nothing happened. Pretty soon it's forgotten."

"He'll have to keep his grades up," Ahern continued.

"That won't be hard for him," Woody said. "He's pretty bright when he wants to be."

"And he has to obey his parents . . . *that* might be harder," Ahern said with a grin. He got serious again. "He'll also meet regularly with a psychologist. If Dick can get some of his mental lines untangled, that will do him more good than anything else."

"What's to happen to the Pooch?" Woody asked his father. "Will he be on probation too?"

Ahern shook his head. "I couldn't do anything for him . . . his record was too bad. They're sending him to the training school."

"They shouldn't send him to jail," Woody said. "The guys who put him up to what he did are worse than he is."

"The training school isn't just a jail," Ahern said. "They'll teach Freddy some kind of trade and keep an eye on him after he's out." He paused, then said, "Getting back to Dick, the problem there is getting him a job. The court felt it would be good for him to have a job, but people are reluctant to hire a boy in Dick's situation."

"I know where he can get a job," Woody said casually.

"Where?"

"At the dairy, candling eggs. I spoke to Mr. Stonelee about it when I heard Dick might be free on probation. If Dick wants his old job back, he can have it."

The Aherns exchanged glances. "What about you?" Mr. Ahern asked Woody.

"I'll keep my clean-up job."

"I thought you needed the extra money for your car."

"I do," Woody said. "But I've known Dick longer than anybody else . . . He's my best friend. I couldn't hog his job when he's in trouble."

"I'm pleased by your loyalty, Woody," Ahern said. "I really am. How will the cutback affect your plans for your car?"

"I meant to talk to you about that," Woody said, trying to keep the casual note in his voice. "Would it be all right with you if I . . . sold my car?"

"I never thought I'd be on this side of the argument," Ahern said, "but why do you want to sell your car?"

"I can't afford to keep it," Woody said.

"I think you can. The shape your car is in now, you ought to be able to run it on one job."

"It can't be done, Dad," Woody said. "It looks good on paper, but you don't know how it is with an old car. I really need another radiator, a valve and ring job, tires . . . as Dan Ilder says, Dad, there's always something."

"I still think you could do it. I hate to see you give up your car just when you've got it going and can get some fun out of it. Don't you like working on your car anymore?"

They looked at him searchingly, and Woody didn't want them to know his true feelings. He didn't want to make a show of a big sacrifice in front of them. He had thought it all out, all through the week of pleasure with his car, and he had made the decision.

"Oh," Woody said, "working on a car is all right, but there's more to life than that. With just one job, I'd be stuck in the garage for the next two years."

"But you worked so hard," Woody's mother said. "It seems a shame to lose the car now."

"I had fun," Woody said. "And it's only a car. You know, Dad, I used to sit and watch the cars go by, and it seemed that everybody in the world but me had a car. It made me feel desperate for a car. But now I look around and *see* all the cars, and I know I'll have a car most of my life. Once I get through school and have a job, I'll have a car. Golly, I don't see how you can *help* having a car in this country. I mean, I'd like to have a car now if I could afford the time and money. But a car isn't the only thing in life. I'd like to have a little cash in my jeans, and play a little ball, and have a little fun now. You know . . . do the things I won't be able to do later on in life. I mean, I want to have a car, but I don't think I have to have one *right now.*"

He talked, not to convince them, but himself.

He looked at his father with such a feeling of resolve and self-pride that he almost looked defiant. He *had* showed them all. Nothing had been able to *make* him give up his car. He'd fought past every obstacle, every setback, every discouragement, and proved he could do it. And now he was proving he could give it up because he wanted to, and not because he had to. He didn't want them to think he was making a big sacrifice, yet he wanted them to understand.

"Woody," Ahern said, "welcome to my squad."

Woody looked at his father and knew, when their eyes met, that his father meant the wartime and not the athletic squad.

Woody got up. "I think I'll go down and see that everything's in order for a sale," he said, seemingly unmoved by the prospect of selling the car. "I thought I'd ask forty dollars plus the cost of the new parts. The labor would be free."

"Sounds fair enough," Ahern said. "It's funny, but now that it's happened I kind of hate to see your car go. I'll miss it."

"What's there to miss?" Woody asked with a grin. "It's only an old car."

He went out into the garage, the grin still on his face but going no deeper. He walked around the good gray-black hulk, running his hand along the car's rough surfaces. As he did, he averted his face, glancing at the car guiltily out of the corner of his eye. All the promises he had made to the car . . . all he had promised to do . . . all the beauty, the glory, the fun together. All the work he had done . . . all the hours he had spent in grimy, lonely labor . . .

He got in and sat under the wheel. His car was for sale. *His* car . . . he clutched the rim of the wheel of his beloved car with both hands, as though he would never let go. He leaned forward, his forehead resting against the top of the steering wheel rim, his eyes closed.

"I'm sorry, Sidekick," he whispered miserably. "I'm sorry, old boy. But Dick needs the job, and I can't keep you running on a couple of dollars a week . . . not with all the things you need . . . goodbye, buddy . . ." And closing his eyes, he wept.

— — —

Woody Ahern stood in the school hallway and looked at a notice typed on a white card that was tacked to the bulletin board.

### FOR SALE

1947 Ford two door. Looks a little rough, but runs good. New brakes and clutch. Ideal for hop-up or custom. Asking $40 plus cost of newly installed parts. Contact Woody Ahern in 10A-2, or at home.

"Any bites yet, Woody?"

Woody looked over his shoulder. "A couple. Some kid is coming over late this afternoon, when I get home from the dairy."

"Speaking of the dairy . . . hadn't we better get a move on? I've got a lot of eggs to candle, and I don't want to be late."

"Okay, Dick," Woody said. "Let's go."

They went out and got into Woody's car. Outwardly, in many ways, Dick hadn't changed at all. He still clung to some of his old mannerisms, but the old harsh cynicism was gone. Beneath the surface he was anxious, unsure, and uncertain, like a person groping in the dark.

"I like this riding to work," Dick said as Woody drove away. "I wish you weren't selling the car."

"I like to ride, too," Woody said. "But I'm not going to kill myself for it."

When they were on the street, Jim Bob passed them in the blue Deuce, honking a loud greeting.

"That's not a redhead next to him," Woody said. "That's a blonde. That car only carries two people, so I guess poor old Sonny is on foot."

Dick laughed, a note of his old mocking self in the sound. "Sonny on foot . . . I guess that fixes him. He'll never get a girl now."

"Oh, I don't know," Woody said wisely. "If a girl likes a guy, he doesn't have to have a car."

"That's how much you know about it."

"That," Woody said, "is *exactly* how much I know about it."

At the dairy, Dick went into his tiny egg-candling room, turned on his radio, and prepared to work. Woody lingered. "Want an ice cream bar before we start?" he asked.

"I'll wait," Dick said. "I want to get a start with the eggs first." He looked at Woody and gave him a wry smile. "I'm not scared to. I'm just trying to learn good work habits. That's what my head shrinker says I need to do."

"What's it like with those guys?" Woody asked. "Do you have to lie down on a couch and tell all about what happened when you were a small kid?"

"No," Dick said, "we just sit and talk back and forth about things. The guy is pretty sharp. We get into some pretty good arguments, and you can say anything you want to and not get in trouble."

"*Anything?*" Woody asked incredulously.

"Sure. You can even call him names, if you want to. I did at first. You know . . . I really told him what I thought about things. Didn't pull any punches, either." Dick looked thoughtful, picked up an egg, and studied it. "You know, I might even take up that line of jazz myself." He shot Woody a questioning look.

"Sounds interesting," Woody said. "I always thought I'd like to do something mechanical . . . maybe even engineering. But since I did all that work on my car, I kind of lost my taste for it as a job. It would be a good hobby, but when it comes to a job . . ." Now it was his turn to look at Dick, and he wondered if he could trust him. "I thought it might be more interesting to work with people instead of things. You know . . . like a coach or something. . . ."

"You ought to be good at that," Dick said, and his voice and grin were friendly. "You're pretty good at having people do things your way."

"I'd better get to the vats," Woody said. "Want to throw some rots for Cokes later?"

"I don't know. I don't want to get in any trouble here."

"We've always done it."

"Even so. I'm out, but with a rope around my leg."

"I'll bet Mr. Stonelee wouldn't care," Woody said.

"We can find out," Dick said. "Let's ask him.

"I don't have the nerve," Woody said.

"I do."

They found Mr. Stonelee in the cold room. Dick approached him and asked if they could throw rots for Cokes at a target in the back lot. Mr. Stonelee looked at them with a grin. "I haven't stopped anybody in all these years," he said. "I don't see any reason to clamp down now."

"Imagine that," Woody said as he and Dick went back to work. "He knew all the time we'd been doing it. I wonder how he found out?"

— — —

The boy who knocked at the Ahern door and said he had come to see about the car was a bright-eyed, eager lad of sixteen. But as Woody led his prospective customer to the garage, he felt years older than the other boy.

"The way it is," the boy explained to Woody, "we have a car club and what we want is an old car that we can use for a project. We want to build up a real custom rod, like all the other guys do."

"It's not as easy as it looks in the magazines," Woody warned. "It takes a lot of time and work and money."

"We figure we can find most of the stuff we want in the junk-yards," the boy said. "And we'll do all the work ourselves. Boy, we can't wait to get our hands on a car. We've been studying about cars for years, so we're not too dumb about rebuilding."

Woody led the boy into the garage and turned on the light. His car loomed massive and black. The boy walked slowly around Sidekick, slapping the sheet metal and kicking at the tires.

"How does it look to you?" Woody asked.

The boy's voice was velvety with longing. "It's just what we've been looking for. It's perfect!"

"Want me to start it up for you?"

The boy looked at Woody with amazement. "You mean it really runs?"

"Runs good," Woody said. He got in and started the car. The boy listened, enchanted. Woody shut off the engine. "I've got a new muffler on," he said. "When I got it all it had was a beat-up old motorcycle muffler."

"It did?" the boy cried eagerly. "Do you still have it?"

"I've got two of them," Woody said.

"Would you sell them to me?"

"You can't use them," Woody said. "The cops will shut you down."

"We can try," the boy said, a reckless gleam in his eyes. "Boy, I can just imagine the tone with motorcycle mufflers."

Woody showed the boy the rest of the car, pointing out the new brakes, brake cylinders, and clutch.

"We'll probably drop in an ohv," the boy said easily. "Maybe a competition type clutch, too, and a tougher gear box. Maybe old Packard, or LaSalle. I want a four-eleven rear end too, and a limited slip differential. Then we plan to paint it purple, with a purple and white Naugahyde interior, and wind up with some striping, or gold flames. By the time the club gets through, we'll have the sharpest rod in town."

"How many in your club?" Woody asked politely.

"Three of us," the boy said. "I'm the only one old enough to have a car right now, but we'll do all the work."

"I'm sure you all will," Woody said, holding back a smile. "Where will you do the work?"

"My dad's letting me use one side of our garage for the summer. That ought to be enough time to get the work done, don't you think?"

"Depends," Woody said. "Depends on how you work and what you have to work with. It takes tools . . ."

"That's why we want an old car," the boy said. "With an old car and a factory manual, you can do an awful lot if you know how to read and can use a wrench."

Woody was suddenly tired of the boy's naive prattle. After what he had been through, it made him slightly sick. "That's the car," Woody said abruptly. "In good running condition and safe on the road. All I'm asking is the forty dollars I paid for it when it was in pretty bad shape, plus the cost of the new parts I put in. I'm throwing in the labor for nothing."

"That sounds reasonable enough," the boy said. He added, a little disappointedly, "I wish you hadn't done so much. You didn't leave much fun for me and the club."

"I'm sure you'll find your share," Woody said with a bitter smile. "Anyway, it comes to eighty-five dollars."

The boy frowned. "I think that's fair," he said, "but all I'm allowed to spend is seventy-five."

Woody hesitated for a moment. "Oh well . . . I'll take it. And if you want, I'll throw in some odds and ends like this extra tailpipe extension, a can of body putty, and some other stuff. I want to keep the tools and the jack stands."

"Gee, thanks," the boy said. He reached into his pocket and brought out a handful of bills. "Here's my seventy-five. Want to give me the key?"

Woody stared at the money, feeling a fierce resentment against this boy who had come to take his car away from him. He looked appealingly at his car, seeking a sign . . .

"You want it now?" Woody asked dumbly.

"Why not? I might as well take it off your hands. My father will come over later to see about the transfer and all that jazz. The key . . . ?"

Woody took the boy's money and handed over the key. He opened the garage door. The boy started up the car and let it idle. There was a look of rapture on his face. Woody came to his window to give him all sorts of directions about how to drive Sidekick and how to treat him. He wanted to cry, "Be good to my car!" But he kept silent, and merely watched the boy settle himself into the driver's seat.

The boy looked at Woody and grinned proudly. "Boy," he said, revving the engine a little, "a real car of my own at last! Too bad you had to give it up."

"I didn't have to give it up," Woody flared.

"You getting something better?"

"No, I just wanted to sell it."

"And not have *any* car?" There was a grin of unbelief on the boy's lips. Nobody just sold a car and went without one if he didn't have to. It didn't make sense.

"We're going to call the car Teen Angel," the boy said. "It used to be a pop song. Like it?"

Woody wanted to protest, *You can't. His name is Sidekick*, but he said nothing.

"Come on, Teen Angel," the boy said fondly. "Let's go home where we belong."

Sidekick didn't protest as the boy backed out of the garage. The headlight eyes were whitish and blank, the chrome grille mouth never quivered. Woody walked out into the drive after the car. The boy backed around into the street, shifted into low with a clash of gears, and started up with a squeak of tires as he lurched ahead.

Woody waited until the last moment for the miracle that never happened. Sidekick did not plead to remain or call back a single sound of thanks for all the work, the heartache, the worry, and the sacrifice of time and money that Woody had dedicated to him.

It was true, Woody thought as he watched the high, awkward car lumber crookedly down the street. His car didn't care who owned it. It went not for love, but for money. It would belong as willingly (or unwillingly) to the next master as to the last. It would not, for the most devoted owner on earth, turn one wheel one inch unless it was paid for, cash in advance, gas in the tank, oil in the crankcase, and fire at the plug ends.

Woody sprinted to the end of the drive and looked down the street, a stocky, forlorn boy with misting eyes. He saw the high narrow rear end of Sidekick moving darkly and erratically out of his sight and out of his life. He raised his hand in a hesitant gesture of farewell, remembering suddenly, with an ache in his heart, the few happy trips they had had together. "Goodbye, Sidekick," he whispered. He hoped the new boy would be good to his car. In the last instant the car turned a corner and the familiar shape disappeared, already a stranger in Woody's eyes.

Woody turned and walked back into the garage. It was huge, empty, dim, and desolate. A few tools lay against the side of a wall. A few pieces of Sidekick's body—a chunk of tailpipe, a piece of rusted chrome, the old master cylinder—were now strange junk in a corner.

Woody stood in the middle of the garage and waited for the full blow of his sorrow and despair and defeat to strike. There was no longer any need for pretense . . . he had had to give up his car.

But his sorrow and emptiness and sense of loss did not decrease. Rather, the little thought came to him, as he stood and strained to produce self-pity, that he had *not* been forced to give up his car. He could have kept it *if he had wanted to*. Yes, he could have kept it, worked on it, and saved, over a long period of time from his one job, for the parts he needed.

He knew that. In the days when he had really wanted his car, no effort, no labor, no sacrifice was too great to make in its behalf. Nothing in the world could have forced him, against his will, to give up his car. And nothing had forced him to give it up.

He faced the truth. He had jumped at the chance to give up his egg-candling job and had been happy to use Dick's need as an excuse to get rid of a car he didn't want. And he had fooled himself into thinking he *had* to give up the car. He knew that.

It was hard to believe, but Woody knew it was true. He was glad the car was gone.

What he had told his father but hadn't believed himself was true. He would choose his occupation, and he would work at it. And, living in the United States and having a job, he would also have a car most of his life. But he didn't really need one *right now*. He wanted one, and wished he could afford to own and operate a decent car, but he didn't *need* one. Not when it cost what Sidekick had cost. It was too big a price to pay for wheels.

Now he could wake up in the mornings the slow and easy way. Now he could loaf a little and not feel guilty over every wasted minute. He could come home without being greeted by the huge, ailing mass of metal that demanded all his time and all his money. He could be a boy again, try out for teams at school, spend some time with his girl when he wanted to, and live his life the way he wanted to.

Woody looked around the empty garage, waiting for the loneliness, the sadness, and the regret to grip his soul. But he could not force his spirits down when, with every passing second, they were rising higher and higher, unfettered and triumphant.

Woody looked at his watch. It was early in the evening. Outside, the sun was still spilling golden light on the fresh, green world. Woody walked outside, then looked back quickly on the chance he might surprise a ghost of Sidekick's image or memory. But the garage was empty, and what space there was belonged to the family sedan.

Woody started away from the house with a quick, springy step. He didn't know where he was going, and it really didn't matter. He could go, and he did not have to look back guiltily.

Woody shoved his hands in his pockets. There were no keys to remind him that he owned, and was owned by, property. For the first time since he had walked into Sam Rizzell's garage, he was free!

# ABOUT RETRO READS

*Road Rocket* is part of a series from Octane Press called Retro Reads, which are reprinted editions of high-quality narrative titles we believe are worthy of the attention of our readers. The series has included several books by Henry Gregor Felsen. With Retro Reads, motoring enthusiasts will delight in familiar classics and discover timeless narratives. You can find Retro Reads and a list of our brand new books at OctanePress.com, where you also can sign up for our newsletter to learn about all our gearhead-related books.

The Retro Reads titles by Henry Gregor Felsen include:

HOT ROD
ISBN 978-1-64234-089-1

STREET ROD
ISBN 978-1-64234-104-1

CRASH CLUB
ISBN 978-1-64234-131-7

ROAD ROCKET
ISBN 978-1-64234-132-4

FEVER HEAT
ISBN 978-1-64234-133-1

RAG TOP
(originally published as CUP OF FURY)
ISBN 978-1-64234-134-8